ABSOLUTION

HEAVEN'S REJECTS MC #3

AVELYN PAIGE

TRIGGER WARNINGS

This book contains graphic scenes of violence, gore, death, kidnapping, drug use, and sexual encounters.

BLURB

She has been through hell. He has clawed his way out of it.

When Erica "Ricca" Delmont learns she has a younger brother in foster care, she is determined to put her life on track so they can be a family. A new city, a new job, and an excuse to run from her feelings for the man she will always want but can never have. It sounds like the perfect new beginning…until it's not.

When Jude "Ratchet" Azzo returns home and finds Ricca has taken off, he is ready to burn the world to the ground. Angry and frustrated and determined to have her, Ratchet pulls out all the stops to win her heart and to help Ricca bring her brother home.

If only it were that easy.

Dedication

This book is for anyone who has lived in darkness and found a way back to the light. Hold on tight and never give up.

Chapter 1

RICCA

"RATCHET?" I whisper into the silence of the room. No one responds in return. Shaking off the drum line pounding in my head from the night before, I outstretch my hand to the spot he had occupied next to me in the bed only hours before. The space now lies coolly unoccupied. My heart drops with disappointment while my body aches with each movement as I turn over to see what my hand discovered. He is gone. He left me here alone without so much as a goodbye.

Should I be surprised? No.

Was I hoping he'd stay after last night? Yes, but even I am not naïve enough to think that after giving into the lingering desire between us, he would stay once he had me. The conquest was over, and the magic of the chase had dissipated. I was no longer unattainable, and with that change in status, I was likely nothing more to him than one of those club whores who lived to serve on their knees. The fall from queen to whore stung, and even though he had never said those words directly, I could feel it in his absence.

I was nothing to him. Just like every other man in my life. I was a bargaining chip, a drug mule, and their whore. When the appeal was gone, so were they.

No man ever stays. I lived my entire life like the discarded newspaper from the day before. Tossed onto an empty park bench, waiting for someone else to come and pick me up. I came from nothing and remain that way thirty-three years later. Happy birthday to me.

Despite what I knew about him, I had hoped Ratchet was different. Maybe hope wasn't the best word to describe the situation I found myself in for the past year.

I *wanted* him to be different.

He was there at my lowest point. He was there when I screamed at the nightmares that spiraled into my mind, refusing to let me go. He was there when I pleaded for someone to just kill me and end it all. He was there, and now he is gone. No other man in my entire life had ever taken so much interest in me, which is why finding him gone the first time I truly let him in hurts so much. Knowing that I meant so little to him and that I didn't deserve enough to get a goodbye before he rode off into the sunset. Was there someone else? Did he ever care for me other than the desire to get between my legs?

The man who rescued me didn't see me the way I saw him, and it sliced me open from the inside out. What do you do when the person who you care about the most leaves you behind? The answer may not seem so simple for others, but for me, it's one that I have experienced more than once.

The answer is that you move on and never look back. Looking back only causes more heartache, and after a lifetime, you just become numb to the world that continues to shit on you. This time I won't forget my umbrella.

Shifting under the sheets, I force my legs to leave the warmth of the blankets covering my nakedness and move into the chilly morning. You'd think that living in a semi-desert climate, the cool morning air wouldn't be so shocking, but even years after taking California on as my second home, I am still not used to it. Back in Kentucky, this time of year is hot to where you'd be cemented to the sheets with sweat as soon as you woke up. Something that I don't miss at all.

Pushing through my soreness, I stand and pad to the bathroom, still hoping to find Ratchet.

I gave in to what we both wanted, and he left. He got what he wanted. Why would he need to come back?

I shake the doubtful words from my mind and

continue walking to the bathroom. Turning on the shower, my reflection in the mirror grabs my attention. I peer into the misty glass, not recognizing the woman I see before me. Years of abuse, drugs, and violence have taken away the glow from my cheeks and the brightness from my eyes, and my will to live after many restless nights of nightmares.

Most mornings, I wake up in terror, reliving the days I spent chained and gang raped by a man who I thought loved me and his crew. Those images flashing through my mind haunted me every night. Their hands touching me as I screamed out for help. The helplessness I felt as they each took their turn at my flesh. How the blades skimmed my skin and the metal from the shackles dug into my wrists as I fought. My soundless screams that reverberated from my swollen throat after days of begging for mercy. The images of them and their demented deeds forever burned into my mind.

Stop thinking about it. It will only bring more pain.

I shake my head to force those memories out of my head, but I know it's futile. They're always there. Within seconds, the panic sets in. My skin becomes clammy, while my stomach retches as my mind relives my time in hell.

"Oh, fuck," I exclaim before running to the toilet. I retch and heave up the alcohol and food I ate the night before until there is nothing left. Bile burns my throat, while my lungs restrict my airflow. Suddenly, the room spins as a panic attack brews.

"You're okay. They're dead and can't hurt you anymore," I mumble and repeat in some stupid fucking mantra to keep the memories at bay. Every morning starts like this. Sure, maybe I needed to go back to my victim group counseling sessions, but I knew the *Kum-ba-yah* mentality they used couldn't help me. The demons in my head were of my creation, and they were never just going to go away by telling others who thought they were like me about them. I couldn't forgive the men for the things that they did to my body, and even with their deaths, my mind could never see the world the same way. They took the last shred of innocence out in that desert, and it was something that I could never get back, even if I had ruby red slippers, clicked my heels, and said it three times.

Life isn't a fucking fairy tale. And no matter how hard I hoped he would be, Ratchet is not Prince Charming. The knight in shining armor isn't real, and he would never ride a white horse to my tower of terror and save me.

I will admit that, yes, he saved me physically that day, but mentally? Never. I've lived my entire life in hell, and that would never change. The only thing in my future was more self-induced pain.

Pain is such a funny word when you think about it. It can encompass a multitude of physical, mental, and emotional things in a person's life. For me, it is a word manifested so deeply into my soul that the lines between normal and tragic blur together.

Flushing the toilet, I step into the hot spray of the shower and into my place of solace. Call me crazy, but after living in shit my entire life, watching the water wash it all away, helped me find a momentary solitude of peace. It cleanses me and resets my brain for a few seconds, watching the filth of the world circling the drain between my feet.

I press my head against the cool stone wall, trying to shut off my mind. While the horrors of my past wash away, the self-doubt and shame replace it. I mentally tick away at the timeline of my life and shudder with each misstep.

My emotional dam breaks, and the tears flow heavily down my face. With each sob, my body weakens until I slip to the floor and just weep. I cry for the pain; I cry for the loss, and I cry for the future I know I don't have. Why would the future want me, anyway? I have nothing to give it in return except for the pleasure of maybe living in it. I would be a waste in its expanse. My dark thoughts continue until the world quietens once more, and the sound of the water soothes me into a state of semi-consciousness.

The water runs cold when a voice startles me back to the present.

"Ricca," a timid voice calls out from the other side of the door. "Are you in there?"

"Just a minute," I stammer out before forcing myself off the shower floor. Reaching to turn off the water, I exit and wrap my shivering body in a towel. I take a deep breath and plaster on my brave face before opening the door to find Dani on the other side. One thing that I have learned in my years is how to pretend that everything is okay. All it takes is a carefully mimicked smile and a shitty attitude.

"You okay?" she asks, trying her best not to pry, even though I'm sure she heard the emotional breakdown outside the door.

"Yeah, sure," I mumble, walking past her and heading for the closet.

"The guys headed out super early this morning, but I made breakfast if you want some," she utters with a hint of nervousness about her. How far we have fallen into our relationship? From roommates to enemies to this awkwardness displayed before me.

"Sure, I'll be out in just a minute. Just let me get dressed," I declare while stepping into the closet. My heart aches knowing that Ratchet left, but at least I can tell myself it was because of club business. Was it an excuse to mask the pain I am feeling? Yes, but anything to make the pain temporarily go away is what I need at this moment. Feelings hurt too much, and I just want to be numb again. Before, I had drugs to make them go away, but now that isn't an option for me. Sobriety has been a bitch to get, and I wasn't about to go back through that hell again.

I think of his brooding face when flashes of the night before the men arrived back at the clubhouse flicker in my brain.

Oh god.

Darcy. The poker game. Ratchet throwing my semi-nude body over his shoulder and carrying me into his room. The heat and passion between us as he fucked me against the wall of his room and in his bed after.

"You're mine, Ricca," he moans as he thrusts inside of me the first time. "This body. This cunt. All fucking mine."

Each memory shocks my system and leaves me breathless.

"Earth to Ricca," Dani chides from the doorway of the closet while snapping her fingers in front of my face. Shit, I didn't even notice she followed me in here. "Are you sure you're okay? You seem a little lost in space."

I plaster on a fake, reassuring smile, knowing that it's the quickest way to get rid of her.

"Yup, I'm right as rain." I smile. "Why don't you go throw whatever you made for breakfast on a plate for me, and I'll be out in a few."

She eyes me before turning and leaving. Dani knows something is amiss, but doesn't want to pry. This has become of our rocky relationship after I shoved her into this kind of life. She's here because of my stupidity. At least her story ended far happier than mine. She has a good man and two beautiful newborn daughters. I've got nothing to show for it except the scars that sting like terrible memories each time I trace their outlines on my skin. The cuts may only be superficial, but they lie far deeper inside of me.

As soon as the door clicks shut, I breathe for the first time. Every smile exhausts me, and I know sooner rather than later, Dani will see through me just like Ratchet did.

Slipping the towel from my body, I toss on a sports bra, hoodie, and a pair of the softest leggings I've ever felt with cute little sugar skulls on them. Walking from the closet, I grab the towel off the floor and dry my long, blonde hair. I make quick work of braiding it and start for the door when my cell phone rings.

"That's weird," I mutter to myself as it continues to ring. I pad over to the nightstand where my phone lays and unlock the screen. A familiar area code flashes as the ringtone continues to sing.

I slide my finger across the illuminated green button and take the call.

"Hello?"

"Hello," a feminine voice responds. "Is this a Miss Erica Delmont?"

"Yes, that's me," I stutter.

"I'm sorry if this is early, Miss Delmont, but I wasn't sure where you lived. My name is Elizabeth Brewer, and I am calling from the Hancock County Coroner's office."

My heart stops. No. No. No.

"I am sorry to have to do this over the phone, Miss Delmont, but your mother has died."

I freeze at her words and remain silent.

"Miss Delmont, are you still there? Did the connection drop?"

"Yes," I reply. "How?"

"Excuse me?" Elizabeth questions.

"How did my mother die?" I forcibly ask.

"An overdose."

Jesus. After all these years, she was still using. Not that it shocked me, but I had hoped after the ten years since I last saw her, she would have at least tried to clean up her act.

". . . your brother is too young to claim her body, so you will need to come in yourself to do that, Miss Delmont," the woman on the phone continues while my mind was wandering.

Wait. What did she just say?

"Can you repeat that?"

"Your brother legally cannot claim her body based on his age. We need you to do that."

"Did you say brother?" I retort. "I don't have a brother."

"Are you sure? I have an Asher Delmont, age eight, listed as next of kin along with yourself," Elizabeth says with a tone of annoyance.

"Are you sure you're talking to the right person?" I question back, confused. "Because the last time I checked, I was an only child."

"Miss Delmont, I'm sorry for the confusion during this troubling time, but the documents I was given regarding your mother's information lists yourself and Asher Delmont as next of kin. I understand you may not have known about your sibling, but we do really need to get the matter of claiming your mother's body settled."

"My fucking mother's body can wait," I snap. "Where is my brother? Is he with a relative?"

The sound of shuffling papers fills the receiver with static.

"That information is outside of my jurisdiction, Miss Delmont. I know this may all be a shock, but we need you here within the next seventy-two hours to claim the body. Can you do that?" Elizabeth asks with an aggravated tone to her voice.

"Yes," I declare before precipitously ending the call.

I stand in shock as I replay the conversation in my head. I have a brother. A brother who I've never met and do not know where he is. What if he was alone? What if they put him into the system, and I never get to meet him? But why do I care about someone I've never met? I have no emotional connection to this kid, but something is driving me to take action.

A sudden sense of urgency hits and strikes my core like a punch in the gut. I may not have been able to save myself, but he might just have a chance to be normal. Something that I was never afforded. I was never granted the chance to have a normal childhood of wonderment. Mine was nothing more than a hellacious period of physical and mental abuse.

My heart beats wildly as I make my decision.

I *need* to save him from the life I lived and to do that, I have to give up everything I have here, including Ratchet. As easily as he left me, he shouldn't be surprised when he finds me gone after he gets back.

My brother needs me, and unlike my mother, I won't leave him behind now that I know he exists.

Chapter 2

RATCHET

"YOU DONE BULLSHITTING ME?" I whisper into the ear of the semi-conscious man tied up in front of me. His hair is matted, while blood drips from the laceration above his eye and broken nose. Just a few short months ago, I would have called him my brother, but today the only word I could use to describe him is traitor. A traitor to our club and to those who lay dead because of guys like him.

He mumbles a garbled response, but it's completely unintelligible.

"What's that?" I antagonize. "You ready to tell me the truth, Hog?"

"Go to hell," he forces out just before spitting blood onto my black leather riding boots.

"Pushing my buttons isn't the best idea. You, of all people, should know that. You could make this so much easier on yourself if you just spit it out. There's no use in stalling since the result will be the same."

"Fuck *you!*" he screams.

It's the puff up my chest like I'm a total badass move that only makes me work harder for the truth. Maybe he thinks it will change my mind, but he'd be dead fucking wrong. When the shit hits the fan, I am the one who laces up my boots and wades in head first for my brothers. Maybe it's my lack of an emotional connection to the consequences of death or the fact that I have a strong stomach, but it's my job and one that I do well.

"Wrong fucking answer, asshole," I seethe. A demented smile forms on his face as my hand balls into a fist at my side.

Keep on taunting me, motherfucker. It'll only make the end more painful for you.

"Raze is a fucking pussy for sending you to do his dirty work while he plays house with that old lady cast-off," Hog fires back, seeming more coherent than before. "That's the difference between me and him. I can handle the dirty work myself. How do you feel about being the puppet of a coward?"

I laugh in his face, and he remains stagnant in his glare.

"A puppet? You were working for the fucking cartel,

Hog. The cartel that is dust in the Mexican wind. If anyone is the puppet, it's *you*. You chose money over your own fucking brothers."

Hog forces himself to lift his head, weak from the beatings and starvation over the last few days.

"The only loser here is you, Ratchet. First your sister, and now your woman. Been gone six months now, and I hear you haven't even tried to find her," Hog chides me as my blood boils. "Seems to me you'd be more careful with the women in your life."

It's one thing to spout off at the mouth in situational anger, but bringing my personal shit into this? That's crossing the fucking line. My sister made her choice, but Ricca is an entirely different story. A story that's been put on hold until I found Hog. He's the last fucking loose end, and his end is so near that I can taste his death on my tongue. As soon as he breathes his last ragged breath, she's my next target.

"I'm guessing from your silence that I hit a nerve," Hog continues to prod. "If you find that piece of Tribe ass, you should just hand her over to me. Even though she's been well used, I'd love to hear her scream underneath me."

Before his mouth can spew any more bullshit, my fist is in the air and connects with his temple. The impact knocks the fight out of him, and I hope he is just unconscious and not dead. The rising and falling of his chest tells me he's still breathing, which is perfect because I want him to feel every agonizing second of what's coming next.

"My sister and Ricca are none of your fucking business," I scream at him before pulling my knife from its sheath on my hip and plunging it right into his groin. He screams as I twist the knife, severing his favorite appendage from his body. Pulling my knife from his flesh, blood spurts as his cock and balls fall a little lower than normal.

"How does it feel to be spineless and dickless, Hog?"

He writhes and wails in pain as I smile, watching him suffer. His admission to knowing my personal issues only goes to show that he's been watching our group long after the Cartel's massacre. The wheels in my mind turn with the angles he could have been working to need such information, but with the bloody mess pooling between his legs, he doesn't have much time left.

"Last chance, Hog. Answer my question, and I'll let you die quickly."

"Go fuck yourself," he screams.

My chest heaves as the anger flows freely through my veins. He just doesn't know when to submit himself to his fate. At least a little information would have made this less painful for him. Well, if it had been someone else down here instead. I have a strict policy on how to handle disloyalty. Zero-fucking-tolerance. You fuck with my family? I fucking kill yours.

"You should have found a better place to hide, motherfucker," I call out to him, knowing he's watching my every move as I turn on my heels. Stalking to the table behind me where my tools lie at the ready, I grab the gas can and return to Hog, dousing him in the fuel. The can falls to the floor with a thud when I toss it aside, and he jumps from the sound.

"You don't have the balls, son. Why don't you call the dogs upstairs down and let them finish up for you? I can see it in your eyes that you don't have the stomach for this shit."

"Balls?" I respond. "Who are you to talk to me about balls when yours are dangling by a thread?"

He's wrong. Hog has always been one of the guys in our club who knew how to spew shit to stall for time. Granted, it was a skill we used from time to time in tough spots, but his usefulness died the moment one of his own named him as being with the cartel. That betrayal stamped his ticket to hell, and I'll be the ferryman to drop him off on Satan's doorstep like a pretty little gift basket. Well, except for the fact that he'll be a little bit less visually appealing, I'm sure that Satan will understand the mess I'm leaving him to deal with.

I pull out the gun seated in the holster at my hip and press the barrel to his forehead. He remains motionless when I pull back the hammer, my chest heaving in a mixture of anger and excitement. There's no denying that I am a sick motherfucker, but I'd wear that shit on a badge every day if it meant my brothers and their families were safe. Sometimes it's just easier to take the smudge of darkness onto my soul than to let those around me suffer in the weight of guilt from killing someone. Good thing for me that my conscience has never been something I cared about.

"Go to hell with the rest of your family, asshole," I declare, pulling the trigger and ending his miserable existence. The force of the shot sends his brain splattering against the wall behind him. Clumps of brain matter stick to every crevice of the wall behind him.

"No one has the right to question my loyalty," I scream at his corpse.

Stowing my firearm and retrieving the book of matches from my back pocket, I look at each one individually before selecting the last one in the pack. Striking its red tip against the grit, it ignites. I watch the red glow of the flame dance for just a second before tossing it onto Hog. His body illuminates as the flames spread, and when they finally reach his face, my body stills. It's at that moment peace fills me. When someone evil is wiped from this Earth at my hand. Some might call me an arsonist or a firebug, but until they've experienced what I have, they'll never truly understand what it means to watch the fire remake something so new again. Fire chars everything in its path, but even in the blackened soil, life can renew.

I only linger a moment before turning away from his now fully engulfed body and gather my tools. Quickly glancing back to make sure nothing is left behind, I leave him alone to burn for his crimes and ascend the stairs to my brothers waiting for me.

I can hear Hero's heavy boot steps pacing on the floor above, so I know time is running short.

"Here's Ratchet-y," Voodoo mimics one of the classic horror movies he's been forcing us all to watch lately as I hit the second floor. "Did someone have fun?"

"It's fucking work, Voodoo. Not fun," I bark back at him.

"Someone pissed in your cereal this morning. I figured you'd be in a better mood with Hog cooking downstairs. Oh!" Voodoo squeals. "Can we stop for BBQ on the way home?"

Voodoo has always had a screw loose, but I think all those hours in front of his computers are frying the brain cells he has left.

I glare at him as Hero takes long strides toward me.

"Is it done?" Hero asks, eyeing the blood on my shirt.

The smoke billows out from the basement below and pools around my feet.

"It's done, and we have about five minutes to clear out before we end up extra crispy like Hog."

Hero nods before turning back to the men with us.

"You heard the man. Time to ride."

Falling out behind Hero, we stalk to our bikes as the fire burns the first floor of the abandoned house we used for our interrogation. Sliding onto the cool metal of my Harley, I pop the kickstand and turn on the ignition. My bike rumbles to life as I turn to watch the flames just one more time before riding out with my brothers at my side.

As soon as we hit the road, the calmness I felt dissipates with each mile ticking away, bringing me closer to the clubhouse and to finding Ricca. I knew before I even opened the clubhouse door, after Mexico, that she was gone. Call it a hunch or intuition, but I just knew. For weeks, she hinted at leaving, so why should I be surprised that she took the first chance to bail? After what she'd been through, I couldn't blame her, but I still wanted to know why. Why she ran after our one night together? Why she waited until I finally broke down her walls to stomp all over the progress we'd made on her past issues? Why she couldn't give me a chance to help her learn to trust again?

All I wanted was a chance to prove to her that even though my monsters still lingered, they would play nice with hers. She could hide her emotions from her time in Twisted Tribe's dungeon, but she couldn't hide from me.

I could see through the façade and look beneath it to find the pain she had behind her beautifully haunted eyes. She was broken like me, and it only made my attraction to her stronger. Unlike other guys, I didn't want to fix her. I wanted her just as she was, a tattered soul that understands me.

But everything would be for nothing if I couldn't track her down again. Voodoo had been hot on her trails for months, while I forced myself to stay behind to clean up Maj's mess. Raze tried for weeks to make me go, but I wasn't the kind of man who walked away from their duties and let someone else pick up the slack. Even with that beast of a guy named Thor that Raze called up from another chapter, it wasn't enough to make me leave.

I still had a job to do, and no one else was going to take my place.

But with Hog on his way to hell, I was free to find her.

And come hell or high water, she will be mine.

Chapter 3

RICCA

I'LL ADMIT I've made a few mistakes in my life.

Who am I kidding?

My entire life has been one fuck up after another, with the blame solely falling onto my shoulders. Those horror stories you see on T.V. specials? Yeah, the kind of things that make you sick to your stomach reading about? I've lived them. Nightmares haunt every waking minute of my life. All because of my unquenchable thirst for bad boys and drugs to numb the pain.

Take my most recent fuck-up, for example. California was my chance to start over, but like usual, I ditched common sense for a hot guy and an endless supply of heroin. When I realized I was in too deep, I ended up in an even worse situation than before. A situation that I still force myself to forget every single fucking day.

But it wasn't always dark. I had some fun between

the shit storms, even if they were only temporary reprieves. Every time something good happened in my life, I would counteract it, just like now. I ran away from the first sliver of hope that I've ever had in my life. Granted, the feeling of hope laid back in California in the bed of a biker who grunted more than he ever communicated, but with him, I felt safe.

Too safe. I knew that my life would come crashing down like it always does. It's my fault. I am the person responsible for the scars, both mentally and physically, marring my body. I am also responsible for the bodies left behind in my wake.

My past may be lined with the ghosts of my mistakes, but unfortunately for me, my ghosts never seemed to stay in the shadows. No, mine liked to wait until the moment I found a piece of happiness before haunting me again.

Those ghosts are why I'm back in the cow shit corner of Willow Branch, Kentucky. Population fourteen hundred, if you count the livestock roaming around the hills. It doesn't even have a gas station or a post office, but we sure as shit had two local honky-tonk bars. It's just another typical old boomtown that was left to rot when the natural gas disappeared. It didn't help that it was filled with people who refuse to give up their country life to move to where the jobs are now.

To most, it was the perfect place to raise a family until

the day my white trash mother brought me into this world. My birth marked a black stain being smudged onto Willow Branch's perfect reputation. Well, at least for my parents. My momma wasn't exactly what you call a respectable woman, and having a daughter out of wedlock with the married local pastor didn't help cement her into the Saint Hall of Fame. Her actions and, of course, my birth broke up a wonderful family, which she blamed me for my entire life. Call it delusional or insane, but she was convinced that he would still want her. Little did she realize she was a play toy on the side for my religious father and that she could be wished away with atonement and prayer. It's almost ironic that I turned out to be just like her. Coming full circle, as you could say.

The images of her withered face on the day I claimed her body pop into my mind. Gone was the beauty she once was, and in its place was the face of a woman who lived a hardened, drug-addicted life. Her creamy, smooth skin had transformed into wrinkled leather. Her hair was all but gone, with patches of dark strands left sparingly over her head. Even her teeth were yellowed and broken into jagged pieces as if she chewed on glass every single day. The last ten years didn't do any favors for my mother. That was the last time I saw her before I relinquished her body to a pauper's funeral and walked away from her. This was never about coming back for her, anyway. My mission and goal were singular and sending her off in a grand fashion was never my intention from the moment they told me she died. After everything that she had done to me as a child, I couldn't stand by her side at the funeral as a mournful daughter. The tears I had for her had long dried up and wasting another minute in her presence wasn't something I had in mind to do any longer than necessary. I wanted it to be done and over. And that's what I did. Never wanting to look at her face again.

A bell dings, snapping me back to reality and the job that I was supposed to be doing.

"Table five's order is up," the cook yells from behind the counter. "Get moving, girl. I don't pay you to just stand around and be pretty," he snaps at me when I don't move fast enough for his liking. "Food's getting cold."

"I'm coming, asshole," I mutter under my breath.

"You say something?" he hollers back over the sound of clanking pans and dishes.

I plaster a fake smile on my face and shake my head no. I never thought I would say this, but this place is a downgrade from Red's back in Upland. Even as handsy as Red could be, Big Joe, the cook, smelled ten times worse and took every opportunity he could to corner me in the diner. He may consider himself a ladies' man, but I never wanted to catch myself downwind from him.

I grab the two hot plates of sandwiches and fries while still holding onto that fake smile. I turn on my heel and nearly run right into Susie, the other server working the lunch shift. This place is about as small a town as you can get, and a day doesn't go by where I don't collide with someone. The plates wobble in my hands but, thankfully, don't come crashing to the ground.

"Shit, sorry," Susie stutters. "I didn't realize that you hadn't seen me behind you."

"It's okay," I coolly utter back to her, sidestepping around her and walking toward the table of customers waiting for their food.

With only five tables and a bar top, we rarely see anyone other than the same locals day in and day out. I hated every minute I had to spend in this place, but small towns don't exactly have a booming job market. The choices and the pay were *very* limited. Between my day shift here and bartending at Wild Willie's at night, I was making enough to keep a roof over my head and food in my belly. The roof may be leaky, and the food isn't exactly gourmet, but I was still making it the best I could.

The two older men clap at my booth as I slide their plates onto their table like it's some major accomplishment. I force myself to not roll my eyes in lieu of losing the tip money I so desperately need. Joe's Diner isn't exactly a five-star restaurant, and neither is the pay, and I needed every penny I could earn.

"Close call there, darling," the man on the left teases. "You know," he says, while his eyes roam my body, "I could use a girl like you down at the construction office. What do you think, Jerry?"

His friend mimics his lingering look over my body and nods at his question.

"Sure do, Billy. I bet this filly here would be great at being a secretary."

The man I now know as Billy cocks a smile as his hand creeps across the table and straight for my ass. I step away from the table just before he touches me, and I smack his hand away.

"Oh, she's feisty," Billy laughs. "I like it when my secretaries play hard to get." He reaches toward me again, and I slap his hand away a second time. He recoils from the hit but only laughs while looking back at his friend.

"Come on, darling. We're just having a little fun with you," Jerry, the other man, chimes in. "Amuse a couple of old guys and give us a little show, will ya?"

"A show, huh?" I coo back while plotting my revenge. "What kind of show are you wanting, handsome?"

Fuck the tip money. No one has the right to touch me without my permission, and I, for damn sure, will not just walk away from these two dickheads. They need to be taught a lesson.

Both men smirk, but it's Billy who makes a move. He grabs hold of me and pulls me into the red vinyl booth next to him. My body tries to recoil, but I force myself to endure his touch, knowing what I am about to do to him. His arm slides around my shoulders, and his hand grazes the top of my breast over my uniform top. I cringe but keep the charade going because Billy is too fixated on my tits and doesn't notice my fingers sliding toward the switchblade I have strapped underneath my skirt.

"You're far too pretty of a girl to be waiting tables when you could work for a guy like me who'd appreciate your beauty more. How about you follow me out to my truck, and we'll have ourselves a little job interview?"

I innocently smile back before flicking open the blade with my fingers. The sound instantly draws his attention to my lap, and shock fills his eyes. I maneuver the blade ever so carefully toward his crotch and stop short of pressing it against his zipper.

"Touch me one more fucking time, and you'll be singing soprano the rest of your life. Do you understand me, Billy?" I press it harder against him, and he jerks at the pressure. A wicked smile forms across my face. I have his attention now. "Be a good boy and let me go because I am not the kind of bitch you want to mess with, old man," I whisper into his ear.

His arm peels away from my skin while his friend looks on in confusion. From his point of view, all he can see is his friend Billy feeling me up and me whispering softly in his ear. I remove the blade from his crotch and flip it closed before sliding it back underneath my skirt into its sheath. Sliding out from the booth, I stand and straighten my skirt to make sure the blade stays covered for the rest of the folks in the diner. His friend continues to look at us both, clueless.

"As kind of an offer as yours is, Billy, I think I am going to have to pass on that job interview." I sweetly smile back. "Can I get y'all anything else?" I add, playing along with the good southern girl charm. Billy remains silent, and Jerry shakes his head no.

I quickly turn from them both and head back to the countertop, where Susie stands, wiping off the bar. It shocks me how content Susie looks in this place, but I am bursting at the seams to get my brother and blow this popsicle stand again. It took less than a month here to remind me why I don't do small towns anymore. Men like Billy and Jerry were lurking around every corner because of my mother and her reputation. Being the bastard child of the town bicycle doesn't exactly paint me in a good light, and the assumptions that I followed her in her career path seem to run rampant in the small-town rumor mill. You'd think they would have run out of rumors to spread about me by now, but sure enough, new ones just keep popping up.

Ripping off my apron, I toss it to Susie as I pass behind her.

"Where are you going, Ricca?" she calls out after me, brushing her long, blonde hair out of her face.

"On break. I'll be back in fifteen minutes," I respond as I grab my jacket from under the counter and head toward the side door. Not even giving her a chance to respond, I am out of the door and into the early spring air. The brisk temperatures suck the air from my lungs as soon as I am away from the heated warmth of the diner. It's usually not this chilly during April, but as they say in the Midwest — if you don't like the weather, blink, and it will change. I'm just glad that it has snowed a little this year because I am not exactly equipped for that kind of thing after living in California for so long. I like the sun and not this cold, gray stuff that is the Midwest in the winter and early spring.

Quickly wrapping my jacket around my shivering body, I rub my hands together to generate more body heat. While most come out here to take a drag off of their cigarettes, I just want a moment to myself. The situation I found myself in with guys like Billy and Jerry has happened far more times than I would like to admit in my life, but now they snap me back to my time in the Tribe's dungeon of horrors. I kept my cool and somewhat of a level head this time, but from the moment I stepped foot outside, my heart began to race in the rumblings of a panic attack on the horizon. The façade of strength that I displayed is only surface glamor. I know how to put on a good show, how to fake my way out of a situation, but the inside of me is filled with fear and nerves. The tough girl part of me died in the desert, where the last shred of my innocence is buried. I emerged from that place a shell of my former self with the ability to play pretend when the situation calls for it.

Leaning against the cool brick of the diner, I close my eyes and focus on slowing down my breathing. The tension in my body slowly melts away over the course of a few minutes. I open my eyes to see the two men who caused this getting in their truck and eventually driving away.

While most would have reported the situation to the local police, I knew I couldn't. The need for a job and to keep my nose clean outweighed the need for justice for those two asshats who thought it was fine to proposition me. I just hoped that the next time they tried to pull something like this, someone much braver than me would turn them in or, worse, sic their boyfriend on them. I just had to wait for karma to come after them as it had for me.

The door next to me flies open with a loud bang, startling me.

"Jesus Christ!" I exclaim, jumping out of the way of the swinging door.

Joe's enormous frame appears in the doorway as he scowls at me.

"Break time's over, Erica. Get your ass back in here and do your job. Susie can't keep covering your tables."

I force myself to stow the one-finger salute I'd like to present to him. Joe may be my boss, but the day I finally get to quit, this joint will go down in history for the best "take your job and go fuck yourself" moment in the history of quitting. Shoving away from the wall, Joe doesn't move and forces me to squeeze past him in the doorway. My stomach roils as I do, but I keep my lunch down while mentally taking a note to wash my work clothes tonight. The greasy food smell is bad enough without adding Joe's unique aroma of body odor and three-day-old cheese into the mix. I doubt even bleach could help him smell clean.

I make my way back to the counter, stow my jacket, and don my apron before diving back into the daily grind of the lunch rush. A few short hours later, I wave goodbye to Susie and head home for a quick shower and change of clothes before heading off to Willie's for the night. At least there, my night of grabby men will come with a few shots of whiskey and a hangover that might help me sleep through the nightmare that is my life.

Chapter 4

RATCHET

IT'S BEEN days since I stamped Hog's ticket to hell, but here I am still at the Heaven's Rejects clubhouse and no closer to finding Ricca. For a woman who has a trail of bad choices behind her, she sure knows how to cover her tracks. To be honest, I thought for sure that she'd leave me some kind of breadcrumb to track her down, but she has always played her cards close to her chest when it comes to dishing out personal information. She was a constant fixture in my room for months before she even told me her middle name or how old she was. It might have been an odd arrangement when you looked at it from the outside, but it made sense to me. She needed protection, and from the first time I saw her at Red's, I knew she was like me.

Try as she did, I could see right through her well-practiced acting. She wasn't happy in her life, even before those Twisted Tribe fuckers took their hands and bodies to her. When I saw her chained to that table in their basement, I sighed in relief. Twisted as fuck, right? I knew she'd been put through hell, but in that instant, I knew she was also still alive. Broken, but still breathing. Feeling her weakened body as I carried her up out of the cesspool, I made a silent promise to myself to keep on protecting her, even if she didn't want me around. She wasn't the first person I'd had to extract from a dangerous situation, but the outcome for her would be different. She deserved a second chance that so many people never get, and it's on me to make sure that happens.

"Earth to Ratchet," Voodoo calls out. "Come in, Ratchet."

I sneer at him before taking another swig of my now-warm beer.

Jesus, how long was I lost in space that even my damn beer is warm.

Voodoo plops himself down next to me at the bar top and motions for Daisy. She smiles and bops her way over to the refrigerator, grabbing a beer and sliding it toward him. Voodoo twists the cap off and tosses it back toward Daisy, who just giggles from his attention. While most of the guys here take up with the free in-house recreation, it was never my thing. Before Ricca, I had a few girls outside the club that would be there when I was in the mood, but she changed all that for me. From the moment she leaned into me during her rescue, I was fucked. I'm not saying that I haven't looked at another woman since because, let's be honest, I have, but none has piqued my interest enough to make a move.

"So," he starts, dragging out his words, knowing that it annoys me.

"Spit it out, dipshit. I don't have all day for your theatrics," I gruffly fire back.

"Well now, someone's in a mood this morning, and to think I was going to share some good news with you," Voodoo chides.

I turn to face him as he takes a hit off his beer with a smile on his face. Voodoo has never been one that's good at keeping secrets, so just by looking at him, I know something is up. I just have to hope it's good news and not bad.

"You know where she is, don't you?" I intensely question without breaking my stare.

The fucker casually takes another drink of his beer before setting it back down on the bar top. His finger traces the lip of the bottle, stalling on his reply. I used to think his games were cute, but being on the receiving end of them, I'm not so sure that I like them anymore.

"You have about five more seconds to answer me, fucker, before I punch that smile right off of your face," I growl.

Voodoo flinches slightly but just keeps on smiling like a goddamn idiot. "Do you need Snickers, big guy? I bet one of the girls has some stashed around her somewhere. Want me to check?"

"You know," I say, "I used to like you. Hell, I even convinced the other guys to let your crazy ass into this club, but now I'm not so sure that I made the right call."

"Ohhhh," Voodoo teases, "delayed blackmail for information. You must really want to know what I have to say." He moves his hands to his face, cradling his chin like a child.

"Cut the bullshit, Voodoo, and just fucking tell me."

"Fine," he sighs with pretend exasperation. "I might have a lead on Ricca."

"You *might*? How in the fuck is that helpful?" I spit back.

"Might is far closer than we've ever been in the last few months, so beggars can't be choosers, ass face."

I know he's right, but I hoped he was going to be coming to me with more of a sure thing than a maybe that could lead me nowhere. We'd have enough dead ends in the search of her. Ricca knew how to hide her tracks even from Voodoo, but even I can admit, I still had hope that we could still locate her.

"What's the lead?" I question, hopefully.

He fingers the lip of his beer again before finally giving in.

"I know this will all sound like computer mumbo jumbo bullshit to you, but I'll tell you anyway because I don't think you appreciate my skills," he says while I impatiently look at him. He has a few seconds before I force the fucking information out of him, and my patience is about to run out.

"Anyway, I embedded a few illegal search alert notifications with her information into the system. It took hours of hard labor and beer, but I did it just for you, big boy."

"Today, Voodoo. Just get to the part where you might have found something instead of giving me the play-by-play of what you do in your electronic device playroom. I don't give a damn about that shit."

"As I was saying," he interjects with a growl, "I got a hit back, but it came from an unlikely source. An obituary dated several months back for a Deborah Delmont, age 52, from a small town in Kentucky."

"And some old broad's obituary leads me to Ricca how?"

"Well, that's the interesting part. Ricca has had a few aliases in the past, and I've honestly not been able to track down, which is her actual name until now. Listed under survivors for dear old Debbie was a daughter, Erica Delmont."

Could it be her? Deep down, I had to have known that Ricca wasn't using her real name, yet why should I have expected her to give me her real name if she had planned to run all along? It's not like I asked or expected her to be a fountain of truthfulness, for fuck's sake. She ran with a dangerous crowd, and lies were second nature to her before this club saved her ass.

"And you think she's Ricca?"

"I didn't at first until I found this."

Voodoo's hand slides from the bar top to his back pocket as a white piece of paper materializes. He slowly unfolds it and lays it out on the bar top for me. Lying before me is a copy of an old black-and-white photograph, from what I can only assume is a yearbook. I scan the faces in each square, and smack dab in the middle of the page. I see her. No longer a blonde, but even a different hair color couldn't hide the face I've studied far more than I care to admit while she slept in my room. Her crescent-shaped, dark eyes that hide the pain behind them, and her heart-shaped lips blare like a spotlight from the page.

"That's her, right?" Voodoo questions.

I stare a few seconds longer before I nod in agreement.

"Look at the name, Ratchet."

My eyes fall away from her beautiful face to the words written beneath the photograph.

"Erica Abigail Delmont," I read out loud. Fuck, at least she didn't lie to me about her middle name.

"The same name listed as a survivor in the obituary."

Relief rushes over me, knowing that for the first time in months, I may know where she is, and I'm one step closer to having her back in my life, or at least I hope she will be. Unlike any of the other women that have been in my life, Ricca understands the way I tick, and after the things I've done, that's not exactly easy to come by.

"Do you know where she is?"

"Like I said, it's a small town in Kentucky, but having confirmation that this is, in fact, her real name, it shouldn't take much longer for me to really pinpoint her location. Give me a few more days, and I'll drum up whatever I can. We'll find her brother, even if I have to sell what's left of my soul to the information black market devil himself. His name is Steve, by the way. Horrible guy. You'd probably like him, though."

Voodoo slides from his chair and heads back to his office with the photo in hand. I know he'll work his tech magic on finding out more information, but knowing her real name alongside the revelation of her mother's death has only opened a question can of worms. Jesus, was I that stupid to think that she was being upfront and honest with me? What else could she be hiding? A kid? A husband? The possibilities of betrayal could be endless, and here I am playing the lost puppy, seeking its old master, hoping maybe she is the girl for me. But lie or not, I will find her, even if it's just to make sure that she's okay in her new life away from me and the club.

With Voodoo working on finding out the information I need, I have only two things left to do. Talk to Raze about leaving and getting my ass on the road. The latter, I know, will take a few days, as Voodoo suggested, but I think it's time to put a check mark next to the first one right now. Pushing away from the bar, I stalk to Raze's office but find it empty. With his newly expanded family with Darcy at home, he didn't spend as much time here at the clubhouse as he used to when Maj was still around. Not that I blame him for trying to stay away from that crazy bitch that was his ex-wife. May the devil have no mercy on her fucking soul, but it would be fucking nice if he were around a bit more in times like this.

"You need something?" Hero asks from the doorway of his office. "I heard footsteps, and I thought it was Raze coming back from getting the boys from day camp."

"Day camp?" I question with a cocked brow.

"Never thought I'd hear Raze and day camp in the same sentence before, but hey, it is what it is as long as the man is happy in his new domestic arrangement," Hero says with a smile and a shrug of his shoulders. "Something up, Ratch?"

While I am almost certain the entire club knows about my situation with Ricca, Raze is the only one who knows the extent of my pursuit outside of Voodoo. While I normally don't hide a damn thing from my brothers, this is different. I may be a cold-hearted son of a bitch with club business, but having a weakness being paraded out for all of my brothers to see, isn't exactly my kind of party. It doesn't help the fact that Ricca played a part in Dani's near-fatal introduction into the Twisted Tribe world. Dani may have forgiven her, but I doubt Hero will ever follow suit.

"It's nothing. Just needed to talk to the Prez about some time off."

Hero cocks his eyebrow, waiting for me to elaborate.

"You going on a trip?" He questions me with a look of suspicion on his face.

"Something like that," I stammer slightly. "Raze and I had talked about it a few months back, but club business got in the way. Not sure how long I will be gone, but with that giant you picked up, I'm sure you'll have enough coverage for the club and the security teams. I just wanted to let him know I was going ahead with my plans, is all."

"How soon are you leaving?" Hero inquires further while analyzing my body language. For a military guy, he sure doesn't know how to hide what he's doing, but then again, he knows this isn't my typical behavior.

"A couple of days. Just waiting on a few more things to fall into place before I take off."

Hero looks me over one more time before he nods.

"I'll let the Prez know when he gets back. I hope the trip is worth the time off," he mumbles before heading back into the office.

"Me too," I mutter to myself. "Me too."

Turning on my heels, I head off to my room to pack for my trip. Between stuffing my saddlebags and checking my stash of cash, I debate with myself whether I am making a huge mistake by wasting so much energy on a woman who left as soon as my back was turned. As much as I want to admit defeat, I can't push the drive and will to find her out of my head. It's almost as if she is calling to me like a siren singing wayward boatmen to our deaths, but like them, I can't resist the chance of seeing her again.

To ask the one question that has been burning a hole in my heart since I realized she was gone.

Why?

Chapter 5

RICCA

"MS. DELMONT," the feminine voice says across from me. "Do you think you could elaborate on those thoughts you seem to be lost in?"

Shit. I forgot she was even here.

I take notice of Dr. Matthews as she eyes me, analyzing me like a lab rat in its cage.

"Sorry, Doc. I didn't realize that I wasn't speaking." I try to play it off with a chuckle and a shrug. "I've spent so much time on my own that I don't notice when I get stuck in my head."

Dr. Matthews forces a smile before lowering her face back down to the notebook she's jotting her thoughts down in on today's session. She brushes away her long, black curls from her face as she continues to scribble her notes. I watch her for a few seconds before I look around at the bright white of her crisp and clean office that screams she's a neat freak and lonely. She has book-shelves filled to the brim with large scientific-looking textbooks and diagrams of some sort of psychiatric mumbo jumbo bullshit. I bet if I looked more closely at her books, they'd have titles like *Ten Ways to Know You're a Psycho* or *Me, Myself, and My 1,000 Unique Personalities.*

Don't get me wrong, Dr. Matthews seems nice, but judging from her office and lack of any personal touches, I'm betting that she doesn't have much in the family's way and friends department in her life. Maybe she is hiding just like me, or maybe she's just a lonely cat lady in need of a vibrator. The possibilities for her chosen life-style are endless in my mind, and it's almost a game for me to think of some new scenario while I pretend to engage in our weekly sessions.

I never thought, in a million years, that I would find myself on the leather chaise lounge of a therapist's office, opening up about the demons hidden in my closet. Well, only the ones who could play nice, anyway. The other ones were locked away in their cages. Group therapy was one thing, but one on one with a certified therapist is a completely different animal. In a group, I could hide away in the background and not talk, but here it's only the two of us, and no talking isn't acceptable for what I am paying her.

Every time one of our sessions rolls around, it takes everything that I have to walk into these doors, but according to my brother's caseworker, I have to prove that I am a fit guardian. I just wish I had thought about that before digging my heels into the idea of trying to save him from the system. Come to find out, it isn't as easy as walking into the Child Services Office and filling out a form to claim him as my brother and bringing him home. Apparently, there's red tape and multiple hoops to jump through in order to even get to meet him. I don't know why I thought it would be as easy as claiming an item from the lost and found, but that goes to show how little I know about the decent part of the world. It's been months since I came back home, and I haven't sniffed at the opportunity to meet him thanks to my previous court records, lack of actual employment history, or permanent residence. It's not like I could put drug dealers and the Heaven's Rejects Clubhouse on my application, which has only added more shit to my to-do list.

Fucking bureaucratic rules.

She continues to write as I sit there like a bump on a log waiting for her next ridiculous question. Lord, I am already using country slang. I need to get out of here before I chew on a wheat stalk and wearing the latest Tractor Supply store clearance rack fashions. As much as this town loves its flannel shirts, wranglers, and cowboy boots — this girl does not.

Returning my gaze back to the good doctor, I can't help but wonder if I were to peek over her shoulder.

Would I find "She's certifiable" scribbled across the pages from our session today? I continue to watch her in the awkward silence of the room, but just when I think about making a break for it while she's distracted with her note-taking, she sets her pen down and returns her attention back to me.

Damn. I wonder how much longer my session is going to be today. It can't be more than a few minutes.

"Let's start with something easy, Erica. How was your week?" Dr. Matthews starts.

"My week?" I snort. "Same shit, different day. I work, and I try to sleep, Doc. Nothing too special about that."

Her brow furrows at my smart-ass response. I know she's trying to help, and I should be more cooperative, but I just don't feel comfortable enough with her yet. The fear that she will have me committed is always lurking in the back of my mind, and that will do nothing to help me with my goal of taking custody of my brother. These sessions are nothing but a check in the box to prove I am not crazy. Sure, it's a lie, but what they don't know won't hurt them. My only concern is crossing the state line with my brother in tow.

"Well, I see talking about your current emotional status isn't something you would like to do today, so let's try something else. Let's try a different approach. I'd really like to drive into what makes you, well, you."

"I'd rather not."

"I rather would." Dr. Matthews straightens up in her chair, drawing her notepad higher on her lap. "Tell me about your childhood? Was it happy?"

I snort again while she asks her absurd questions.

"Is something funny, Ms. Delmont?"

I shake my head, trying to curtail my laughter.

"You obviously aren't from around here, Doc," I tease, straightening myself up on the leather sofa across from her. "Do you want the full version or the Cliffs' notes?"

Her eyes narrow. "What's the difference?"

"About two days and a bottomless bottle of whiskey," I fire back while she frowns at me. "Okay, judging from that look of yours, you want the short version," I declare before inhaling a deep breath.

"Mom was a whore. Dad ignores my existence. I grew up in a trailer park here in town, probably not a surprise there, while my momma whored herself out. From the time I was nine, I did odd jobs around the trailer park to keep food in my belly before my momma decided my body was better served in her line of work. Men like them young, or so she liked to say."

Dr. Matthews sucks in a deep breath and looks on in horror. No doubt the imagery from my personal hell is filling her mind.

"Your mother forced you into sleeping with men for money?" she questions. "How old were you?"

"Thirteen. It was sell my body or starve to death on the streets," I coolly reply while forcing those memories back into the dungeon. I try to lock them down in. "And before you ask, I went to the police, but it was already too late for me."

"Too late for what?" she questions.

"Why would they believe the daughter of the town slut when she comes to beg for help? Not that half the police force was on my mom's clientele list. If I took her down, they'd go do with her. What would their wives and families think?"

"But, Ms. Delmont, you can't possibly believe that's true. How could they not protect a child?" The horror on her face no longer hiding.

"The truth is simple, Doc. The rumor mills run this town. Everyone knows everyone else's business, and as long as that business stays away from their family life, it's fine. When it doesn't, well, it's never their fault. Women like my mom were always the problem. Never their cheating or abusive husbands."

"But, I–," she blurts out before the timer on her phone chimes.

Saved by the damn bell.

"Sorry, Doc. I'm going to be late for my shift."

I dart from my chair, fling open her office door, and bolt before she could even dismiss me. It's not because I don't like Dr. Matthews, but spilling my soul out to a complete stranger leaves me rattled by the time our sessions were over. I've sat in her office three times a week for the past two months, and I don't feel anywhere close to finding absolution for my past.

I shut the door to her office building behind me, taking in my first deep breath since starting my session with her. Talking about this shit is supposed to give you peace, but it only makes my anxiety even worse. Had this not been a strong suggestion from my caseworker, I doubt I would have ever stepped foot in her office, but I need to see this through. Not for me. Not for closure. But for the life I am trying to save.

I rush to my ride, throwing open the door and sliding into the worn leather seat. I knew the day I left the clubhouse that taking the car that the club had provided for me wasn't an option. It could be reported as stolen, and I didn't want the heat from the club on my ass while I tried to take care of my family business. So I took a page out of Dani's escape plan playbook and bused it to Kentucky instead. No way for them to track me down, and it bought me more time to handle things on my own.

This beat-up pickup truck may not be easy on the eyes, but it gets me where I need to go, and it doesn't hurt that it came at the right price. Free thanks to some schmuck who my mother probably conned it out of for the pleasure of her company. Even now, after looking through the pictures she had in her trailer, I couldn't understand her appeal to the men of the town. They all knew what kind of woman she was, so either these men were desperate or just plain fucking stupid. But hey, I have a free ride, thanks to her. Herby, as I have named him, isn't exactly fuel efficient, but broke bitches can't be choosy in my position.

The biggest hurdle I had once I got here was finding a place to stay, but thankfully for me, my mother left me yet another gift. Her trashed as fuck trailer. It took a lot of cleaning, but it was finally livable. I'll be honest when I say that I was shocked to find out that she actually owned that piece of shit on wheels since she never seemed to own a single thing in her entire life, but it was a welcome surprise. I know in the long run; it was just a temporary solution, but until I could afford something better, it's what I called home.

Turning the key in the ignition, I let the engine creak and grumble like an old man. Saying a silent prayer for the damn thing to turn over on the first attempt — it actually does. I pull away from the curb and cruise down the tiny streets of my hometown. This place hasn't changed a bit since the day I turned my back on this part of my life for a fresh start. I should have known then that no place was ever going to feel like home for me, but I was young and naïve enough to believe that happy endings really existed.

My destination is the same every weekday around

this time. A place where my heart breaks more and more with each passing day. My truck dies as soon as I pull into the secluded spot of the parking lot just before the school bell rings. Kids pour out of the doors like the place is on fire, but it's one child I am looking for amongst the crowd. It doesn't take long until his mop of curly, dark hair comes into view. My brother Asher steps out of the front door of the school, chatting with another kid. The moment I set my eyes on him, I knew he was my brother. His smile lights up the moment he is free from the confines of the school day, just like mine did at his age. I've spent the last few months studying his face from afar, and each day I notice another similarity between us.

His face turns to the sunny sky and soaks up the rays before a horn interrupts his propitious moment. His smile instantly fades as a black town car pulls up to the curb and honks. I watch as a tall man exits the vehicle and greets him before ushering him back to the car.

His guardian and my father, Ronald Boatman. His hardened, wrinkled face has not changed since the last time I saw him. I was an abomination to him, and the thought of him being the foster parent to my brother only strengthened my resolve to get him back. Even after my mother publicly outed him as my father, he continued to shun my existence and me, like I was a figment of his imagination. Pray as he might, his blood was in my veins. Unfortunately for my mother, she didn't have the strength or the will to fight him for child support when the state already paid a handsome sum to her as a single mother on welfare.

By the time I could take care of myself, she saw me to get more money from the state and through charitable groups. I was just a burden to her that came with paycheck perks, food, and gifts around the holidays. Even now, I don't think she saw me as her daughter, but as a hindrance to her lifestyle. What man would want to slut it up with her when there was a child in the house? There were only so many times a kid could watch the same cartoon VHS tape before getting bored and wandering into her room while she was in a compromising position with her latest financial mark. After that, my new "uncles" stopped coming by, and my mother disappeared for long periods of time. Hours turned to days and then two weeks before I learned to just fend for myself. Well, until I became attractive to men, and I could earn my keep by lying on my back.

The way my skin crawled as they touched me. The vile words slipped from their mouths as they tried to sweet-talk me into giving them possession of my body. And the sheer utter fear of not being left alive the next time while also wishing for death every single night those men came for me. Obviously, I wasn't in a mentally stable place. Visions of those horrors flash through my mind before the honking of the horn brings me crashing back into reality.

I watch as my father ushers my little brother roughly into the waiting car. He slides out of view, and my emotional dam shatters as heavy tears streak down my face while the town car pulls away. The one person in the world who never wanted me, his own daughter, now has the one thing I want most in the world, my brother. The world has a funny way of dishing out a sick and twisted sense of irony.

I thought my mother had only made one mistake in her life, but I couldn't be more wrong. She may have set me on a path of self-destruction, but I'll be damned if I let the same thing happen to my brother.

One day soon, he won't have to go home with that monster.

It may not seem possible now, but that day will come.

Chapter 6

RATCHET

AFTER TWO DAYS of waiting for Voodoo to work his computer wizardry, I finally got to hit the road heading to Ricca. Most men would have taken the fastest route possible, like a plane, for a matter such as this, but I needed time.

Time to think.

Time to plan.

Time to figure out what the fuck I was going to do if I found her.

Voodoo's information tracked her down to a small town just inside the Kentucky/Indiana state line, but who knows if she is even still there? It's been months since she took off, and this could all be some wild goose chase. I couldn't sit by and wait to see if she would come back to the club and to me. I owed it to myself to at least try.

The club may have saved her life and sheltered her, but she knew a debt like that could never be paid back. As a man, that is something that I would never ask of her, and neither would the club. It's not a minor task to bring someone back from the brink of death and get them back on their feet again. I know what it feels like to be lost, hungry, and broken. There's no coming back from that kind of pain and leading a normal life. There wasn't for me, anyway.

Our clubhouse was the only place she could find solace in her past, and she knew that, but she still ran. While I had hoped that her mother's death might be the cause, I wouldn't allow myself to explain it away so easily. She has her demons, and I knew that going into whatever this is between us. It had always been a flight-risk relationship, but I stupidly thought after she'd been there a year that it would never happen — until it did. Assuming she felt safe with the club and I got me nowhere until now. Her running fueled the fire inside of me again and gave me a purpose. Find the answers to my questions and try to reach her again. Long shot as it may be, I had to at least try one more time — for her sake and my own.

The plains of the Midwest zoom by as I ride Route 66 toward Kentucky. The ride was smooth with decent weather, but Mother Nature was about to give me the finger. The blinding sun, when I started my day on the road, quickly faded into storm clouds. I rode for a few miles and watched the lightning in my path strike the ground, one hit after another. With the way this morning had started out, I had hoped to make it to Kentucky before sundown, but the storm ahead was about to rain on my fucking progress for the day.

Realizing that the storm to the east of me would not play nice and move out of the way, I pull off onto the roadside and grab my rain gear from the saddlebags. I unbuckle my helmet and lay it on the seat of my bike. Tossing the raincoat over my head, I feel large, wet drops pinging off the metal of my bike and hear them sizzle from the heat of the running engine.

Shit. I need to move faster.

The rain grows in intensity as I pull off my boots and slip on the rain pants over my jeans. I replace my boots, but my socks are already soaked. That fact alone is going to make this last leg of the trip less enjoyable. Not like arriving at my destination could be called "enjoyable," especially if I walk into the fiery storm of a pissed-off Ricca. Honestly, the odds were twenty percent for her not trying to clock me for tracking her down, but hey, I'm a betting man. I'll take what I can get.

Thunder claps as I strap on my helmet and mount my bike.

"Shut the fuck up, Mother Nature. I don't need a damn reminder of what shitstorm I am riding into. I already know," I mumble under my breath as the thunder rumbles through the air again. "I already fucking know."

I pop my kickstand and head straight into the storm, cussing the entire way.

Hours later, a tiny road sign with white letters gives me the first sign of hope that I am getting closer to my destination.

"Ten more miles to go," I say to myself. "Ten more miles to see if she kicks or kisses my ass for showing up here."

The sun has long since fallen, and the darkness of night settles into the quiet of the country road that I travel on. It's been miles since I've seen a single house or gas station. It's a reminder of how stupid I might be for even trying to do this. The only person who would run to a place like this is someone who doesn't want to be found. Am I making a fucking mistake by driving all this way to see her? Self-doubt creeps in just as the illumination of a small town comes over the hilly horizon. As the lights grow brighter and closer, my heart races.

Calm the fuck down. You don't even get this jittery when you're killing some dumbass motherfucker.

I force myself to shake whatever the hell is going on with me off just as I enter the small town. Tiny houses and trailers are alternating on either side of the streets without a soul to be found outside. The rumble of my bike's engine echoes off the dark houses as I pass by.

Shit. Does anyone even live here anymore? This place looks like a fucking ghost town.

Passing a few more dark streets, I finally see signs of life. There are neon signs of two neighboring bars flashing ahead. I pull into the conjoined parking lot and kill the engine of my bike. The parking lot is nearly half full, which would explain the lack of people roaming around town at this time of night. I mean, shit, just because it's ten o'clock at night doesn't mean that it's time to roll up the sidewalks and roads until the next day. I can't even imagine Ricca staying in a place like this. Then again, the two bars gave her options, at least.

In the year or more that I have known her, she's been a night owl. Rarely did I ever come back to my room and find her asleep before three o'clock in the morning. Hell, half the time, it was almost dawn before she settled down. She would get so pissed at me when I'd purposely make noise to wake her up, but it was a part of the fun I liked to have with her. Ricca would scrunch up her eyes as soon as I turned the light on and huff at me. Even pissed off, she was still beautiful, sprawled out in my bed. Her long, blonde hair used to fan over to my side of the bed, and just having time to smell her on my pillow was enough for me while she healed. I took the chances she gave me, and this time I had a game of chance to play myself.

Taking off my helmet, I survey the two bars, trying to decide which one to try my luck with. She worked in a bar the first time I saw her, so I imagine she would try her luck here in the way of getting a job again. It was a fifty-fifty chance, but at least I could try again if I guessed wrong.

The first bar on the left looks like something out of the old west. Weathered wood paneling exterior with oddly painted green shutters lining its windows. The bright red neon sign spells out *Rusty's* over the wooden door. Judging by the look of the place, it's the local old-timer's bar, which I confirm as two older men stumble out of the front door with an older male bartender hot on their heels.

"Get your asses back here," the bartender twangs. "Y'all haven't paid your tab, and you, for damn sure, aren't driving home in that condition." I watch closely as the bartender catches up to the men and snatches the keys away from one of them.

"Your wives would skin my hide if I let you out on the streets like this. Y'all come inside, and I'll call Missy to come get you."

The men obey and follow him inside as I turn my attention to the other bar.

Wild Willie's, according to the sign, and it was about

as opposite as you could get to Rusty's. Instead of a wood panel, this one was obviously the newer establishment, with brick walls and LED lights shining from every single windowpane in the place. The people I watch over several minutes, coming in and out of the place to smoke, seem younger. I look between the places before I make the call and dismount from my bike.

Wild Willie's it is.

Removing my rain gear, I tuck everything back into my saddlebags and flick the lock closed, just in case. This might not be the big city, but shit still gets stolen in small towns. Stepping away from my bike, I head toward the bar. Music slowly pours from the place and hits me like a brick wall once I step inside. The room vibrates from the sounds pumping from the speakers on the ceiling. Black plastic booths and tables line the room, with the bar top seating toward the back of the place. I start toward the crowded bar top when a server in cut-off jean shorts, a white wife beater that strains against her big tits, and a red flannel shirt steps into my view, blocking me from scanning the place for Ricca.

"Hey there, sugar," she coos, with a slight southern accent. "You eating or drinking tonight?"

"Both," I coarsely answer. It's been a long day on the road, and I need to eat and relax before I try to find a place to crash for the night.

"Well then, let's get you settled at a table and get you

whatever you need," she flirts back while looking me up and down.

Big Tits leads me to an empty booth and slaps down the plastic-covered menu on the tabletop as I sit down.

"Now, my name's Brenda, sugar, and I will serve you whatever your heart desires tonight," she says while popping her hand onto her hip. "You go on and look at that menu. If you see nothing you like, you just let me know. I'm sure I can find something to satisfy a guy like you."

I force a smirk on my face, but it's as fake as her tits. Don't get me wrong. She's got a nice rack, but a quick fuck on the side isn't what revs my engine anymore. If this had been any other time before Ricca fucked with my head, I'd have already shoved her to her knees and given her what she seems to dead set on running from. Unfortunately, strange pussy was permanently off my menu, and no matter how hard she tries, it's never going to fucking happen. Ricca had invaded my mind, and with her invasion, it had put me off other women until I knew where we stood. Even my dick settled for my hand without her there. It was a one-pussy man on principle until Ricca told me otherwise. Call it pussy whipped or being soft, but the time she was with me opened my eyes to the possibility that one-night stands weren't all that special. The excitement fades, and so does the impulse.

"Hey, Brenda," someone from the bar top calls out. "Order's up."

"Shit," she mutters. "I'll be right back."

As she walks away, I almost audibly sigh in relief that the one-sided flirting is over for now. I glance at the menu in front of me and randomly pick out the greasy spoon meal that will fill my belly tonight.

Brenda roams the room with a tray in her hand before coming back over to me.

"You find something that will tickle your fancy?" She smiles.

"Cheeseburger with everything on it, fries, and two bottles of Budweiser," I stoically respond.

"That it?" she hopefully questions.

"That's about all I see in front of me I want," I retort. "Make it to-go on the food."

"Okay," she stutters before walking away, stunned at my crassness, but her hurt feelings don't matter one lick to me. I'm here for food, a cold beer, and maybe some hints about Ricca's whereabouts.

Brenda stops back by with my beers, but she ignores my presence completely, reading my lack of interest in her loud and clear.

I take a swig of my brew, and the cool liquid hits the spot. It's been a long couple of days on the road, and this is the first time that I've stopped for more than a piss or a quick meal. A few more swigs later, a commotion damn near silences the room as glass shatters, followed by shouting. I see people sitting around sliding out of their booths toward the noise. I crane my neck around the corner of the booth to see the fight happening near the bar top, but there's a crowd gathered around them.

"I said hands off, motherfucker," a woman's voice cuts through the room. "No means fucking no."

"Come on, doll face, I was just playing around," a man slurs, noticeably drunk by the sound of his voice. "I just wanting to see what she's got hiding under that shirt of hers."

"And I'd like to see what's inside that brain of yours, Johnny. You've been warned before to keep your damn hands to yourself. Didn't your mama teach you any manners?"

"Willie," the woman screams, "get your fucking ass out here, and get this piece of shit off my barstool."

Heavy footsteps belonging to a large man move past me and toward the crowd that parts for him. He emerges with a man horse-collared under his arm who struggles to break free.

"I's not drunk, Willie," he chortles. "That bitch made it all up. Her momma was a whore, and so is she. You can't fault a man for trying to get a free sample."

Willie growls and cuts off the man's air even more.

"Johnny Monroe," he bellows, "if you show your

damn hide in this bar again, I'll let her have a shot at you. Pretty face or not, she'll knock your ass into next Tuesday."

He protests as a siren wails from outside the building.

"Deputy McDaniel is waiting for you outside. Time for you to sober up, son."

Johnny struggles as Willie releases him and shoves him out the door. The flashing blue and red lights of the local police reflect off the front door glass as they barrel into the parking.

The bar owner watches as the officer takes Johnny into custody and then stomps back up to the bar as the crowd disperses. My eyes follow Willie as he approaches a brunette from behind the bar. I watch as his arm slides around her shoulders, and I instantly tense at the sight of him touching the woman.

Why the fuck am I reacting this way to a man comforting one of his employees?

The longer he has his arm around her, the more the tension builds in my body. Her face remains hidden as another female bartender joins them in the huddle, comforting her. It couldn't be her. Could it?

My heart stops when I realize the source of my tension as the brunette turns around and reveals a familiar face.

Ricca.

My body instantly freezes into place, unwilling to move in case this is all a daydream. Months apart, and her presence still affects me like she'd never left. Her crescent-shaped brown eyes have haunted my every dream. The perfectly placed curves of her body. Even the scars that dotted her skin like battle scars screamed out for me to kiss each one of them. She was my everything back when I could call her mine. My beautifully damaged creature. My siren.

Every night I felt her calling to me. Screaming for me to find her. Begging to come to her. Yes, I know that thought is fucking bat shit crazy, but I know what I felt. It's hard to describe something that has never existed until she walked into my life. Walked being a relative term that could describe her. Ricca was more like a delicate flower with thorns. Delicate and beautiful until the need to strike hit her. If you brushed her petals the right way, she was soft and loving. But brush them the wrong way, and she would leave you bleeding and writhing in pain. She was the embodiment of a vengeful goddess, and she was mine.

My eyes stay on her, watching her every move and every touch she is given by her boss. A low growl settles into my throat as the scene plays out before me. It took me months to get where he is now. Maybe this was a bad idea after all. I get up and walk away, but she skirts around the edge of the bar and finally gives me a full glimpse of her. It's at that moment that I know, no matter how hard she pushes, that I'll never leave. Not without seeing her first.

Years of abuse and fighting to stay alive dulled her radiance. Yet here, she shines like the face of the sun on the longest day of the year. Her hair has remained long, beautiful threads, but its light blonde color has now been replaced with a chocolate brown, which, thanks to Voodoo, I now know to be her natural color. The shade of her hair has never mattered more to me than it does at this moment. The dark color encircles her face like an angel's halo, and I love it. Her face is natural and lacks the war paint that most women cling to hide their flaws. The make-up she wore back in California was her own version of camouflage. It hid her pain, but no matter how much she wore, I still saw through it. She didn't need it, and seeing her like this was like learning to breathe again after someone stole your breath away.

The lean tone of her body has been replaced by even more beautiful curves. Her hips are more rounded, and her perfect ass teases me as she sashays back behind the bar. The tight jeans she looks to have painted on sends my hardening cock rubbing deeper into my zipper. I try to adjust myself, but even I know it will not diffuse the critical mass situation happening below. As much as I want to rush to her and fuck her back into her senses for leaving me, I stay. She may not even be mine anymore.

Jealously coils inside of me when a dark thought flourishes in my mind. Did she need to leave me to find herself again? Did this place bring her shine back? How could I take her away from this place if she's happy here? Question after question fills my head, rooting the seed of doubt further.

Every bone in my body screams at me to go to her, but I force myself to wait to see if she senses me here. The last thing I want to do is to scare her off. Patience may not be a virtue of mine, but I need to take this slowly. I watch her intently as she shivers from the touch of her boss, which I know made her uncomfortable, and my reaction suddenly makes sense. While the surrounding others may not have noticed it, I did. I spent months observing her and making a note of the little things about her, just like her aversion to the touch of anyone outside her circle of trust. And trust me, it's lonely in that circle because until she took off, I believe I was the lone male member in the group alongside Dani. It took months for Ricca to be comfortable with me staying in the same room with her after her time with Twisted Tribe. Those fuckers tried to leave her for dead, but she wasn't meant to die in that basement. Anger courses in my veins just thinking about how she looked when I found her. Blood soaked everything, and her skin was more bruised than the beautiful tanned hues she sports now. How she survived, I will never know. She slept in my bed while I took the ratty couch I had dragged in from one of the outer garages. It wasn't exactly comfortable with the spring that dug into my back, but she needed space and time to heal. It was the least I could do to give that to her.

Her eyes remain downcast as she pours a draft beer into a glass for the customer to her left. She slides the glass with ease across the bar top before motioning to the other bartender. She mutters something to her as she flips up the counter of the bar and walks out from behind it. She walks away but stops. For the first time since I spotted her, her eyes lift to take in the room, almost as if she was searching for someone in the crowd. She stands still for nearly a minute before shaking her head in likely disbelief. With one last look around, she stalks out of the side exit, giving me my opportunity.

Tossing a twenty-dollar bill down on the table for Brenda, I slide from the booth. My stomach grumbles in a mix of protest from the lack of food and nerves, but food isn't what will satisfy me now that I've finally found her. She is what I've hungered for the last six months and will be the only thing that satisfies the gnawing pain inside of me.

It's now or never Ratchet. Take it slow and let's see how things go.

I stalk toward the side door she escaped from and open it quietly. I look to the left and find no one, but when I turn right, I see her profile illuminated in the dark by a neon sign above her head. The quiet creak of the door closing behind me doesn't startle her. I take a deep breath before I move a few steps closer. Her tall and curvy form leans caressed by the night against the wall. Had I known it was her who was touched without permission, Johnny Boy wouldn't have walked out of this place. No man deserved to touch her smooth skin. Even me, but for some reason, she allowed me into her world for just a split second.

I watch as her chest heaves up and down in a panicked reaction from her encounter in the bar, like I had seen so many times before during her recovery process at the clubhouse. Even the slightest touch or accidental brush from one of my brothers would send her into a panic attack. At first, it killed me to watch her attacks as a spectator, but as she let me in, I became a source of comfort for her. Seeing her like this again, my body riots for me to jump in and soothe her.

Just do it, pussy. Pull the Band-Aid off, and talk to her.

Shrouded in darkness, I approach her, but she hears me, and her head snaps in my direction.

There goes quietly approaching her. Smooth move, asshat.

"Johnny, if that's you, your ass better get to stepping

the fuck on out of here. Willie will kill you if you darken his door again."

"Johnny boy won't be bothering you anymore, Siren."

Her body tenses and her eyes grow wide before she gasps.

Chapter 7

RICCA

"RATCHET," I squeak, staring in disbelief that he is even here. The sound of blood rushing through my body fills my ears, deafening me until I get my nerves under control. My biggest regret that I left behind in California is here, looking like he wants to devour me whole.

"Siren," he coolly responds, stepping into the light radiating from the bar windows.

My heart races like a runaway train, about to derail, as reality sets in that he's really here in front of me. This isn't a dream or a hallucination. He stands before me, and I honestly do not know what to do. Do I run? Do I jump in his arms? Do I do both at the same time? Indecision and excitement battle inside me, freezing me in place. How could one man have so much hold on me?

That question was easy enough to ask, but our past was as complicated as our present state of affairs. He was the man that didn't even realize how much I cared about him before he left. He held the keys to my heart and never cared to even use them. I wanted to be his, but that was just a broken dream left behind in California.

He's the man who drives a woman crazy from trying to figure out the way his brain ticks. Just like now, my heart and my mind are at war on whether to be angry or ecstatic to see him again, like two families facing each other on the battlefield. Neither side will win the war without losing something in return.

The panic attack from my boss, Willie, trying to comfort me doesn't even compare to the cyclone of emotions coiling inside of my body. Part of me is jumping for joy inside, knowing that he tracked me down, but the dark side of my mind is filling my head with doubt and suspicion.

He's here to take you back to work off your debts to the club.

You don't know his intentions or his reasons.

He's here to kill you for betraying him and just leaving.

Give him the benefit of the doubt. He'd never do that to me.

You're naïve enough to believe that night meant something to him.

Stop listening to the devil on your shoulder for once.

Listening to me is the only way you'll survive.

My eyes stay trained on him as he shifts closer to me.

With each step he takes, a warmth flows over my body in response to his being so near. It isn't until he's face to face with me I can finally break free of my stunned muteness. His massive body shrouds mine like a child compared to a full-grown adult. He's always been bigger than me, but now I can feel every inch he has on me. It's nerve-wracking and exhilarating all at the same time. His expansive chest has grown since the last time I saw him, and his defined arms look like sculpted cords of smooth marble. If I had to bet, the gym had become his new best friend in my absence. While I've never known him to have a full beard, his chin sports a thicker-than-normal layer of hair. His dark hair is cut close to his scalp, but it's his eyes that freeze me into place. Their dark, brown hues bore into my soul with every passing second, and right now, they are trained on me.

Fucking asshole. I leave him, and he gets even better looking. Resist him, Ricca. This isn't the time or place for this.

"Why are you here?" I blurt out, not knowing what else to say to him.

Smooth, Ricca. It's been months since you've seen the man, and you're acting like a fucking teenage girl talking to her first crush. Dismiss him. Don't encourage him to show weakness. You're not a wounded deer, for Christ's sake.

"I'm here for *you*," he intently declares. His hands move toward me, but I recoil, trying to keep the distance between us. I waver as my body tries to force me to move closer to him, and he catches it. After everything that has happened, my body still betrays me. Ratchet takes his chance and moves closer. The smell of his woodsy cologne driving me to snuggle deeper into him. To bury myself in his warmth and stay there where I know am safe. A slow-motion version of a prey and predator dance before the predator charges in for the kill.

I try to step away from him, but my back lands against the wall. Ratchet moves to catch me as I fall backward, but I shirk away from his touch again. My eyes widen as I see him flinch at my rejection.

"Please stop," I protest his closeness. "Please, Ratchet. Not so close."

"Siren, I—" he starts before I bring my hand between us, stopping the conversation from where I think it's going. I can't hear this right now. I have a purpose for being here, and not even he can distract me. My focus needs to be on Asher, and Ratchet being here will only complicate things even more.

"You can't be here. You aren't supposed to be here," I stammer out, knowing that I sound so fucking stupid, repeating myself. It's as if my mouth and brain are refusing to work together to make a coherent argument out of shock. If I could mentally face-palm myself, I would have already done it.

Ratchet cocks an eyebrow and, in a flash, slaps one of his hands next to my head on the brick wall. The impact sucks all the breath out of my lungs, making me yelp. I know this wasn't a move on his part to hurt me. He's not the man who would ever lay a hand on a woman. It was a move to garner my full attention and nothing more. An alpha male shock and awe campaign to stun me into submission. Too bad for him. His presence alone took care of that for him.

"Not a good time, Siren?" he quips with a hint of annoyance in his words. "When would have been a good time? Would that have been before or after I came back from handling club business to find you fucking vanished from the clubhouse? No note. Not a fucking clue why you left. Just gone."

I try to dodge away from him, but he presses his chest into mine, trapping me where I stand. My erect nipples graze against his chest, and I shiver from the contact. He smirks when he notices. The fucker knows my body is reacting to him being here, and he is playing it to his advantage. Of all the people who know how to play dirty, Ratchet is the master, and I am his willing puppet.

"I left?" I argue. "I wasn't the first person to leave. That was *you.*"

"Jesus, Ricca. Is that what you think I did? That I left you," he hisses. "I had club business, and I thought you understood that comes first. It will *always* come first."

His hot breath trails down my neck as his lips move closer and nearly brush mine.

"I don't give a shit about your club business. You had your chance, and you blew it. Now, leave," I demand, standing my ground. My posture goes rigid.

"Nice try, Siren. This whole posturing up to seem big and bad doesn't suit you," he says, looking me up and down. "You forgot I know who you are, what your tricks are, and how your mind thinks. I know you better than you know yourself, and right now, you're pushing me away to protect that fear of yours. The fear of feeling something for a change."

"Leave," I demand. "I don't want you here."

"Is that what you really want? After everything I've given you."

"You haven't given me shit," I recoil. Why does he think he was the one who gave me the world? He may have made it a bit more tolerable, but everything that I have ever been given in this world came with a price that I paid for pounds of my flesh. The only thing that he has given me is a reason to stay here.

"Are you fucking kidding me right now? What have I given you? I've given you the space that you seemed to need. I've given you time to figure your shit out. Do you know what I haven't done?" he yells, as my body trembles from his vicious tones.

I sheepishly shake my head in response when no

audible words spill from my lips in the response that he's waiting to hear from me.

"I haven't figured out what made you run away from the club, from Dani, and especially why you ran from me."

He's purposely baiting me into giving him what he wants, but I know once I tell him about Asher that he'll never understand why I am going to such lengths to get him.

The club is his home.

The men who ride beside him are his brothers.

Those are the things that matter to him.

His family was forged in fire, while mine lies tattered in the winds of abuse and betrayal. This is a concept that only someone who has lived through it would understand. Asher is my chance to have a piece of what an actual family should feel like, and I want to hold on to that splintering thread as hard as I can. I may not even know Asher, but he is my blood, and that's all that matters.

If I told him, Ratchet would only push his way into the situation, ending any chances that I might have of getting custody of Asher. A biker and my checkered past would only ensure that Asher would stay in the hands of my father for the rest of his life. It was a risk I wasn't willing to take.

"You don't understand," I mutter before he cuts me

off again. He objects, but the side door swings open, and out steps Willie.

"Ricca, your break ended twenty minutes ago," he yells out before seeing me pinned to the wall by Ratchet. Willie's body tenses, readying for a fight. "What the hell is going on out here?" he drawls as his fists curl up at his sides. "He messing with you?" He starts toward us.

I shove Ratchet away, and this time he moves. The farther he is from me, the better chances he has of Willie not trying to kick his ass. Willie might be the heavyweight champ of ass-kicking in his bar, but Ratchet would wipe the floor with him. Something I want to avoid entirely. Willie saunters his way over to us, settling next to Ratchet's side.

"It's fine, Willie. Just a friend from a past life, saying hello."

Ratchet narrows his eyes as soon as the word friend leaves my lips. We both know that word doesn't even describe our relationship on even the basic level. Truthfully, I don't even know if there is a word in the dictionary that could describe it. We're just us. Two complicated, dark souls trying to find a place in each other's presence without self-destructing.

"You sure that you're okay?" Willie questions further, watching Ratchet intently.

"I'm sure. He just wanted to say goodbye before he took off. Isn't that right?" I nervously respond, urging him to follow my lead before we both land in hot water with my boss and the local authorities.

"That so, young man?"

Ratchet stares at me while I smile back and shake my head, pleading.

"I think I might just stick around longer," he retorts, sending my face spinning toward his. "It's been a long time since I've had a quiet place like this to do some soul-searching. Maybe I'll even take in a bit of its history, since my girl here seems to like it so much."

Willie assesses him again before dismissing him as a threat.

"Well then, why don't we let Ricca here get back to work so you and I can have a chat about this place? I've lived here my whole life, and if it's history you're wanting, I'm your man." Willie declares, slapping Ratchet roughly on the shoulder. The impact doesn't even make him jostle a single inch. Ratchet just smirks at my boss. He knew exactly what this exchange was. A who's the bigger badass pissing match. Willie smirks at us both before turning on his heels to move toward the door. He stops just as he opens it and looks back at us.

"Sugar, the customers are waiting."

"I'm going, Willie," I say, but Ratchet grabs my wrist and pulls me back against him before I get too far.

"This isn't over. We're going to have a talk later. You best believe me, Siren," he whispers in hushed tones. The vibration of his words against my skin sends a wave of goosebumps prickling on the surface.

I push away from him and head into the open door Willie has hanging open. Ratchet follows me in, but Willie leads him back over to one of the bar tables.

I watch them both the entire rest of my shift. Ratchet and Willie talk and periodically laugh for over an hour before the customers finally start trickling out after I make the announcement for last call. I duck back into the kitchen to take a container of dirty glasses back to our dishwasher, but when I return to the bar top, Ratchet is gone. An exacerbated sigh escapes my lips, both in relief and nerves. Ratchet isn't one to give up easily, and for him to disappear on me without trying to get his answer again has me on edge.

Grabbing a clean rag, I wipe off the bar one last time when a noise startles me.

"Shit, sorry, sugar," the other bartender Missy says as a glass falls from her hands. "I didn't see that glass sitting there. Damn drunks never seem to put the damn things in the right spot at last call."

I mumble an unintelligible response to her, not really paying much attention to what she just said.

"You know," she questions. "You seem to be jumpier than a long-haired cat in a field of mouse traps, Ricca. Everything okay?"

I continue cleaning the bar and plaster a fake smile on my face.

"I'm fine, Missy. Just been a shit day between the diner and the crowd tonight. I'm good," I lie.

Missy saunters up beside me, planting her elbow on my nice, clean bar, and stares at me. Her closeness sends a shiver down my spine, and I jerk away from her.

"That so?"

"Yup," I squeak.

"So, it doesn't have to do with that cool drink of water that came in here tonight?"

"Nope. He's just someone from my past that came to visit unannounced. He'll be gone soon enough."

Missy rolls her eyes at me, not believing a damn bit of what I am telling her from the smirk on her face.

"Sugar, if that kind of man came looking for me, I'd be riding him like an express train instead of rubbing the same damn spot on that bar repeatedly."

My eyes drop to the rag when I realize she's right on at least part of that. I have been cleaning the same damn spot. Fucking Ratchet. He's been here a few hours, and he's already turning my brain into mush. He's a fucking distraction, just like I thought he would be.

"Why don't you go on home and find that man of yours," she teases. "I'll take over from here before you wear a hole in that new countertop."

Missy snatches the rag from my hands and bumps

me with her hip, effectively moving me out of the way. I stand and watch her before she turns around and glares at me.

"I said get going, Ricca. Don't let that man go to waste before someone older and wiser like me steals him from right under your nose."

I stifle a laugh at the mental picture of Missy trying to seduce Ratchet. He may not be a young buck anymore, but I doubt even Missy could inspire him to sample the cougar side of life. Reaching down below the bar, I grab my purse and head toward the door. I step outside and inhale a deep breath, letting myself relax for the first time all night. The air is cooler after the round of storms that went through this afternoon, and the humidity is finally tolerable. The cold tingles against my shin, making me shiver just a little.

Finding Ratchet isn't on my to-do list tonight, as much as my brain is screaming at me. All I want to do is crawl into bed and wake up tomorrow to find him still gone. If the situation didn't involve my brother, my reaction would have likely been different. It kills me to plaster on this indifferent façade, but I need every advantage I can get for Asher. Ratchet is bound to have a record, and that's something I don't need when the caseworker comes knocking on my door. I think about the look on their faces when I swing open the door of mom's old doublewide trailer and introduce the biker, who likely has more blood on his hands than I have on my own.

Since the night that I kissed him at Red's, he had me. The bond between us took root the night that I accidentally invited Dani into the underbelly of the motorcycle club world. I was in an abusive and manipulative relationship with Enrico but at that moment, I betrayed him for a stranger who made me feel for the first time in years. A stranger that has now invaded my life with no intention of going quietly and will travel down the dark rabbit hole of being near me. My actions nearly cost Dani her life, but I was willing then to make her collateral damage to save my hide. Something I regret every single time I see her with Hero and her children. I nearly cost her that happiness.

It was a mistake that I could never let happen again.

As badly as I want to embrace his presence, wishing him away, for the time being, is the course I must take.

I have to stay strong, but how can I when Ratchet is a tornado hurtling right toward my safe space? He is chaos, and with chaos, nothing is safe in its chosen path.

Chapter 8

RATCHET

WATCHING her leave the bar that night nearly killed me. Every fucking inch of me wanted to follow her home and claim her again, but I knew that wouldn't bring me any closer to getting her back. This was going to take time, and lucky for me, that was something I had. As I talked to her boss, I kept my eyes trained on her when she wasn't looking. She moved between the customers, but unlike most bartenders, she didn't make small talk or flirt for tips. The surrounding air seemed different from I remembered before she left. She was on edge constantly and short-tempered, but nothing like this. Every touch seemed to send her spiraling into a panic attack. Not that I minded knowing that no one has touched my girl while she's been gone. I just didn't like that she had suffered in the last few months.

She let no one close to her, which was a good sign for

me because that meant there wasn't someone else she ran off to be with. Something I could definitely cross off on my "why she left me" list.

One down. A million more theories to go.

Yet, I could tell that she was off. While the panic attacks were worse, Ricca's guard was up higher than ever. She's protecting something. Maybe someone. Whatever it was, she was on edge when I saw her tonight. She would never stay in a place like this unless there was a good fucking reason. There was something else keeping her here, and it pisses me off that she's keeping it from me. Try as she might, she can't push me away now that I am finally here.

Last call gave me my opportunity to slip away and give her space to leave. After she left the bar, I slid from my hiding place in the dark alley and stalked my way back to my bike. Sure, I could have followed her home, but I needed sleep before I tried to talk to her again. Her protesting and reluctance outside the bar on her break were frustrating to me. Add that in with exhaustion from my long trip out here, and you get a volatile situation. I needed this to be a slow burn and not a towering inferno to get somewhere with her. The comfort she had with me before had all but disappeared. I was going to have to put in more effort to get her to let me back in, and as much as she will hate it, I will wait until the opportunity comes knocking again.

Thanks to the tip from Willie, I found a decent place to kick off my boots for the rest of the night. It wasn't much, but it's all I needed. The patron wasn't exactly good with a rough-looking biker knocking on her door at nearly three o'clock in the morning, but mentioning Willie's name was endorsement enough to get me in the door. Vickie, the owner, slowly walked me to the room at the back of the house and opened the door for me. Besides the old bed, the room just had a dresser and mirror. Nothing fancy, and that was fine by me. A place to sleep and the communal bathroom was all I needed because if things worked out my way, I wouldn't be staying here long before taking Ricca back to Upland. A few days at max, by my guess.

I dumped my saddlebag by the bed, topping it with my cut, and pulled off my riding boots and socks before I hopped into the bed.

Even exhausted, I was a fool to think that my mind would shut up long enough to get some shut-eye. For hours, I laid in the creaking, old bed of the Willow Branch Bed and Breakfast as my mind processed every damn detail of our brief exchange at the bar, analyzing it like V analyzes his damn computer code. Every syllable. The dips of her tone. The way her eyes lit up with that familiar fire that I loved. All this time away from her, and no matter how pissed off I am with her running off, she still had me by my fucking balls. My mind had a way of overthinking at the wrong fucking time. Add in Ricca, and it sends that part of me into overdrive.

How did I not know about her family? Not once had she ever mentioned her mother or any other family, for the matter. If family mattered that much to her, she'd have said something to me, or even maybe Dani. Wouldn't she? We were the closest people to her, yet if I would bet if I called Dani right now, she would be just as clueless as I am. I knew about her mom only because of what V found, but without hard evidence or the words coming out of her mouth, the proper answer was completely up in the air. Uncertainty at its worst. One of the few fucking things I loathe.

After dawn, I passed the fuck out, but the noises of the town blare through the thin walls of the place a few hours later. I pop open my eyes and glare at the sounds of people moving about the surrounding town. The engines of heavy farm equipment and trucks grumbled at the stoplight just outside my window, and as hard as I fucking tried, the chance of going back to sleep was pointless.

Fuck me. They should have put that rise and shine shit on the town sign.

"What the fuck is wrong with you people?" I curse at the noise, forcing myself awake. I know no one could hear me, but protesting the efficient work ethic of this damn town helped satisfy my urge to flip the entire town the bird for waking me up. "Who the fuck gets up this early willingly?"

I shove my legs off the bed and stretch my aching muscles. The long ride stiffened me, and the only thing that was going to fix that shit was a hot shower. I slip my dirty shirt over my head and toss it on the bed behind me, reminding me I need to hit up the local laundromat within the next few days. Standing with another stretch, I rummage through my saddlebags and find a clean set of clothes. My aching feet protest with each step toward the door, but better things lie ahead, with hopefully a hot shower just down the hall.

I step into the hallway, but Vickie runs smack into my bare chest. Her hands fly out in front of her, but when she sees what object she's run into, she stammers an apology as she sidesteps me. I laugh off her embarrassment when I see her looking back over her shoulder at me, knowing that the entire town will probably hear about her run-in with the half-naked biker in the hallway. No doubt the embellishment will have me being completely naked, but hey, I'll let her have her fun.

I step into the bathroom and get the shit done quickly. The hot water did the trick for my muscles, but I hurried to avoid opening up the curtain to find a panting Vickie on the other side of it. Women of a certain age are fucking crazy when it comes to pursuing men, and that's not the crazy I need or want in my life right now.

Though I'm sure some of my brothers would take the chance in a heartbeat.

Slipping from the bathroom, fully dressed and on cougar watch, I hightail it back to my room. Just as I reach the door, a familiar ringtone blares from inside. I shake my head as some striptease pop singer and her "Hit Me Baby One More Time" lyrics play through the door.

Fucking Voodoo.

That fucking nerd started a game of hacking the club member's phones and putting the most ridiculous songs as ringtones for all the club brothers. I thought Raze was going to lose his shit when some bullshit pop song interrupted church. Voodoo thought it was hilarious. Raze, not so much.

The door swings open as I turn the handle and take long strides to the dresser, where my phone lies.

". . . Hit me, baby, one more time," Voodoo sings as I answer.

"Oh, I'll hit you fucker, the next time I see you," I growl into the phone.

"You're such an angry little elf this time of the morning," Voodoo chides as I hear the voices of my brothers laughing in the background.

"Speakerphone, really?"

Loud laughter erupts through the speaker, forcing me to pull my phone away from my ear.

"Sorry, Ratchet," Hero laughs. "V's been waiting for days to call you just to hear your reaction. You good?"

I roll my eyes, knowing the fucker planned this. Payback is a bitch, and I doubt he'll be laughing about my brand of revenge. Those precious little toys of his might just go missing for a few days.

"I'm good, brother. I'm assuming he filled you in about why I'm here?" I question.

"We're all in the know. You could have told me that's why you needed to leave. I'd have understood. Hell, I'd have been hot on Dani's goddamn trail if she took off on me."

"You have any luck finding her?" Raze asks.

"You could say that."

"Uh oh," Voodoo's voice teases through the earpiece. "Trouble in paradise?"

"This shit was never paradise, V. It's not like the missed connections bullshit you troll on Craigslist. She wasn't exactly happy to see my ass."

"Hold, please," Voodoo says before hushed tones fill the receiver when what sounds like a hand goes over their end of the line. I hear Raze growl and boots hitting the floor in the background.

"Hello?" I yell into the receiver. "What's going on?"

"Gotta go, brother. Trouble may have just walked in the door. I'll fill you in later," Voodoo says before immediately hanging up.

What the fuck is going on? Shit, going down while I am a thousand miles away isn't exactly what I had in mind. My body immediately tenses, readying for a fight. My brothers and club come first, and if I had to leave to take care of business, I would risk Ricca taking off on me. Nothing is fucking easy for my club, and maybe this is a sign that this shit with Ricca isn't meant to be. My brothers seem to balance their club and family lives, but my job was a different story. I am the cleanup man who comes back covered in blood, guts, and gasoline when the shit hits the fan. I deal out death like a pharmacy deals out pills to anyone with a prescription. It was my job and one that I was damn good at. Even the club whores cringed at the sight of me after one of my sessions of please confess your sins and die. How would Ricca react to seeing that with everything she's been through?

You should have thought of that shit before you rode all the way out here, dumbass.

I wait by the phone for over an hour before my stomach protests the lack of food in it. Sitting here and waiting will not change the fact that something is happening with my club and that I am on the outside for the first time waiting to be filled in. Stuffing my shit in my saddlebags, just in case, I head out the door toward the front of the Inn. Vickie is thankfully tied up on the phone when I walk by, allowing me to get by un-groped.

The front door chimes as I open it, but she doesn't even look up. The red and chrome of my bike shines in the sun, reflecting into my eyes. I grab my shades from my saddlebag, slip them on, and make the sun shut the fuck up with its rays of happiness. Settling the bags on my bike, I swing my legs over the warmed metal and flick on the ignition.

The engine idles between my legs as I try to map out my destination on my iPhone. Google doesn't fail me and finds a diner just up the road. I think this is the first time that I have ever wished for a Walmart to be close by, but the closest one is nearly an hour away. The citizens of this town must have a secret because I have no fucking clue how they survive this far out of civilization. No major hospitals or businesses outside of the bars and diner. Do people just drop dead, and that's it?

I pop the kickstand and head toward the diner, hoping the entire time that the food there is edible. I smell the place before I see it. The air becomes thick with the scent of fried food and lost dreams. I might exaggerate on the latter, but one look at this place and the people who live here are self-explanatory. Just a few blocks into the ride, the diner comes into view. Much like the rest of the town, it's stuck in the nineteen fifties. The old boxcar design built into the front of the building doesn't do a damn thing for the place, but I doubt that this town cares much. This is the place that city dwellers would die over for its rustic aesthetic. Me? I don't give a flying fuck about materialistic things. Only my brothers, my club, and this damn woman are all I need to be happy. Nothing more. Nothing less.

I note the local LEO's squad car parked in the first spot by the door. Their presence is both a good and a bad thing for me. Good in the sense that if they are eating here, the food won't kill me. The bad part of it is that I stick out like a Goth at a pop show in this place. Nothing screams trouble like a tattooed biker riding into town. Just as I pull into an open spot, the local cop steps outside the diner and heads straight to his car. His head is turned to his walkie-talkie on his shoulder, so he doesn't notice me. I watch as he drives off and dismount my bike.

Stepping into the place, the air conditioning smacks me in the face as people stop talking once I enter. Every eye is trained on me, an outsider to their small town, and every move I make is monitored closely. A whispered laugh leaves my lips while I smirk at their reaction. And they say small-town USA is the friendliest part of this country.

Scanning to find an open place at the bar, the sound of breaking dishes and glasses startles me. A collective gasp from the crowd around me draws my attention to the source of the noise.

I smirk even more when I find Ricca staring at me like

a deer in headlights with broken plates surrounding her feet on the floor.

"Morning, Siren," I chide to her before crossing the room and settling onto the worn red plastic of the barstool. The hushed murmurs of the other diners fill up the place as Ricca quickly bends to clean up the mess.

I have to say, judging from her reaction, that I know how to enter.

The other server, a pretty blonde thing, rushes to her side. She kneels beside her as a large man steps from the bat-looking wing doors of the kitchen, his hands firmly crossing his chest.

"That's coming out of your check, girl."

Ricca looks up at the man towering over her, and I see her shiver at his dominating presence. She remains stone silent, trying to quickly clean up the mess, but the guy doesn't take the hint. The blonde stands abruptly, moving away from the scene. I have a feeling is about to take place.

He reaches toward her, grabbing her elbow and hauling her off the ground roughly.

"Don't pretend you didn't hear me, Ricca," he hisses as I spring from my seat, charging toward them both. No one touches my girl like that without her permission.

"Get this fucking mess cleaned up, or you're fired," he screams, shaking her.

"Big Joe—" she stammers before I cut her off when I

move between the two of them and force him to break contact.

"This ain't any of your business, *pal*," he snarls. I shove Ricca behind me and then get into this fucker's face.

"Keep your fucking hands off her," I growl. My hands fist at my sides as the man postures up to me. Rage courses through my body at the vision of him touching her again. She may not want me, but no one needs to shove around a woman like that.

"What I do with my employee is my business. Why don't you go sit your out-of-town ass back on that stool and let me handle my business?"

He reaches for her again, but I step into his path and shove his hand away.

"Ratchet, please," Ricca begs from behind my back. "It's fine."

"See," the man says, gesturing to Ricca, who shivers behind me. "It's none of your business. Now get to stepping."

Wrong move, dickhead.

I swing wide, connecting a right hook to his face. He stumbles back, falling into the bar top. A few men from the diner jolt out of their seats toward me. I turn, staring them down. They back down immediately, and I pivot my attention to Ricca.

"You okay?" I question, looking for redness forming

or emerging bruises from his grip on her arm and a sign that it's okay to touch her. I lift my hand to her jawline, caressing her soft skin with my elbow, and she leans into my touch.

"I'm fine," she mutters, just as I am jerked backward. The man wraps his forearm around my throat to choke me. Unfortunately for him, it doesn't work. I angle my back, releasing the pressure on my neck enough to head butt him. He stumbles back again, and taking the chance, I turn, kneeing him in the stomach.

He gasps for air and falls to his knees. His eyes fall on Ricca.

"Get the fuck out of here," he gasps. "You're fired."

"No!" she exclaims, glaring at me. "Big Joe, you can't do this."

"Get OUT!" he screams while wiping blood away from his lip. Knowing the fucker is bleeding brings a smile to my face. He should be happy that a bloody lip is all he received after pulling that kind of shit on my girl.

Ricca shoves past me toward the bar, gathering her things from underneath the countertop. I try to stop her, but she rushes past me and right out the door. Big Joe still gasps for air on the ground below me. I swipe a rag off the countertop and kneel before him.

"You don't fucking touch what's mine," I warn him, tossing the towel into his face. "If you so much as breathe in her direction, I will end you."

I rise from the ground and stalk out of the place without so much as looking at the people gaping around me. It was a risk getting physical with the guy, but no one touches her or any other woman like that in front of me. I may be a cold-hearted killer for my club, but even I know that rule. Women and kids are off-limits and should be protected. A lesson I wish my mother had learned prior to being my incubator. Some people were never meant to be parents, her included.

Just as I step through the door, I see Ricca peeling out of the parking lot in a truck. Dust fills the air, clouding her escape. I look around, surprised by the lack of red and blue lights. Knowing the patrons of the diner were smart enough to not get the police involved eases the tension of the possibility of staying the night in the gray bar hotel for assault. I've done the jail thing before as a teenager, and I'd rather avoid that shit happening again. Apparently, taking orders is just not something I am equipped to do unless it comes from my Prez and the club.

I smirk, watching her leave, because this cat-and-mouse game is only just beginning.

Chapter 9

RICCA

"FUCK!" I scream as soon as I slide into my truck. Anger courses through my body like raging rapids. Ratchet has been here less than twenty-four hours, and he's already got me fired from a job I desperately need. That son of a bitch thinks he can bulldoze his way into my life and expects me to be fine with it.

It's not fucking fine. He nearly cost me my job at Willie's last night with his back-alley rendezvous, "You are mine" bullshit. I was honestly surprised that Willie bought his fake as fuck story and let him back in the place. Thinking about him talking with my boss while I worked makes my blood boil.

The nerve of that man to do this to me under the guise of protecting me. I don't need his protection anymore because with it comes a price that I don't think

I will pay again. My heart on his platter, just waiting to be devoured.

My hands beat against the weathered leather of the steering wheel while my chest heaves and my heart beat wildly.

Why was he even there? Is he following me? I know it's a small town, but after last night, I had thought for sure that he'd have left by now.

There was no sign of him this morning, even though a part of me wished to find him outside the shit hole I temporarily call home right now, but that's beside the point. My feelings be damned. He is butting into my plans and making this entire thing harder than it should be. I was dead fucking wrong in my assumption, and now, I am paying for it.

My mind replays the entire scene over and over in my head, and it frustrates me even more. The images flutter by before focusing in on him as I pulled away. His lips pursed as he watched me peel out of the parking lot like a bat out of hell. He didn't budge from his spot there in the dusty aftermath of my theatrics. Not him. Instead, the bastard *smirked* at me.

Smirked.

He fucking ruined a piece of my plan, and he fucking smirked while doing it. It took everything I had in me not to throw this truck into reverse and run over his pretentious ass. To think, I was happy to feel his light touch on my cheek. Happy that he was protecting me from Big Joe's unnecessary tirade, but in the end, that got me fired, and now I'm fucking pissed off.

I was already on Big Joe's shit list after being over an hour late for the start of my shift. I tossed and turned all night, reliving my encounter with Ratchet outside of Willie's. Even as I dozed, his face haunted my dreams. His eyes drawing me into him. His body joined with mine in a passionate embrace of intertwined limbs and screams of passion. His hands touching every inch of my body and making me feel alive again. Just the two of us without the pull of the world trying to tear us apart. Now that I am awake, it's only worse.

I try to slow my breathing by exhaling and inhaling deeply, but my breathing exercise is cut short by my cell phone ringing in the seat next to me. Its chimes continue and abruptly end as soon as I pull off onto the shoulder. Far too many accidents have resulted in using a cell phone while driving, and California laws forbid its use without a Bluetooth device. Old habits don't fade easily, and because of my one-rule-following nature, I miss the call.

"Shit," I mutter while reaching over for my phone. I quickly unlock the screen and pull up the missed call. Seeing the familiar number, I curse. I throw my head back against the headrest of the bench seat and release an exasperated sigh. It was the caseworker for my brother.

With a flick of my finger, I hit the button to return her call.

The phone rings as I force my heavy breathing to quiet. The tone rings four times before someone answers on the other side of the line.

"Kentucky Cabinet for Health and Family Services. How may I direct your call?" the operator says in a clipped tone.

"Nicole Wild, please," I respond, trying to ease my nerves by tapping my fingers on the dashboard.

"One moment, please," the woman responds before the transfer goes through.

"This is Wild," my caseworker gruffly declares.

"Hey, Nicole," I stammer. "It's Erica Delmont returning your call."

"Ah, Ms. Delmont. I'm glad you called right back. Listen, I am about to step into a meeting, but I wanted to check in about the status of your application."

"About that," I stall, knowing she will not like my excuse. For nearly a month, she's been after me about finishing up the application to petition the courts. I stalled the best I could to get things and myself in a better standing, but as my caseworker, she is about as impatient as one can get. I understand that my brother being with my asshole father isn't an ideal situation, but things needed to be in place so that the courts don't have a reason to tell me no the first time around.

"Until we receive your two-hundred-dollar payment to initialize the filing with the courts for a relative adoption, I cannot proceed any further."

"I understand that, Miss Wild. I had some unexpected changes to my employment, but I am working on getting the filing fee to you soon."

I hear shuffling papers in the background, which annoys me instantly. I get she is busy, but her insistence on keeping working while we are talking strikes me as rude.

"I understand, but we cannot proceed without it. I need to clarify one other thing with you. I have in my notes from our phone conversation that you listed you are unmarried. Is that still the case?"

Why does that even matter?

"Yes. That's right," I curtly reply. "It's been three weeks since I last spoke with you, Nicole. It's not like good men grow on trees around here."

Or anywhere. The men around here are way too old or way too poor. Neither of which would serve me any bit of good when it comes to a paper marriage for the sake of Asher. There are only so many things I would do to get him back, but marrying someone is likely at the bottom of that to-do list.

"I see," she coolly replies, while the noises from the paper shuffling intensifies, only adding more to my annoyance with her.

"Is that a problem suddenly?"

"While it isn't impossible to adopt as a single parent, the court typically enjoys placing children in a two-parent home. It provides a better structure and a constant level of supervision during the transitional and bonding phase of adoption."

My patience breaks. The bureaucratic bullshit that has come out of this ordeal has given me a healthy reminder of why walking the straight and narrow is so hard. My former way of life would have had Asher already in my custody by now, with a few threats and an exchange of a wad of cash. Unfortunately, that's no longer an option, even with Ratchet in town. The Heaven's Rejects had moved away from their underbelly of the world dealings and walk the straight and narrow path for the first time in club history. I doubt, even for the sake of an innocent boy with no ties to their club, would make them stray from it. Not all good deeds are worth time in jail over.

"Are you telling me that after I go through all of this, the courts could decide against me because I don't have a husband?"

"It has happened before," she recalls. "With his age and your intent on returning to California after the adoption goes through, the state is quite strict on the requirements. Legally, I cannot advise you to marry, but it would help your case."

"I can't believe this," I growl into the receiver.

"I'm so sorry, Miss Delmont, but I really have to get to my meeting. Please call me as soon as you have made your payment to the clerk's office, and I'll get the ball rolling on my end."

Before I can even respond, she hangs up the phone. My head hangs as I sob into my hands with the phone still pressed to my ear. I thought that getting fired was the biggest of my worries today, but that has been shoved into the meaningless bullshit pile in comparison to my caseworker's revelation.

Marriage. An institution that I barely believe in, and in order to get my brother, they want me to find a man to check the box. This is so fucking unfair. Of all the things they could have asked of me, it had to be this. Something that would require me to sell my body and soul to the highest bidder to satisfy the government's outdated ideas of how a family structure should be. The only gain would be my brother in return. It's too much to ask and makes me feel as if this entire thing was doomed from the start. Maybe this was all a farce of a fantasy, and I was the leading lady of the dramatic interpretation of how life fucks Ricca yet again.

Life has never been easy for me, so why did I assume that handing over some cash would give me my brother? The outdated family values of the Midwest were going to fuck me over, and my only choice was to take the licks they give me and keep trying until there was no other option left. I've sold myself to the devil far too many times in the past to even remotely consider doing it again, even if it was for a good cause.

My mind swirls and pounds with the beginnings of a headache. I lean my head against the warm leather of the steering wheel and close my eyes. Focusing on my breathing, I try to force my body to relax. I feel a shift to a more relaxed state after nearly thirty minutes of quiet. The headache still lingers, but relaxing has helped ease the sudden pains from tension and stress. Just as I lift my forehead from the steering wheel, a loud knock on the glass and the rattling of the handle startles me upright.

"What the fuck!" I scream out, my eyes wild from shock. They finally focus, and I find Ratchet glaring from outside of my door.

He raps his knuckles against the glass again, motioning with his hands for me to roll down the window. I hesitate momentarily, but decide that he'd just break it if I didn't.

"It's not safe to take a nap on the side of the road, Siren," he coarsely declares. His eyes search my face, analyzing my every feature for injury. Whenever he's around, I always feel like I am a slide underneath a microscope, like you see on television. It's as if he is trying to look into my black soul and find something unexpectedly there.

His gaze makes me uneasy, and with my unease comes my mistimed attempt at humor to diffuse the tension and break the silence.

"I'll nap where I want, Ratchet. Without your permission."

I roll my eyes at his incorrect evaluation of the situation laid out in front of him, and he growls again.

"Don't you roll your eyes at me, Siren. You know I don't like that shit."

I do it again just to spite him before he reaches inside through the open window and pulls up the lock. He rips open the door. I try to scoot away from his grasp, but I don't make it in time. His large, calloused hands grasp me and pull me out of the truck. I try to fight him, but I know it'll only make what's coming worse. When Ratchet wants something or someone, he doesn't give up. Clear enough because he tracked me down to Kentucky. No additional proof required.

As rough as it might look to someone on the outside, he's way gentler than Big Joe was early this morning. My hips hit the edge of the bench seat of the truck before he stops. He releases my arms and goes for my feet, pulling them to my left and out of the car. Ratchet watches me, looking for what is likely a sign of panic before he reaches inside the truck and removes the keys from the ignition. He slides them into his back pocket before returning his attention back to me.

"I'm tired of the cat-and-mouse game, Siren. It's time we had a little talk."

I cross my arms in front of my chest, putting a barrier between us. As much as I want to reach out and touch him, I can't give in to temptation. Not yet. Not when my association with a biker and his club could affect my already slim chances of getting Asher.

"Not sure there's much to talk about," I respond sharply. "I left, and you seem to follow me. That about sum it up?"

Ratchet hisses at the sting of my words. His hands jolt from his sides as his fingers wrap around my hips. He uses his strength to pull me all the way out of the truck to my feet. My chest crashes into him, and my body instantly reacts to his closeness. The warmth of arousal builds at my core.

My eyes lift to his, and that fucking smirk forms on his face again.

"You didn't just run, Siren. You left for a reason, and I want to know why."

I try to cast my eyes downwards again, but his fingers pull my gaze back onto his face.

"I just left, okay? I needed to get away from the violence of the club," I mutter.

"Bullshit. You have never been a good liar to begin with, but even that was pathetic. I want the truth. Try again."

I try to shove away from him, but he grips me even tighter.

"Fine, you want the truth?" I yell at him. "I met someone else."

"Strike two, Siren. No man with any claim to you would ever let you out of his sight. A lesson I've recently learned myself," he growls. "Last chance."

"I left because I felt trapped by you," I retort. "I couldn't breathe when you were around. I needed to put distance between us." My heart aches as the last word slips from my lips. As hard as I tried to forget him, I couldn't, and spilling those half-truths hurt me more than it would hurt him.

His eyes narrow before he lingers, his face closer to mine.

"Strike three. You didn't run from me. You can pretend to believe that horseshit all you want, but your body is telling me a completely different story. I can sense your arousal, Ricca. Your goosebumps and flushed cheeks are giving away your lack of indifference."

Pretend to hate him. It'll be easier to apologize to him later than to face the consequences of having him here now. Just do it, Ricca. It's for the best.

I force myself to smile and laugh back at him. He cocks his head at me, trying to figure out the source of the sudden emotional change.

"We fucked, Ratchet, and it was great. Just because

my body liked the things you did to me doesn't mean that I am yours. We scratched an itch that was a long time coming, and I moved on. End of story."

"Bullshit," he protests. "Keep telling yourself those lies, Siren. You might just start believing them."

"It not a lie —," I stammer before his mouth crashes onto mine. His tongue parts my lips as my unwillingness to give in to his kiss melts away. He kisses me like he's gone for years without a drink of water, and I am the only fountain that can quench his thirst. My tongue slips out of my mouth and caresses his. A soft moan escapes my lips as his hands fall onto my hips before reaching under my ass. His fingers dig into my flesh when he lifts me back onto the truck seat, putting my jean-clad pussy against his rock-hard erection. I nearly moan from the feeling of him being so close to me and wrap my legs around his waist.

The contact alone brings back memories from that night we shared, and it sends vibrations of warmth tingling all over my body, crashing back to me. Our entangled limbs. The heat of our bodies moving together. The screams ripping out of my mouth as he brought me to my third orgasm in a single fuck session. Each memory sends a more intense wave of arousal crashing into my core.

My legs wrap around his waist tighter, forcing my pussy harder against his cock as the kiss continues. He removes his mouth from mine, trailing kisses along my jaw, and then he licks down my neck.

"You're mine, Siren," he whispers against my neck, his breath ragged. "*Mine.*"

His mouth travels lower toward the top of my breast. My head falls back as he inches closer to my pebbled nipples. A soft moan escapes my lips when he reaches the edge of my bra, just as the horn of a car blows as it passes us.

"Get a room," someone from the car yells at us, breaking the moment.

Ratchet smiles at me as I lean my face against his chest, hiding my embarrassment. My body shakes with a mixture of overstimulation from the ensuing battle of arousal, excitement, and fear inside of me. I was so close to giving it all to him on the side of the road, regardless of everything else I have been through and still going through.

With one kiss, I sealed my fate.

I just invited the Devil back into my life with the master key to my heart.

I am *so* fucked.

Chapter 10

RATCHET

IN HINDSIGHT, letting her drive off after the incident at the diner wasn't my best idea. Hell, it didn't even register on the top one hundred good ideas list. I knew, watching her drive away, that she was pissed, and I needed to leave her alone, but, her call was blaring for me to track her down. I leaned against my bike for nearly twenty minutes in an internal battle with myself about whether to go after her before I finally made my decision. In her state of mind, she could be dangerous to herself as well as others on the road. When Ricca lets her anger and fear get the best of her, she lashes out to anyone within firing distance. Myself included. It was better for me to become the asshole once again than to watch her fall apart after fucking her life up again.

For once, my brain had a good fucking idea because as soon as I saw her truck pulled off to the side of the road, my heart stops. I'd have patted myself on my back, but I could feel the pain she was in.

She didn't budge as I approach the truck. Something else had happened in the time since she left the diner. I tried to keep myself in check, but the line of questioning poured out of me like I didn't know how to shut the fuck up. I could see her pain and frustration with every lie that came from her mouth until I couldn't take it anymore. I needed to feel her lips on mine.

I don't know why I did it, but having her leaning against my chest right now felt right. For the first time since I rode into this tiny ass town, she let me in. Well, I shoved myself in, but she didn't kick my ass back out again. This was the moment I needed to embrace before her walls came hurdling back up again and effectively locking me outside in the cold. It was a win that I was proud to claim in my column.

She nuzzles against me as I feel my shirt become wet and notice her quiet sobs.

Tears.

That's not exactly the reaction I expected after such a fucking good kiss, but with her, I'll take her tears instead of her running away from me again. The dark side of me wanted to taste her tears, while a tiny part of me wanted to actually be a decent human being and comfort her. It's fucked up, but what else is new for me?

"You okay, Siren?" I whisper against her ear. Her body instantly tenses again.

So much for relaxed. Why do I feel like she is about to shut me out all over again?

"I'm fine," she sobs, pushing away from my chest and wiping her tear-stained face. "Listen, Ratchet—."

I place my fingers on her lips, hushing her. She's about to tell me some reason this can't work. Another lie. Her reaction to the kiss tells me she wants me, but her heart or mind is resisting the idea. Her eyes widen when I hush her again.

"Unless you're telling me to stay, I don't want to hear it. I know that kiss changes nothing, but I'd like just one more pleasant moment with you before it all goes to hell again."

She blinks without saying a word.

"I know you have your reasons for being here, but you owe me the truth. The whole truth, Ricca. Not some sugarcoated fucking lie. And until you can give me that, I will wait."

I watch as Ricca's body shivers in response to mine while she hopefully processes what I just said. I waited six months for this woman. A few more days wouldn't kill me, or so I hoped.

"Just tell me you'll think about letting me in, Siren. I did ride all this way out here to see you," I say to her, running my thumb across her cheek as a stray tear slides down. She smiles at my joke. A genuine smile that doesn't hold back pain and misery behind her swollen, just-kissed lips.

"I did lie to you," she starts before hesitating. "And I'm sorry for that, but I need space and time, Ratchet."

I consider her words internally before answering. One wrong phrase, and I would put this all at risk because I hurt her.

Think of a solution, fucker. Equal ground. No ultimatums.

"I can live with the time, but the space is a hard no," I demand, squeezing her closer. "I want nothing between us. Not even air should be able to slip between my grasp on you."

Congratulations, shithead. You just broke the no ultimatums rule.

She gulps and blushes at my terms. Her attempt at holding me at arm's length ends today. I may deal her a hand that she may not be willing to play with just yet, but space will not make her lay it all down on the table and bet against me.

"Is this about your mom?"

"I thought you said you wouldn't pry," she rebukes, shoving my own words back at me.

"I said I will wait, Siren. I didn't say a damn thing about not asking questions."

She huffs and uses her hands to put space between us.

"Do you actually think I am here to mourn that cunt of a woman?" she sharply declares. "I'm happy she's gone."

I must have hit a nerve. While I admit to a bit of curiosity about the relationship with her mother, that's not exactly what I am here to find out. That she called her mother a cunt was a big enough clue to tell me she hated the woman. A suspicion I had from the very beginning. With everything that she had gone through over the years, you would have thought that she would have clung to a familial connection had there been a good relationship there to bring her peace. Yet, she didn't. She stayed with the club that saved her and with me. Maybe I was just a source of protection for her, but I felt more between us.

"And what the fuck does that mean, exactly?"

She fidgets in her seat, trying to stall me, but it doesn't work. My eye is on my prize, and she won't be able to wiggle away that easily when I am so close to getting my answers.

"Time's a wasting, Siren. Tell me the truth."

She sighs, turning her beautiful eyes toward me. "My mom is part of the reason I'm here, but she's not the reason I stayed."

I stare deeply into her eyes, silently pleading with her to continue, but her phone interrupts us. She sighs in what I can imagine is an outward display of relief for cutting this conversation short. She reaches behind her, patting the seat for her phone. Her eyes widen when she looks at the screen.

"Shit," she curses before silencing her phone. "I have to go."

"Hot date?" I tease her before I realize she is being dead-serious about her need to leave. She looks at her phone again as it chimes once more. She mutters under her breath, but I can't make out what she says. She uses force to move me. I firmly stand my ground, and I don't give her an inch of backpedaling. Ricca may not be the tiniest woman on the planet, but even she can't move me that easily. Tough girl or not, I don't move unless I want to move.

"Ratchet," she yells. "Fucking move already. I need to leave."

"I don't fucking think so, Siren. We still have some talking to do."

She drops her phone and swivels into the truck. She goes for the ignition before remembering that I have her keys. Something I don't regret doing since she's trying to run again.

Not today, Siren. This doesn't end here after that kiss. You want this just as much as I do.

"Give me my keys, Ratchet," she coarsely demands. I watch as the wheels in her head turn as she looks for a way out of the situation that likely doesn't result in her having to hot-wire the damn truck. A skill I'm almost certain she has in her toolbox.

"No."

"I'm not running, if that's what you think. I need to be somewhere."

I step into the open door of the truck, reaching for her. Her chest rustles, and her breathing becomes heavy.

"The only place you need to be is here with me," I fire back at her. Tasting her lips is only feeding the monster I have inside of me. Even an inch is too far of a distance for my liking.

"I'm serious, Ratchet. Please give me my keys," she pleads.

I pull her keys from out of my pocket, spinning them around my pointer finger to annoy her. She reaches for them, but just as her fingers nearly grasp them, I pull them away.

"Too slow." I smile. "Do you want to try again?"

"God dammit!" she swears. "What do I have to give you, so you'll stop being a bastard for one fucking second of your life and give my keys back?"

Her insults don't affect me in the slightest. Bastard has become nearly a term of endearment when it comes to my line of work with the club. What does pique my interest is her sudden thought I need something in order to give in to her. Little does she know I would gladly lie down in traffic just to make sure she is safe. The male in me has another list of demands that start with her mouth around my cock, but that will not help my cause at this point. Answers first. Fucking her raw comes later.

"Tell me the truth, and I'll give them back. That's it."

She growls and reaches for the keys again, but misses them yet again. She huffs back into her seat and glares at me.

"I can't tell you, Ratchet. You wouldn't understand," she starts. "But I can show you. Give me my keys and let me go to my appointment."

Her eyes plead with me to give in and take a chance that the Queen of Lies is telling me the truth. Everything inside of me screams to rip her out of that truck and fuck her into submission in the bed to show her what happens when she lies to me. The visual of my sick and twisted form of punishment only makes my cock scream louder to go through with that devious thought, but I force myself to shove that idea aside until we are some place a little less public.

"You'll show me," I repeat back to her while handing her the keys. "You lie to me again, and I am going to enjoy reddening your ass with my hand, Siren."

She gulps again as her hand moves the keys to the ignition. I note the slight tremble in her hands as she twists the key, and the truck barely turns over. She really needs a new fucking ride, and I make a mental note to handle it for her. Not that I expect her to agree or happily thank me for doing it, but I don't give a shit. I won't let her ride in some piece of shit truck that could break down and explode at any minute.

She pushes me back, closing the truck door behind me. I watch from the outside of the window as she shifts the truck into drive, but she hesitates. Her lips mouth a curse word before she reaches over and rolls down the window.

"If you really want to know why I am here, meet me at Willie's around three o'clock. I'll show you why I left," she tells me before pulling away from me.

Her truck turns left as she heads back toward town and passes me on the side of the road.

"Dumbass," I chide myself aloud.

Was it a smart idea to put my trust in someone who has run from me more than twice in just a matter of a day? No, but I have to prove to her I'm not here for a quick suck and fuck. She means more to me than a warm cunt to put my dick in, and I need her to realize that.

My boots shuffle on the dusty shoulder of the road before I kick the dust and head back toward my bike.

I didn't come all this way to chicken out now.

Hit me with your best shot, Siren. I'm ready.

Chapter 11

RICCA

"SHIT, SHIT, SHIT," I curse as I fly down the road at least thirty miles an hour over the speed limit. My truck speeds around the corner, flicking up rocks and dust as I skid. I mutter silent prayers that the police don't see me driving through town like I'm a Tokyo drift stunt driver on a practice run. Jail is not where I need to be for reckless driving, but if I don't make it to my appointment with my therapist, she might just throw me into the psych ward for being late. Neither of those options would bode well for me. I'm not big on padded rooms or jail cells. It's just not my cup of tea.

"Come on!" I yell as a car pulls out in front of me at the last minute. The white minivan creeps along at a glacial pace. "It's not even fucking Sunday! Move!"

As the seconds tick by, the white van continues its

course in front of me until my patience snaps. My hands clasp the steering wheel, and I jerk out to the left of the van. My eyes bug as I see the coast wasn't clear and a large semi is barreling toward me.

"Fuck!" I scream.

I jerk back over behind the van as my heart pounds wildly. The woman behind the wheel of the minivan flips me the bird and pulls over to the side of the road to let me by.

I wave half-heartedly, apologizing as I zoom past her. My fucking rage at Ratchet could have killed us both had I not swerved at the last second. Just one day here, and Ratchet already has me on the borderline of stupidity-induced suicide. That fucking man has come crashing into my world, making unreasonable demands and destroying every single shred of common sense that I still have left. All in one fucking day. Really?

My destination quickly approaches as I shut down the mental bitch fest I am having with myself. How could I be so fucking stupid to agree to let him into my plans here? Why would he want to stay when he finds out? Ratchet doesn't exactly scream family man to me, and putting my brother on the line shouldn't have even been an option. Yet, I offered my reasons on a silver platter, with the long shot of his reaction being a positive one. The idea is the complete and total opposite of my expectations. Maybe Dr. Matthews should have me committed after all because, apparently, I'm insane enough to think Ratchet and Asher would be a good idea to mix.

Maybe his knowing would solve one problem for me. He'd leave, and I could go on without his interference. Two birds with one stone. The odds may be stacked pretty heavily against me at this point with everything else, but this one might actually go in my favor.

Skidding into the parking lot of Dr. Matthew's office, I find a place and park. I almost jump from the truck before it completely stops and dash for the door. Being late isn't an option for me in the eyes of the law. They need to see that I am committed to fictitiously working through my problems. It might not be real to me, but it would be to them on a piece of paper. Had it not been for my prior convictions as a juvenile for drug use, I wouldn't have even needed to go through with this farce of a recovery program. Thankfully for me, my other past discretions were below the involvement of the law, thus saving me from being one hundred percent completely fucked. I doubt the state would look too kindly on being prostituted out by your mother, drug trafficking, and being an accessory to multiple murders thanks to the man who had gang raped me along with his club for his own pleasure. I am so fucking glad he's dead, or I would kill him myself all over again.

The waiting room lies empty, and I sigh in relief that

no one saw my rapid-fire barrel roll into this place. Signing in on the piece of paper at the front desk, I hear someone clearing their throat. In an instant, I can feel the eyes of someone watching me, and for a split second, I fear Ratchet has followed me, but it's not him. I peer up from the sign-in sheet and find Dr. Matthews leaning against the doorframe of her office. Her furrowed brow and tightly pursed lips tell me all I need to know. She had seen the entire display and is pissed at my tardiness.

"Hi, Doc," I sweetly reply, hoping that my act of innocence pays off.

"Erica," she nags. "I wasn't aware that NASCAR was recruiting drivers here in our little town."

My eyes fill with horror. There's no way I'm getting out of this one. I don't stand a snowball's chance in hell.

"About that," I stammer. "Something came up, and I lost track of time. I promise I won't be late again, Dr. Matthews."

She shifts from her rigid stance in the doorway and waves me into her open office. Though she seems to be a patient and understanding woman in our sessions, I feel that she might not be the sunshine and rainbows kind of person who I had originally pegged her to be.

Brushing past the doc, I make my way toward the couch of misery, as I named it after my last session with her. Ever since my great revelation to her that my childhood wasn't gumdrops and rainbows, she seems to have taken an unhealthy interest in that period of my life. Not that I blame her because, unlike most people in this town that would come to see her, my problems didn't revolve around the local gossip and church ladies' luncheon drama over who stole whose casserole recipe. The latter made for quite an interesting week at the diner, as I had the privilege of listening to the women cackle about it.

Dr. Matthews quietly shuts the door behind her and heads toward her chair. She pulls a notepad from her side table and clicks the pen, ready to hear my confessions today.

"How have you been since our last session?" she begins, her eyes focusing on me closely. "Any recent developments?"

"Nope," I sharply reply. "Nothing new in the land of me."

Her eyes narrow, and a look of disbelief settles on her face.

Shit. What does she know?

"It was my understanding that a new arrival has developed quite an interest in you. Wouldn't that classify as something new?"

"God, I hate the rumor mill in this place. You can't take your trash out without someone alerting the rumor mill media about it," I exclaim. "Don't any of these old broads have anything else better to talk about?"

"The day those women stop gossiping is the day this

world ends." She smirks. We both share a quiet laugh, but the momentary amusement is short-lived. She plasters her game face back on, and I feel she has an agenda today.

"Is this man a friend of yours?" she bluntly asks, looking for more of an elaboration.

I sigh before answering her. Ratchet and his storm-the-gates entry into this town has already cost me my day job, risked my chances at getting full custody of my brother, and now is invading my therapy sessions. What's next? Will I go home to find him already moved in and demanding a home-cooked meal?

Shit, I shouldn't have thought about that. The way things have gone today, I may have just wished that thought into existence.

Dr. Matthews clears her throat and brings me back to reality.

"He's an acquaintance, yes."

"An acquaintance?" she teases.

"That's right. He's practically a stranger to me," I lie in hopes she ends her interrogation.

"Being found pinned to the wall by this acquaintance outside of Willie's bar doesn't accurately explain a lack of familiarity with this man. Is he a boyfriend or, perhaps, an ex-lover by chance? If his presence here is uncomfortable for you, I'd be happy to inform the police so you can file a restraining order."

I internally laugh at the idea that the good doctor thinks a restraining order would keep him away from me. I'm almost positive that someone could bury him ten feet underground in a cement-covered casket, and he would still find a way out and back to me. He's never been one to give up easily, and I doubt the trait will ever fade away.

I fold my arms across my chest and huff my displeasure at how this conversation has turned from her interest in me to her interest in finding out if the gossip is true or some fabrication of a bored stay-at-home parent.

"All the above," I offer, knowing how much a vague answer will frustrate her. One thing that I have learned in as many of these therapy sessions that I have attended over the years is that non-specific answers are like kryptonite to psychiatrists. The meaning being they will drive them off the wall. It's a sick little game, but when she has the power to commit me at any moment, it evens the playing field. "Why such an active interest in my relationship with this man, Doc? Are you inquiring whether his bed is occupied?"

Before the words finish rolling off my lips, the image of Ratchet and the doctor tangled up in bed together hits a nerve. The thought of Ratchet with another woman sends a wave of nausea straight toward my gut, making it a churning mess of confusion and jealousy.

"Of course not. I am simply concerned for you as

your doctor since you did not find his presence here enough of significance to mention when I asked the first time."

"His being here is a temporary situation, which I hope to remedy later today."

"I don't think that's actually what you want. His leaving, I mean. I can tell by the change in your body language that this man means something to you. Even implying to yourself that he is unattached has made you visibly shaken. I can assure you, Miss Delmont, that my curiosity is simply regarding your mental and physical well-being. After our last session's revelations, I have a significant concern about your past derailing your recovery progress."

"He may derail me in many things, Dr. Matthews, but if anyone was going to keep me on the path of righteousness, it would be him."

"Please elaborate on that."

For nearly forty-five minutes, I retell my story. Just a general overview, of course, but I explain how he saved me. Dr. Matthews doesn't say a word as I speak candidly about how Ratchet saved my life and helped me get clean. Because of respect and a healthy dose of fear that I have of the Heaven's Rejects, I leave them out completely. They are the last people I want hot on my trail for exposing their club secrets about the recent bloodshed and war between the cartel.

As I finish telling my story, Dr. Matthews remains quiet for several minutes. Her face remains neutral. The sound of the ticking wall clock is nearly deafening before she breaks the silence.

"I have to tell you, Miss Delmont," she starts as she removes her glasses and sets aside her notebook. "For the first time since we began our sessions, you have truly opened up about a piece of your past. The fear and the anger that usually lace every word you speak were gone. This man means more to you than someone who merely helped you recover from your past traumas and addiction, and I think that deep down, you know that to be true. While I wouldn't normally say this, I think he's the person who you need in your life right now."

"You don't know him, Doc. He's not the man that you can bring home to your parents and have family dinners with. He's more of a cave dweller who imposes his will upon you until you succumb to his side of the argument," I protest. "He saved me, but he's not the person I need around right now."

"Is that you talking or your fear of giving up control to see what the two of you could become?"

Where in the hell is all of this coming from? It's as if she's shoving me toward him. Not that he would mind, but I do. I may need a push in the right direction sometimes, but his direction is the opposite place I need to go. At least for the time being.

"Trust me, Dr. Matthews. Ratchet isn't the answer to my problems. He's the catalyst to new problems."

"Ratchet?" she questions. I note a flash of recognition in her eyes when she repeats his name. Could she possibly know him? I mull over that thought before I quickly dismiss it. Because how could she know him living here? It's not like he's a frequent flyer through these parts. Maybe my brain is finally losing some of its marbles.

"I know," I laugh. "Not the best name in the world for a guy, but it's his nickname. I think."

It hits me suddenly that I don't even know the real name of the man who I shared so much with. How is that even possible? Then again, nothing about my relationship with Ratchet has been remotely normal.

The session timer chimes just as Dr. Matthews asks another question. She quickly rises from her chair and ushers me out of the room with a sense of urgency. What in the fuck just happened?

The entire trek out to my truck, I think about the odd exchange. It's almost as if the mention of his name triggered a panicked response in Dr. Matthews. I can't help but wonder about it with each step I take.

I fling open the door and slide into the truck when something else completely pushes into my train of thought once I notice the time on the dashboard clock.

The flashing numbers remind me I have another meeting today that I have left to deal with.

As far as the score of today's accomplishments goes, it is Ricca - zero and life - two. I guess it's time to see if my promise to Ratchet will be my third strike.

Chapter 12

RATCHET

"THANKS," I grumble to the server as she hands me my meal. After Ricca left me on the side of the road, I decided that after two attempts at eating in this place, I needed to give it the old college go again with her not distracting me. Thankfully for me, Willie's was open for lunch since I was probably no longer welcome at the diner anymore. Now I just had to make sure I didn't piss him off, or I'd be starving for the rest of my stay here.

The smell of the steak in front of me makes my stomach grumble impatiently. It's been over twenty-four hours since I've actually eaten something, but my cravings were singular compared to the woman who keeps eluding me. I can only hope the promise that she left me with on the roadside was actually the truth and not another lie. Unfortunately for her, she wouldn't be able to run far, thanks to the tracker that Voodoo packed for me. With a flick of my finger, I could see her every move in that truck. Was it invading her privacy and illegal? Of course, it was, but I'm not about to let her slip away so easily this time. The trust between us needs to be rebuilt, but call me a fool for keeping my skepticism about it. I just had to pray that she doesn't find out about it because that kind of fight could draw a good payday if I sold tickets for it.

Grabbing the knife and fork, I cut into the steak and nearly groan at the medium-rare perfection on my plate. The first bite melts in my mouth. The second and the third go down as quickly as I can shove it in. I eat like a man starved for months, and that's exactly what I am. Starved for Ricca. As I reach for my beer, I feel a vibration coming from my pocket. It could only mean one of two things: Ricca left the city limits, or it's one of my club brothers. Setting the utensils down on my plate, I reach into my jeans and pull out my phone.

It's sad to admit that I sigh with relief when I see Hero's name on the screen.

"Hero," I state plainly as I answer the phone. Music pounds in the background until his muffled voice finally breaks through the commotion.

"Celebrating, VP?" I inquire. "Sounds like there's quite the party happening at the clubhouse."

"You could say that," Hero declares with a hint of exhaustion in his voice. "It's been a long night."

"Do you need me back?"

A muffled sound comes through the receiver, along with whispered voices I can't understand. My instincts heighten knowing that something is wrong.

"Hero," I call out. "You still there?"

"We've got another club here at the moment, and we're about to get into some heavy shit. Raze is tied up in meetings right now, but he wanted me to call to let you know."

"This isn't your version of the if you don't hear from me ever again talk bullshit, is it?" I ask, hoping that I am wrong about the gut feeling I have. I'm helpless here, so far away from my club, and that is not a feeling that I particularly like having. The club has been my life since Jagger brought me into the fold, thus saving my life. When they call, I answer no questions asked. I have never not been there for a fight, and it's gnawing at me, knowing that this could be the first time experiencing the shit hitting the fan from the outside.

"It could be. Our old buddy Rex apparently started trafficking local pussy. One of the girls he has belongs to a club in Texas. They showed up, guns blazing."

"Sounds pretty heavy, man. Are you sure you don't need me to come back? I could be there in less than six or seven hours if I caught a flight right now."

"Raze was very specific in his instructions for you to stay put. Besides, we have their numbers to help us end this problem for the last time," he replies, but the pull inside me to be there for my club continues to nag at me. There are a few things that I have remained loyal to in my life: my club and Ricca. The hard part of having two priorities is that one may have to be sacrificed for the good of the other, but I don't think I am equipped to make a call like that just yet. Raze, being the good club president that he is, isn't asking me to do that, but that time may come, and when it does, the decision will have to be made.

"Are the women and the kids taken care of?" I ask. Hero pauses before answering.

"That's not the shit I expected to hear coming out of your mouth, Ratch. I'm not sure if I like this softer side of you."

"I'm not soft, asshole. We've got more people than ourselves to think about now, including your woman and kids. We protect our own, and that extends to them," I growl back at his surprise.

"I appreciate it, brother. It's nice knowing that should shit go south that you'll still be around to watch after them. Not all plans work out the way they should."

"No shit," I mutter. "So, I'm gonna ask again. Do you need me?"

"No, we're covered. How are things going on your end? Any progress?"

A laugh rumbles from my chest unexpectedly. How in the fuck did two grown-ass men get to the point in their lives that we talk about the women in them? Jesus, maybe being here with her has turned me into a fucking pussy.

"Slower than expected, but with a little luck, that might change today."

"I wish you luck, brother. Women are complicated creatures," he teases. "Trust me, I have three of them under my roof right now."

"Twins keeping you busy?"

"You have no idea. Fucking hell on wheels, times two. Nothing is safe in my house."

We both share a laugh before I notice the time. Ricca should be here soon enough. Hero talks about his daughters and Dani, but I tune him out while I wave for the server to bring me a to-go box for my meal. Instead of bringing it, she takes my plate with her. I try to reach out and stop her, but she slips past me and stomps off with my half-eaten dinner. Let's hope she comes back with it because this time, I would not take a chance of leaving with an empty stomach on the off chance Ricca gets me blacklisted from this place. Convenience store food fucking sucks and the chance of her actually being a decent cook is slim to none. I've seen her so-called cooking skills, and we're just lucky she hasn't burned down the clubhouse kitchen yet.

"Hey, man, I've got to run. Let me know how things go, and if the status quo changes, I'll be there to clean up the mess you make. Just don't let Voodoo near a gun. He might blow a foot off instead of taking care of business."

He chuckles before disconnecting the call. The pretty red-headed server comes back with a box in her hand. I leave her a hefty tip for a good job and slide from the booth. Willie waves at me from behind the bar as I exit the building.

At least Willie likes me. For now, anyway. After watching him manhandle that Johnny kid last night, I'm sure he could hold his own against me. Something that I hope never has to come to fruition.

I hold my breath as I scan the parking lot and sure enough, Ricca's truck sits waiting in the far corner next to my bike. Score one for me on the promise scale today. A sigh of relief hits me as I notice she didn't run my bike over. Yet another sign pointing to yes on the Ricca version of the Magic Eight Ball.

I stalk over to the truck, takeout box in my hand, and knock on the passenger side glass. She startles at the sound and stares a hole through me before motioning me to hop in.

"This isn't a stakeout, Ratchet. You didn't need to

bring a snack," she sasses as I open the truck door and set down the box on the bench seat.

"Funny thing about eating in this town," I retort back to her, sliding into the truck. "I don't seem to get to finish my meal without having to rescue your ass."

I smile back at her, but her face turns angry. I would never admit it to her, but seeing her eyes narrow and her chest heave like that turns me on. Fucked up, I know, but I like what I like. It leaves me to wonder what hate sex would be like with her. I make a mental note to test the theory. She's already a wildcat, but a pissy kitty might just make me bend a knee and submit to her.

"I do not need rescuing, asshole. It's your fault that I got fired today, or do you not remember that fact?" she sneers.

"Yes, that one is on me, but your boss needed to be taught a lesson. Good thing the first one is a freebie. The second lesson won't be so nice."

Ricca glares at me and just shakes her head at my joke. I watch her throw the gearshift into drive and head toward the street. She maneuvers into the light traffic but remains silent. I drum my fingers on the dashboard, hoping to annoy her enough to break the silence. It doesn't. Shifting in my seat, I turn and notice that her knuckles are gripping the steering wheel so tightly that they are completely white. What in the hell does she have to show me that is making her this scared? Have I given her any reason to think that whatever the fuck it is would bother me that much?

"So, what's this secret of yours?" I blurt out.

Did you not learn from the first time you tried to force something out of her? She's like a gold vault at Fort Knox. Impenetrable until unlocked. I just need to find the right key to get her to lower the gates and let me back in.

"It's not something that I can explain yet. You need to see it for yourself."

"You aren't driving me out to the country to kill me, right?" I tease her, trying to make her break the hardened look on her face. She side-eyes me, but she smirks just like I wanted her to. Another point in my win column already. This day might just shape up to be a decent one.

I settle back into the bench seat of the truck and just let her drive. The narrow streets filled with small homes and trailers zoom by until she finally slows and makes a left turn. She quickly turns again, and my eyes fall in disbelief when she pulls up next to a school building. The thought of one of my fears punches me in the gut. It can't be true, could it? Was there a kid I didn't know about?

She cuts the engine and unbuckles her seatbelt before turning to face me.

"I can see your wheels turning already, but stop jumping to conclusions before I can explain."

"Explain what exactly?" I question.

"Just wait. Once I show you, I'll explain."

She settles into her seat with her eyes trained on the front door of the school. An awkward silence settles between us. I try to think of a way to break it, but every time I try to open my mouth, she shushes me. If it wasn't so frustrating, it would be kind of cute. Ricca looks at the clock on the dashboard, and her eyes flash with delight. The sound of a bell ringing echoes off the brick walls of the surrounding playground as she watches intently. I lean forward, studying her face. As the kids come out of the school, her eyes dart from kid to kid until they stop completely. I follow her gaze and see what has her so locked-on in interest. A young boy stands at the corner of the building. She turns to me, and I realize this kid looks eerily similar to her.

"It's not what you think," she blurts out.

"So that's not your kid that I am looking at right now?" I hiss. "Because that kid looks just fucking like you, Ricca."

Her eyes dart between mine and watching the kid again in an unwavering panic.

"He's not my kid, Ratchet," she declares with a look of sorrow on her face. "He's my brother."

"You honestly think I am going to believe that kid is your brother? A kid that has to be nearly twenty years your junior. Do you think you can play me for a fool?"

It takes seconds for me to realize that the only fool in

this situation is me. The pained look on her face tells me everything that I need to know. I've hurt her deeper than I could have ever imagined possible. The fucking broken word filter between my brain and mouth may have just shut me out of the picture for good, and there is nothing I can do about it.

Chapter 13

RICCA

"YES, asshole, he is my brother. That's what happens when your mother is a fucking whore. You know, like the women who flock to your club and beg for attention on their knees with open mouths," I recoil at him with tears welling up in my eyes.

"Ricca, I didn't mean it like that," he stammers out, but I have nothing left to give him. I gave him what he wanted, and he's spit the trust I put in him back into my face.

He tries to move closer to me, but I barricade myself with my outstretched arms.

I'm emotionally drained, and having his touch enveloping me won't solve anything. It will only confuse my heart even more. Why was I so stupid to believe that he would understand? That he would just accept it at face value. The part of me that wanted him to leave is reveling, because I did this to myself. This is my misery.

"No, don't you dare try to play the pity card with me, Ratchet. You wanted the truth, and there he is."

Ratchet flops back into the seat and watches along with me as my brother disappears into the town car with my sperm donor. I could have mentioned that to him, but he didn't care enough to ask. He's made up his mind, which also helped me make up my own. We aren't strong enough to be together and probably never were. The realization hurts as the dreams of my future shatter into pieces.

Without a word, I turn on the truck and barrel out of the school parking lot. When we reach Willie's, I skid into the open spot near his bike and kick him out of the truck. He tries to protest, but his words fall on deaf ears. Before he can even latch the door closed, I speed off. The door slams shut as I take the corner hard.

I can't deal with this anymore. The need to be away from him and everything else is almost overwhelming.

I try to drive around town to ease my anger, but nothing helps. The former addict who lives inside of me screams to find a hit to dull the pain. To give into temptation because, in the end, it's easier to forget the pain than to live with it.

No, I won't give in. That isn't my life anymore. It will never have a hold on me ever again.

I finally give up and head back to mom's trailer. I bust into the door and head straight to the nearly bare refrigerator. The only thing my mom apparently kept in here was beer, and for once, I am thankful for her vices. As much as I want to drink myself into oblivion, one beer should be enough to take the edge off and help me clear my mind of Ratchet and the drugs.

I pop the top of the beer on the cheap countertop and take a few swigs before I manage to spill the fucking shit all over myself. Setting the bottle down, I rip off my beer-covered shirt and toss it to the ground. The clock over the stove catches my eye, and I swear out loud. My shift at Willie's starts in a few hours, and I reek of beer. I've lost one job today, and there's no way I am going into my last one smelling like a saloon. Willie would fire me in an instant if he thought I was drunk on the job.

Deciding it's easier to shower than it is to take the chance, I make my way back to the bathroom. The hot spray from my shower helps release the last wisps of anger that were not taken care of by the beer, but relaxation is as short-lived as the hot water supply in this place. Wrapping the towel around me, I pad into the bedroom and slip on a pair of panties and a bra when I hear the door of my trailer swing open.

Fuck, I'm being robbed, and I'm fucking naked. Just great. That'll make the perfect headline for the local paper. "Daughter of town whore found naked and burglarized." That's exactly how I want to go out in this world.

I search for my switch knife, but I realize that it's out in the kitchen in my purse. The only way I am going to get to them is to go out there and face whoever is in my house. I reach down for the towel, wrapping it around me like paper armor. It won't protect me, but at least my dignity can stay intact for the coroner to identify my body if this goes south.

I quietly pull open the door and peer out. My feet make tiny steps down the hall, and I pray that the floor doesn't creak under my weight. The corner to the kitchen comes into view, but I stop dead in my tracks when I see who the intruder is.

Ratchet is in my goddamn house.

"Get out of my house," I scream at him. I eye a beer bottle on the counter and consider throwing it at him to emphasize my point.

"Don't you even think about it, Siren," he booms. "You throw that bottle, and I will paint your ass red."

"Get out. I don't want you here. You got what you came for, and now you can leave," I yell back as my hand grasps the bottle. My fingers curl around the smooth neck.

Ratchet's hands come out in front of him in a submissive gesture, like he's the china shop, and I am the bull wreaking havoc.

"We both know that's a lie. You would have never shown me that *boy* if you wanted me gone. You want me here, even if you think you don't. I make you feel safe, and that's exactly what you need right now."

"I don't need you for shit, asshole."

His face is visibly frustrated at my lack of submission to him. Do I want him here? Yes, and no. Being near him is like toeing the line between heaven and hell. Lean a little too far on either side, and it's too late to save yourself.

"Jesus, Ricca. I am trying to apologize here, and you're not even giving me a fucking chance."

"Nice try," I chide him. "You were pretty clear you wanted nothing to do with this. You accused me of lying to you, and now you want to apologize?"

Ratchet inches closer to me with his hands still in front of him.

"I was an asshole, but you didn't exactly give me time to process the situation. This isn't what I was expecting you to be hiding from me."

"Well, it's not what I expected either, but it's the hand I've been dealt. Not that you would understand."

Ratchet winces, and for a second, I see a pain in his eyes that I have never seen before.

"I would understand more than most. I came here knowing you'd be pissed, but I've seen that look on your face before. The last time I saw it, I spent nearly a week at the hospital with you as you detoxed. I couldn't let you walk away without trying to save you from yourself. That isn't the road you want to travel back down now that you have someone else depending on you."

"Thanks for your concern, but I will *never* subject myself to that shit again. As much as I wanted to find the nearest dealer, I couldn't bring myself to do it," I admit with a trace of weakness in my voice. The fact he recognizes my weaknesses is both shocking and soothing at the same time. It's as if he knows me better than I know myself anymore.

"You could have told me, Siren, from the very beginning, but you ran and hid this from me. Do you know how it makes me feel knowing that you've been dealing with this alone when I could have been here helping you? That you've been working in seedy fucking bars and restaurants with fucking piss ants trying to get into your pants. You did this to us, Siren."

"Like you would have came here with me," I scoff. "This isn't your problem. It's mine."

Even as angry as I am with him, he's right. His presence, although aggravating, is calming to me. He makes me crazy, but it's moments like these where he opens up and shows me only what I get to see, his heart.

"That's where you are wrong, Siren. If it involves

you, it has everything to do with me. Why do you think I came all this way? I came here for *you*."

Ratchet moves closer and takes the beer bottle out of my hand, tossing it on the couch. My heart is beating way too loud when he stops directly in front of me.

"Have you missed me, Siren? Missed the things that I can do to your body?" Ratchet teases. His hands trace the edge of the towel wrapped around me before slipping it away from my body. His gaze slips down my nearly naked form, taking all my curves in. Unease settles around me, and I suddenly can relate to being a slide on a microscope.

Ratchet steps forward and grabs me by the waist, pulling me toward him.

"Eek," I squeak.

"You didn't answer my question," he recalls, pulling my flesh flush against his. The bulge at the fly of his jeans tells me one thing, he still wants me. Part of me wants to resist his seduction, but I can't. I want him. I want to feel human again, and only he can give me that.

"Yes," I moan when his hand moves between us and slips inside my panties. His fingers circle my sensitive flesh before slipping inside, just grazing my clit. He strokes me slowly, knowing how crazy that makes me.

"Your body remembers me," he declares, pressing harder against my clit. "So wet for me already." His voice is thick with a lusty desire. "You've missed me, haven't you? Missed what I can do to you."

My head falls back as a small ripple of arousal vibrates around his touch. Though his hands are rough, his touch is gentle. Ratchet continues to fucking tease me by circling my clit. My hand trails down my body, grasping his to quicken the pace.

He breaks the contact from my clit as he removes my hand.

"Six months," he growls at me. "You have six months to make up for, and I will not have you rushing this. I want to watch you come undone on my fingers, my mouth, and my cock. In no fucking particular order. This is my time, and you will follow my rules. Do you understand me?"

My body screams to comply, knowing that as soon as I do, his touch will return. He watches me squirm and likely enjoys every second of it. I reach out for his hand, but he steps away.

"Just fuck me already."

"Rush me one more time, and I will fuck you until this bed breaks."

My eyebrow arches in response.

"That's not a punishment. That's an incentive."

Ratchet growls at my offer and swiftly moves forward, grasping me by my hips. His mouth crashes onto mine, and his tongue forces my lips to part. I raise my arms and wrap them around his broad shoulders, pulling him in closer. His fingers dig deep into my hips, and even though I know they'll be bruises there tomorrow, I just don't care. I moan into his mouth before he suddenly breaks contact.

"Do you want this? Me, I mean," he asks, searching my eyes for a sign of hesitation.

"Yes," I respond, my voice urgent with need.

Ratchet smirks before beginning the kiss again. His hands lift from my hips and slide upward to my bra. He unclasps it and pulls it away from my flesh, exposing my nipples. He pulls away from the kiss, leaning forward and taking one into his mouth. Each second he sucks and nips at my pebbled bud, my legs grow weaker. He looks up as he places a light bite on my nipple, watching my reaction. The initial pain stuns me but is quickly replaced with another feeling, arousal.

I moan louder when his free hand pinches my other nipple, doubling the pain and pleasure sensations. He breaks contact again, and I want to scream out in protest. Ratchet suddenly lifts me and carries me to the bedroom. He drops me on the bed, and the springs creak as I land hard, but he only smiles as he takes in the scene in front of him. I am almost completely exposed and vulnerable as soon as I gave him the confirmation he needed to move forward.

"Take off your panties," he commands as he unbuckles his belt from his jeans.

My hands reach down to my thighs, slowly slipping the thin pink fabric from my body. I try to tease him in return, but he rips them the rest of the way down, tossing them across the room.

"No more panties while I am here," Ratchet teases me. "I don't want a single boundary between us."

I try to respond, but the movement of his hands distracts me.

"Is that belt for me?" I question, imagining how the smooth leather would feel stinging my flesh.

"Not today, Siren, but soon."

I prop myself up on my elbows and watch him unbutton his fly. He smiles at me and plants his gaze firmly on mine. His jeans hang low on his hips, but the head of his enormous cock moves out of the material, restraining it. My pussy vibrates once again, seeing the sexiest fucking cock I have ever seen. Thick with veins wrapping around his hard length. He slides his jeans from his hips, and his cock finally springs completely free. I lick my lips again as his cock twitches in response.

"Keeping at me like that, Siren, and this ends far faster than either of us wants."

I push off my elbows, trying to touch him, but he shoves me back onto the bed.

"No," he declares, "as much as I want to watch this

sexy fucking mouth around my cock, I have other plans tonight."

His knees fall to the edge of the bed, and a sense of being his prey overwhelms me. I shiver at the thought. Ratchet grabs my thighs and pulls me closer to him. In a flash, his mouth is on me. His tongue slips between my slit, heading straight for my throbbing clit.

"You taste like pure fucking sin," he murmurs against my pussy.

A moan is my only response. His tongue moves slowly from top to bottom repeatedly, only stopping to nibble and suck my clit. I tremble at every pass he makes. His speed increases, and my back arches in response, pressing him harder against my apex. My hands clutch the cheap sheets around me as my breathing becomes shallow.

"So close," I moan. "So fucking close."

"Not yet," he growls. "Not fucking yet." His assault continues until every nerve in my body is on fire, begging for my release. Ratchet swipes his tongue up my entire core before laying down a light bite on my clit. The sting fading away instantly.

"Stop fucking edging me." I growl. "This is torture."

"This is what the last six months felt like to me, Siren." He doesn't stop. Ratchet brings me to the cusp of toppling over the edge and then he bites me again.

"Wondering if you were okay. If you were safe. Pure fucking torture."

"I'm sorry," I cry out. "Please." My voice cracks under the weight of my orgasm.

"Come for me, Siren," he whispers against my flesh. The command enough to send me toppling over the edge.

I squirm as he quickens his pace once more. I feel his finger pressing against my tight hole before he slips one inside of me. A second and third quickly follow behind. My walls clench around the intrusion, but the sensation throws me over the edge as I ride his fingers. My orgasm hits hard, like a punch to the gut, and my legs squeeze tightly around his head as I ride the cresting waves of pleasure. I collapse in a boneless heap on the bed, panting for air.

He removes his fingers while emerging from between my legs. I peer down at him as he smirks back at me with wetness gleaming on his lips. He slowly licks them back and forth, and I shudder, watching him enjoy my taste. Ratchet rises from his kneeling position and slides onto the bed. It dips from his weight as he positions himself above my hips, and his massive cock falls to my lower stomach.

"I thought you wanted to take this slow," I pant in anticipation.

"Slow is for the fucking birds."

He shifts farther down my body, taking his hard cock in his hands, and positioning himself at my entrance. I can feel the head of his length pressing against me, and I impatiently shift, trying to push him into me.

"You want this as badly as I do?"

"You have no idea."

"I know it's a little late, but are you still clean?" he asks me. Normally, I would be pissed at his insinuation, but he knows my past better than anyone else.

"Clean."

He guides the tip of his cock in slowly. My body protests his girth, but he doesn't force himself in until I adjust to his size.

"You okay?" he checks.

I nod my head as he pushes farther inside of me. It isn't until he's fully inside that the prickles of pain finally fade away.

"Fuck," Ratchet moans. "Your pussy feels so fucking good, Siren."

He stays still inside of me until he notices I begin moving my hips against him. He pulls out slowly and re-impales me faster this time. He repeats the motion until I'm fully adjusted. Six months without sex has made me tight, but even with the soreness that will come tomor-row, the sensation of him inside of me is more than enough to satisfy me.

He stays at his slow pace, but I need more.

"Faster," I beg of him. "Please, Ratchet."

He smiles down at me and doesn't move any faster. Taking matters into my own hands, I slam my hips harder against him and drive his cock deeper inside of me.

"So greedy," he moans, just before grabbing my legs and hoisting them over his shoulders to deepen himself farther. My body cries out in a mix of pain and pleasure, and I swear he's going to hit my cervix if he goes any farther.

He pounds into me harder, our bodies moving in unison.

Screams rip from my lips as a second orgasm begins it build inside of me.

"Don't stop," I scream out.

"I won't stop until your neighbors hear you screaming my name and know who you belong to." Ratchet lifts my ass from the bed, bringing me closer to him.

"Oh, God," I exclaim. "Fuck, fuck, fuck."

"I'm not God," he huffs. "Say it, Ricca. Tell the world who this pretty little pussy belongs to."

"I belong to you," I force out.

"And who am I?" he questions as he increases his speed. "Say my name, Siren. Who do you belong to?"

"Ratchet!" I scream as my orgasm crests over the edge. "I belong to Ratchet!"

He only grunts in response. His balls clench against me, alerting me he is getting close. My orgasm bursts free, and he follows quickly behind, a few thrusts after me. His hips buck forward as he spills himself inside of me. My body goes limp as I gasp for air.

We both stay silent as the adrenaline rush of our orgasms fades to exhaustion. Ratchet slips out of me and slides off the bed. Shifting to my side, I grab one of the pillows and press it against my front. I watch as his tight ass leaves the room and pads down the hallway. His footsteps come back, and I laugh into my pillow.

"The door is on the left," I call out to him, knowing he's searching for the bathroom. This place may be tiny, but its design isn't exactly obvious when it comes to what door goes to what room. A few minutes later, I hear the flush of the toilet, and he reappears in the room. The bed dips from his weight when he settles in behind me. His arm slides across my midsection, and he pulls me closer to him. I nestle against his warm body and enjoy the quiet moment we are sharing.

"Shit, what time is it?" I swear, looking for the clock. "I have a shift tonight at Willie's."

"No, you don't," Ratchet mutters against my back. "I told him you needed the night off, and before you start another argument, it wasn't because I expected this to happen. You needed a break, and I wanted you to have it."

"Bastard," I laugh.

"Yeah, but I'm your bastard."

My eyes become heavy as I drift off to sleep, but resting only lasts a short while before Ratchet wakes me up for rounds two and three before we finally pass out for the night.

The devil may own my heart, but after tonight, I think I might own his in return.

Chapter 14

RATCHET

THE FEELING of Ricca shifting in her sleep against me wakes me up far earlier than I had planned, but it is not an unwelcome intrusion. She's still here with me, and that's all that matters. By giving me her body, she sealed the bond between us. Even if she ordered me to leave, I couldn't. As soon as her lips declared she was mine again, she agreed with the devil that never expires. She is mine and always will be. As the sun's rays shine into the room, I am taken aback to the last time she was in my bed.

That day I made the hardest decision of my life. I left her to secure the safety of my club and her safety as well. She took down her walls and gave me a piece of her that so few had likely ever seen: her soul. Ricca may not have had a perfect life, but that night, just like last night, she bared it all for me. I watched her for hours that night, battling with myself how to say goodbye. The chance of not coming back after that trip was the highest it had ever been. I was forced to go all-in with no guarantee that the outcome would be in our favor. It was an impossible situation, but for my club, it was what had to be done. Ricca was a completely different story. How do you tell someone that you love that this may have been the one and only time that you had together?

My answer was that I couldn't.

Instead, I left her without ever telling her how I felt. It was the thought of her waiting for me that kept me going throughout that entire trip, but the faith I had in her wasn't reciprocated. At least until now, it wasn't. I let my pride and sense of responsibility get in the way, and this is where it landed me months later, trying to pick up the pieces. Would things have been different if I had said goodbye that morning? No one will ever know.

She shifts again, and my attention turns back to her sleeping form. Ricca's beautiful curves fit perfectly against the hardness of my body. My finger traces down her back, and she wiggles closer to me. I smile, knowing that even in her sleep, she still seeks me out. It's a beautiful sight to behold, and I am one fucking lucky man to get to experience this a second time. Will she have the same feelings that I have the morning after? Maybe not, but last night was only a taste of what I am going to give her.

Ricca tosses around before turning to face me. Her long lashes flutter when I sweep a piece of hair off of her face. Her hand reaches out toward me, but instead of touching me, she grabs the pillow from under my head and tucks it against her body.

I stare in disbelief at her. How in the hell did she pull that off while still asleep? A chuckle leaves my lips, and I reach over to steal the pillow back. Her lips purse as she mutters angrily. My fingers wrap around the edge of the pillow, but as I pull, she swings wildly and clocks me in the face.

"What the fuck!" I yell, releasing the pillow and moving my hand to cover my eye.

Ricca doesn't move an inch and a smile forms on her face, still completely passed out.

"I see how this is going to go," I whisper. "You get all the pillows, or I get punched in the face. Seems fair."

She smiles before wrapping a leg around my stolen pillow and snuggles back into it. All I can do in this situation is just laugh. How is it even possible that I could love her more, even after she's decked me for trying to steal my own pillow back?

Seeing that she's not ready to wake up just yet, I try to fall back asleep myself, but just as my eyes close, I hear my phone vibrating in my jeans pocket. How that damn thing isn't dead already is a mystery, but Voodoo knows how to pick them, I guess.

Slowly shifting out the bed, I pad over to my jeans and retrieve the phone. It's Raze. Shit. I grab my jeans and head for the hallway to avoid waking her up. I make it to the front room before taking the call.

"Prez," I answer. Putting the phone between my ear and my shoulder, I slip on my jeans with a hop to get them over my hips. I leave them unbuttoned and flop onto the couch. A thick plume of dust flies up around me.

"Hey, brother," he responds with exhaustion clear in his voice.

"Things go okay?"

"Yeah, it's done. Rex is officially no longer our problem."

Rex had always been a thorn in the club's side since the time I was a prospect. He trafficked women like Audi sold high-end cars. If the money was right, he did the job, and for a time, our club helped him transport them. Not my proudest moment of Heaven's Rejects membership, but I didn't have a choice back then as a prospect. I needed the club to survive, and I could not say no. The guy was scum, but because of him, our club still existed. Raze's dad had put us in a shitty position with a drug runner that, much like our own deal with the last cartel, had put our heads on the chopping block. Rex and Raze made a deal to no longer be involved in the business sense in exchange for his help. A part of that deal was not trafficking local girls, and apparently, Rex decided it wasn't a good enough business deal for himself anymore. Decisions like that are what get people killed, just like Rex.

Our club has dealt with a lot of shit, but when we make a promise, we keep it. Leniency isn't in our nature, and once you break that trust, it is definitely no longer on the menu. Dealing death may not be the easiest to handle, but it is a far easier solution than living your life looking over your shoulder every single fucking day.

"That's one funeral that I won't be attending. Casualties?" I quickly ask.

Raze goes silent on the other end of the line, and my heart nearly freezes mid-beat.

"The other club lost one," Raze admits. "Sad ass shit. He was the brother of the girl we went after. She made it out okay, but her rescue ended up costing him his life in return. The new guy, Thor, got beat up pretty bad in the aftermath, but Doc says he should recover."

I sigh in relief that it wasn't one of my brothers with a toe tag, but I feel for the other club. Jagger's death hit me hard, so I can sympathize with them. Collateral damage is never an easy pill to swallow when you are trying to right a wrong.

"Give their club my condolences," I offer.

Raze clears his throat. And I know this call wasn't just about the club business. Something is on his mind.

While Jagger used to be his sounding board when shit hit the fan, I think I have filled that role for him. Unlike the others, I listen more than I talk. Sometimes you need someone you can unload on to make sense of an unpleasant situation. Just the amount of times I've played therapist for Hero would have made me a millionaire if I had charged him. You need someone like that in your life, and it's a role I don't mind filling for my brothers.

"You sound like you have something on your mind, Prez. Care to explain?" I question, hoping that I haven't overstepped my bounds.

"Yeah, you're right. There is something else I need to talk to you about," he starts, but then pauses. An awkward silence builds up between us before he finally breaks it. "I know this is probably shit timing but I need to know if this trip might be a one-way ticket."

Raze damn near stuns me with that question. Logically speaking, I would have probably asked the same question in his place. One of the most loyal members of his club takes off after a woman with no reassurances of coming back. It's unusual even for me, and he knows that the possibility could be real.

"You trying to get rid of me?" I tease back, trying to break the tension.

"I would never do that, brother, but man to man, I have to ask. I've never seen you go after a girl this hard, and coming from someone who's been there, I get the draw to be on the outside of what happens when you're a part of an MC."

"I fully intend on returning, but the situation is more complicated than I expected. There's a kid involved," I bluntly say, laying it all out on the table for him.

"A kid? Shit, Ratchet. That is not what I expected you to say. Is it hers?" he asks.

"It's her brother. She just told me about him last night. I'm not sure what her intentions are with him yet, but I need to ride this out. If she intends to bring him home with her, I will make sure that happens."

"I understand. Fuck, do I understand. I am happy to know you want to stay with us. It just wouldn't be the same around here without you."

"Yeah, who else would bust V's balls?" I smile. Raze's laugh fills the phone, and I laugh with him.

"If there's anything that you need me or the club to do, please let me know. Keep me in the loop where you can."

"Will do, Prez," I tell him. "So, tell me how our good friend Rex met his maker."

Raze tells me about the activities of the last night when a stack of papers on the coffee table in front of the couch catches my eye. I scoop up the pile and study the words on the first page as Raze talks about burning Rex's business to the ground with him inside of it. I should have been pissed that someone else got to handle my job for the club, but this new information has me engrossed.

The paper in front of me is the application to file for custody of the boy whose name I know now is Asher.

Does she intend to make this a permanent stay?

My eyes read line by line, and I notice that she's left only one portion blank. Marital status.

Thank god for small favors.

I flip to the next page and find a handwritten page with her to-do list with a neatly organized row of check-boxes. The first line simply reads, *find a job*, with a broad check mark next to it, but the rest are blank. The other items on her list are a bit more sporadic. The next line mentions a therapist, and the rest detail the things she needed to do based on the application I saw first. The biggest item that stands out to me is her task of paying the court administration fee and filing the actual paper-work. It hits me like a punch to the gut, knowing she's constantly working just to scrap together two hundred bucks. This could have been taken care of far sooner if she had just let me in from the beginning. I may not be rolling in serious cash, but everything that I have earned from the early backdoor dealings of the club and my legitimate job through the club's security business has been saved. I grew up with nothing, and after starving and living on the streets, I made a promise to myself to not waste whatever I was given. In my own way, it was a guarantee to never go without a roof over my head and food in my belly.

A swell of pride hits me when I realize how serious she is about getting her brother, and no matter the cost to me, I want that for both of them. But even I have to admit that the odds will be stacked against her. After spending countless years in the system, I know all too well the requirements of getting custody of a relative or adopting a child. While it might be different here than it was in Florida, married couples with disposable incomes and enormous houses always get priority. It pains me to think that her effort to get him may all have been in vain. She's a single woman with a small income and a trailer that is falling apart around her. She would be seen as a risk by the courts. Not to mention the fact that she might have a criminal record a mile long thanks to the men she clung to during that dark period of her life. Something that I don't blame her for since I know all too well the sacrifices that it takes in order to survive.

A crazy idea pops into my head, but I need to look into the local laws before I go through with it. My idea could come with consequences should the Kentucky state law stars align. She would be pissed, but if it expedites her case, it's a risk that I will take.

"You still there?" Raze asks.

"I'm here, Prez. I think my girl is waking up, but

when Voodoo leaves his computer bat cave, have him call me."

"Will do. Be safe, brother."

"Same goes for you. Get some sleep, old man."

I disconnect the call and toss my phone down next to me. With Raze not distracting me, I look over the paper again. This confirms what I have only assumed since she told me about her brother. She wants to adopt him, and what my girl wants, my girl gets. I will, for damn sure, make this happen.

I make myself a promise before heading back to bed with my girl.

That no matter how much she fights me, I will fight for her and Asher even harder.

Chapter 15

"WHAT THE FUCK have you done to my truck?" I yell out the door of my trailer. Ratchet looks up from the heap of car parts lying around him and just smiles.

"Good morning to you, too, Siren. How did you sleep?" He smiles while cleaning off the engine grease on his hands with a rag from his back pocket. He tosses the rag aside and just smirks back at me.

"Don't you dare try to play this off, Ratchet. Why are these engine parts all over the ground? I may not be a mechanic, but even I know that doesn't go there."

"It needed a tune-up, amongst other things," he coolly replies. "The brakes were shot, the alternator was about to go out any second, and I don't think the previous owner changed the fucking oil since the day this thing came off the dealer's lot. It's a miracle it's still running."

It should have been a warning sign when he came to me a few days ago with a copy of the truck's title in hand and demanding a copy of my mother's death certificate that he had plans for the old beater. How he even found that is beyond me, but he did. My mother did actually own this hunk of junk. Ratchet had me sign the title, amongst other documents, before whisking them away in the promise that he would handle the Department of Motor Vehicles for me. Maybe I should have asked more questions, but if it kept him occupied for a few hours, then so be it. I hated that place; even here, it wasn't as bad as California. If I didn't have to go to the one government office that was modeled after the pits of hell, it was fine by me. But this was just way too much.

I just stare at him in shock. It's been a week since I let him into my life, and he has taken it upon himself to just impose on every facet of my life. First, he fixed the plumbing on the trailer. Then it was the roof. After that, he convinced Willie to switch me to the afternoon shift, which I protested. The money was better at night, but Ratchet's overprotective ass didn't want me around that kind of a crowd after what he witnessed the night with Johnny. And now, he's fixing my truck. Well, at least I hope he's fixing it.

It's not that I don't appreciate the work that he's doing, but it is all so unnecessary. This trailer would have better served as ash once its purpose was fulfilled, but he didn't see it that way. Ratchet took one look at the place, and his inner handyman came out. I think if I hadn't distracted him the last few days, then this place would have looked like it belonged on the front page of Redneck Home Weekly.

The house was one thing, but the truck is a completely different story. It's my only means of transportation, aside from his bike. Now that I think about it. Maybe that was his intention all along. If I was dependent on him, he could invade everything in my life. Fucking asshole.

"You could say thank you. I'm trying to make this thing safer for you," he suggests, slamming his hand down on the metal exterior.

I glare back at him in return. His intentions of stranding me here are as clear as day on his face. Every time that I have tried to leave for work, he's tried to use his dick to keep me here. Not that I minded, but, I needed to make money. Without that, Asher would have to stay in my father's care another day longer than necessary.

"And how will I be getting to work?" I question him. "This doesn't exactly look like I will drive it soon, Ratchet."

"About that." He smiles, wiping the sweat from his face with the sleeve of his shirt. "I didn't think that it was going to be this bad until I started really looking at it. It's going to be a couple of days before I finish up."

"I guess I could take your ride."

"I'll take you, Siren. Not a big deal," he replies, without a clue at what I just said. Autopilot answers are about to bite him in the ass.

"That's not what I meant."

He cocks an eyebrow at me as confusion clearly paints his face.

"I didn't mean taking your bike as in riding with you. Since you took my ride, I am going to take yours."

I step off the porch, heading toward his precious ride. He stands stoically, trying to figure out if I am bluffing or not. It isn't until I swing my leg over the warmed red metal tank that he y takes action. He strides across the driveway toward me with a look of concern plastered on his face. Playing along, I run my fingers toward the ignition switch just as he reaches me.

"This is how you turn it on, right?" I innocently ask before turning the switch. The engine roars to life between my legs, and his eyes widen. Moving my hands to the grips, I outstretch a finger across the brake. "And this is the gas."

"Hang on just a fucking minute, Siren," he yells over the sound of the engine. "You can't take my bike."

"Well, you took my truck. It's only fair."

Ratchet reaches down and switches off the engine.

"While I would be happy to teach you how to ride, this isn't the bike you try to learn on. You need something with less power and weight to it. Had you popped that kickstand, I would have had to haul this thing off of you."

"I think I could handle this bike just fine," I argue, knowing that this is going to annoy him even more.

"If you're going to handle anything, it's going to be me. Now, why don't you slide right off that seat and let me show you how we handle things around here."

"That an offer?"

"Get your ass off my bike, and you'll find out, Siren."

I smile back and do as he asks. As I pass him, I can feel the arousal radiating off of him. As each day passes, the passion that I feel for him grows exponentially. For the first time in my entire life, I feel loved. Though he has never said it aloud, I know he feels the same way. He may never say it, but as much as I am his, he is mine. One heart beating in two different bodies.

I get a few feet away from him and bolt for the door. The chase is on, but he soon catches me. His arms envelop my body as his mouth descends on mine in the hallway to the bedroom. I rip his shirt over his head, and he undoes his jeans.

My fingers trace the edge of his boxer briefs before sliding inside. I wrap my hands around his thick cock and begin to stroke him, feeling the quickening pulse of his arousal. His head falls back with pleasure, but he quickly snaps back and looks at me.

"As good as that feels, I want your mouth first and then your pussy. My cock has seen enough of my hand in your absence the last few months."

I smile and release him, lowering myself to my knees as he works his briefs over his hips and down his legs. His cock is rigid with his need. It might be an odd thing to say, but Ratchet's cock is a work of art. The veins wrapping around his thickness are like a beautiful piece of architecture, and every time I see it, it makes me pause to admire it.

I look up at him as I take his cock into my mouth. The tip slides against my tongue, which sends a moan slipping from his lips as his head falls back again. The tip of my tongue flicks against his frenulum, and I feel the veins of his cock pulsing against my lips in response to the touch. It's a minor act that drives him crazy. I let my teeth lightly graze his sensitive flesh while I pull his cock from my mouth before taking it back in. His hands fall to the top of my head as I quicken the pace. With each motion, the pulse from his cock vibrates more and more until he suddenly pulls himself from my mouth with an audible pop.

In one swift motion, he hooks his hands under my shoulders and lifts me to my feet. He urgently grabs my leggings, and I give him a knowing warning not to rip them. He just smiles before dropping to his knees and sliding them off of me. He nuzzles me against the wall, spreading my legs with his hands. His mouth plunges straight to my aching, wet pussy. I cry out in pleasure, forcing my hands to run through his short hair. His tongue laps at my clit, biting and sucking until I nearly come undone against the wall.

"I'm so close," I protest when he removes his mouth.

"The only way you are getting off is around my cock," he demands.

His devilish demands make me smile as he stands, but before I can protest, he hoists me back around his waist. His cock teases at my wet entrance before he pushes himself inside of me, stretching and filling me to the brim. I press my back against the wall and wrap my hands around his neck. His smile beams as he thrusts hard.

"If you're smiling, Siren, then I am not doing my job correctly."

I smile back, but it soon fades to pleasure within seconds as he quickens his pace. With each movement, he continues to increase his pace, his hands digging into my ass to where I know his fingerprints will be bruised into my flesh. But I don't care. All I want is for him to fuck me until I can't take it anymore. As weird as it sounds, the aches I feel, with each step at work, remind me just who I belong to.

"Fuck me," I murmur. "Harder, please."

He smirks as his pace increases more, with sweat dotting his brow. Just a few seconds more, and I feel the vibrations of my impending orgasm. I try to force it down to prolong our time together, but with each thrust, my back scrapes against the wall, roughly turning me on even more.

Note to self, wall sex is super-hot, but this wallpaper shit has got to go next time. I'm pretty sure that the floral pattern on this wall is about to be permanently tattooed onto my back.

"Siren," Ratchet moans. "I know you're holding back. Give it to me. I need to feel you come."

He leans down, taking one of my nipples into his mouth, knowing exactly what it does to me. His teeth nip my sensitive flesh, sending shockwaves straight to my clit. He releases my nipple, adjusts my hips one more time, and thrusts deeper into my core. My body shudders as my orgasm takes hold. My pussy clenches like a vice around his cock, when I feel his own release inside of me. He thrusts a few more times before his forehead falls to mine and our chests heave from the exertion.

"I love you," he whispers before pulling his cock out of me and lowering me to the ground. "You don't have to say it back."

I answer him, but he shakes his head. "I wanted to say that to you so many goddamn times, but I was too chickenshit to tell you. For the first time in my life, I found something good, and I knew, I knew that if I pushed you too hard. You'd run."

"But, I ran."

"That's in the past. No more running. For either of us." My eyes flick to the clock on the wall, and he catches me looking at it.

"Come on," he says, pulling me by the hand. "Just enough time for me to get us both cleaned up before I need to take you to work."

"And maybe a round two?" I tease back.

"Jesus, woman. You are insatiable."

He makes good on my request, but the high of the second orgasm is short-lived before it's time to head to Willie's for my lunch shift. Ratchet sits on the edge of the bed as I braid my wet hair in a tight plait against my head in the mirror he installed for me.

He slides off the bed, stalking closer to me, and wraps his arms around my waist. He places a kiss on my neck and looks up at our reflection in the mirror.

"I do love you, Siren. I know I have a shit way of showing it sometimes, but I do."

"I know," I respond, leaning into his embrace. The sweet moment between us lingers a little longer before he pulls me away. As we ride toward the bar, my mind relives that moment. He told me he loved me repeatedly, like a song on repeat. The affirmation of his feelings leaves me walking on cloud nine my entire shift. Even Willie noted how happy I looked as I clocked out after my shift ended.

"Happiness is a good look on you, sugar. It's nice to see you smile."

"Thanks, Willie," I respond back. "I'll see you tomorrow!"

"Be safe, sugar!" he calls out in return.

Stepping outside of the bar, I instantly notice that Ratchet isn't here. Reaching inside my purse, I retrieve my phone and notice a missed call and voicemail notification on the front screen from a local number. With him running late and having a bit of extra time on my hands, I click on the bubble, and the voicemail instantly plays instead of waiting until I get home to take care of it.

"Hello, Erica. My name is Marissa Myers, and I am calling from the Hancock County Family Court office. I wanted to verify that you are available to attend the hearing regarding the custody of an Asher Delmont that is scheduled for next Friday at ten o'clock in the morning. Please let me know if that time doesn't work for you."

I look down at the voicemail translated text to make sure that I didn't mishear the message, but sure enough, it has everything I heard clearly written on the screen. A wave of confusion washes over me.

"This has got to be some kind of mistake," I tell

myself as I search through my contacts and click on my caseworker's number.

"Kentucky Cabinet for Health and Family Services. How may I direct your call?" the operator answers. I ask for Nicole, and I'm immediately transferred to her.

"This is Nicole Wild. How can I help you?" she answers automatically.

"Hi, Nicole, it's Erica Delmont," I hurriedly state. "Listen, I just got a voicemail from the family court office regarding a court date for my application for Asher next week. Is that correct?"

"Let me pull up your file," she casually responds. I hear her clicking on her computer before she comes back onto the line. "Yup, that's right. Next Friday morning. Do you have a conflict with the time?"

"I don't understand how I could have a court date if the paperwork and the payment to get a court date are still sitting on my coffee table at home. How is that even possible?"

"Oh, your husband dropped it off to me a few days ago."

"My what?"

"Your husband. He came by the office on Monday and dropped off the completed application, your marriage license, and the payment for the court filing."

"That son of a bitch!" I seethe into the receiver.

"Is everything okay, Mrs. Azzo?"

Azzo? That's his last name? Oh, dear god, I don't even know his real first name. How in the fucking hell did he do this? How is this even possible?

"Mrs. Azzo. Are you still there?"

I see red, but I find the power to answer her without shattering my phone in the process.

"Yes, I'm here. I was unaware that my *husband* did that. Let me check my work schedule, and I will get back to you if there are any problems."

"Sounds good. Congratulations on your marriage," she says before ending the call. "You're a lucky woman."

"Yup, sure am." He'll be lucky to still be alive once I'm done with him. When I get my hands on that asshole, I am going to murder him. I don't even care that I will go to jail because I think the judge would rule it as a justified killing for marrying me without my fucking knowledge.

Chapter 16

RATCHET

PULLING UP TO WILLIE'S, I can already tell that my goose is cooked. Her body language lets me know that my crazy idea has been spilled to her, and she is not happy about the development. Not that I blame her. It's not every day that you wake up and find out that the man sharing your bed married you without your knowledge or consent. They say that Hell has no fury like a woman scorned, but I doubt they factored in the woman standing in front of me. If looks had a thousand words, I am betting this one is declaring a bounty for my body, dead or alive.

Anger radiates from her as she grits her teeth and clenches her fists at the sight of me. Every single thing about her screams that my death is imminent. For the first time in my life, I feel an ounce of the pain that I have doled out to others for the sake of my club. Does it make me remorseful of my past actions? Of course not because it was in the name of protecting those around me, but explaining this to Ricca will not be easy.

"We're married!" she screams at me, charging toward me with her fists flying.

She swings and nearly connects her fist to my nose. The motion knocks her off balance, and she tumbles toward me. I reach out to grab her while trying to maintain the balance of my bike. How I support them both without bringing us all to the ground is a miracle. Ricca regains her balance and straightens herself upright. Without a second word, she rears back and slaps me hard across my face. She repeats the motion, but I stop her hand mid-swing. She growls at me, but once was more than enough to get her point across. Breaking free of my grip, she moves away from me.

If that didn't scream, "I'm fucked," then I don't want to know what else would. The couch and I may become very acquainted if she doesn't understand my reasoning behind it. Not that I don't deserve the bedroom banishment and no sex penalty.

"Get on the bike," I demand. "This isn't the place to be having this conversation. Do you want to be arrested for public disturbance?"

"I don't give a flying fuck who's watching me," she roars. "I am going to *kill* you for this."

"Pretty sure I already figured that one out, Siren," I

stoically respond. "But this will not be solved in the parking lot of a fucking bar." She huffs in response to me, but I tread forward, hoping she'll see the logic of my relocation request. "Just get on the fucking bike, and I will explain when we get home."

She starts to argue with me again, but I grab her and pull her onto the back of my bike. Ricca makes sure to let me know she's still pissed when she digs her knees into the base of my spine, as if I couldn't tell she was still mad. The entire ride, she keeps her hands off of me and on the grips on the back of the bike. Yet another bad sign.

I consider taking the long way back to the trailer, but it's only delaying the inevitable tongue-lashing that I am about to be on the receiving end of. Pulling into the drive by the trailer, she's off the bike before I even get the kick-stand down and stomps off toward the door, slamming it closed behind her.

Well, this is going to be fun. I get my bike squared away, and for a brief second, I consider wearing my helmet into the trailer for fear that she is lying in wait with a cast-iron skillet for my head. It's not a bad idea, but it would send the wrong message. I need to remain calm and try to talk myself out of this shit wreck I caused.

My hand slowly reaches for the door, and when I grasp the handle, I listen for signs of my impending doom via a cast iron-induced skull fracture. No sound comes from inside. I take a deep breath and jerk open the door, stepping out of harm's way. I slowly stick my head in and find that the front room is empty. One foot inches into the door, followed quickly by the next one until I'm fully inside. A crash comes from the direction of the bedroom, and I bolt toward it.

"Ricca," I call out, announcing my presence. "You okay?"

She doesn't respond, and the crashes only continue. I kick open the bedroom door and find her halfway underneath the bed with her ass in the air. The few belongings that I have here are piled up in the corner of the room.

"Planning to burn my shit while you're at it?" I question.

She startles when I speak and hits her head on the bed frame with an audible thud.

"Son of a bitch," she yells, pulling herself from underneath the bed.

I walk over to her as she cradles the top of her head in her hands. Thankfully, I see no blood pouring down her face, so I know it's not anything serious, but I need to check her out for myself.

I try to remove one of her hands, but she throws a punch toward my crotch.

"Don't touch me," she seethes.

"I get it. You're pissed as hell at me, but I am going to

check that wound, whether or not you like it. Move your hand."

"I'm fine."

"Yeah, and I'm a saint. Just let me look at it. Do I have to say please?"

She rolls her eyes but begrudgingly complies with my request. As I suspected, there's no laceration to her scalp. At least karma didn't add a head wound to the list of shit I have made happen today. If marrying her didn't get me killed, brain damage while trying to apologize just might.

"You're fine," I tell her, helping her off the floor.

"I tried to tell you that, but of course, you had to be the macho man in the situation and pretend to care," she says, mimicking my voice. "I'm capable of taking care of myself."

"Yes, that I am very much aware of."

"What's that supposed to mean?" she questions with an arched eyebrow.

"Nothing," I mutter under my breath. "Come on out to the kitchen. You need a bag of frozen peas and an explanation."

She knows that I'm right, but fights against me out of principle.

"I don't need anything from you except for your ass to get out of my home."

"I guess the honeymoon is over then," I fire back. She screams and finds the nearest object, throwing it at my head. The glass vase whizzes past my head and crashes on the wall next to me. Her chest heaves with exertion and anger as she watches my reaction. My face remains unchanged, and it only infuriates her more.

"Fine, you stay in here with a splitting headache. I'll be in the kitchen waiting on you to be more reasonable."

I start for the doorway, but her heavy footfalls soon start after me. She hesitates as we both get to the door at the same time. I wave for her to go on, but she stands her ground. Giving up, I start out the door. She shoves past me in the hallway and heads straight for the newly stocked freezer. While she may not have an interest in cooking, a week's worth of bar food has taken its toll on me. She was shocked the first night she came home from the bar, and I had a home-cooked meal on the table waiting for her. I may not look like much from an outside perspective, but life has dealt me many lessons, including how to cook decent meals.

I lean against the edge of the hallway as she makes a show of getting the frozen bag of peas and slapping them to her head. She winces at the change in temperature and contact. Pushing away from the wall, I go to her side. The bag balances against her head as she inhales and exhales, trying to soothe herself.

"Give me that," I advise, removing the bag. A towel dangles from the front door of the old stove, and I snatch it. The bag is too cold, and the shock of it against her already inflamed skin isn't going to do her any favors. Wrapping the towel around the bag, I gently re-lay it against her head.

"That's better," she comments, leaning into my hand. "How did you know how to do that?"

"Life skills, Siren. One of far too many I had to learn the hard way."

I give her a few minutes to soothe the bump on her head before I take her by the hand and lead her toward the couch. The feverish anger that she had earlier still lingers under the surface, and what I'm about to tell her is going to make it go either of two ways. She'll understand, or she'll explode into a million tiny pieces. I'm hoping for the latter to not be the case.

She lowers herself down, but I decide that it's probably better if I am not within striking distance, so I take the chair that I found buried in one of the other rooms across from the couch.

"I know you're mad," I start, but she instantly cuts me off.

"Mad doesn't even begin to cover it, Ratchet. It isn't even in the same ballpark. How in the fuck are we married?"

"When two people love each other very much," I tease before she glares me into stopping. Okay, leading in with a joke didn't go over as well as I thought it would.

"Cut the bullshit. How did this happen without my knowledge? I may not have the best idea of how normal people live their lives, but isn't there supposed to be a white dress and a church?"

"Yes, that's the gist of it. You can probably guess as to the how portion."

"Voodoo," she growls. "He helped you, didn't he?"

"Yes, but at my request. Do you remember that stack of papers I had you sign earlier in the week? Most of that was about the truck, but one of them was a marriage license."

"I signed what!" she shrills loud enough to make me wince in reaction. "Let me get this straight," she says, pulling the bag away from her head. Her hand rubs across her face as she tries to grasp what I just told her. "You took it upon yourself to obtain a marriage license, have me unwillingly sign it, and then had Voodoo hack the system to upload it. Do I have that right?"

"Yes, that's about it."

"How did I not know this was going on? This whole thing took serious planning, and you did it right under my nose," she spills out. "It doesn't make sense. Not one bit of sense."

"Siren, please understand that I did this all for you. Should I have involved you first? Yes, but there's nothing that I can do to take that back. It's done." Hard truth, it is. "We're married because you needed a husband to help your case for Asher."

She sighs and looks away from me. My heart breaks knowing that I have done this to her, but it was only in the idea that it was all to help her. The impulse to protect her has been ingrained in me from the moment that I saw her at Red's, and this situation has only made it worse. My heart beats, and my soul yearns for her happiness, and along the way, I still find ways to continually fuck it all up.

"What I did was reckless. That, I fully admit. But without that piece of paper, you may have never even gotten a chance to meet Asher. The adoption system isn't as easy as it looks, and I wanted to give you the best chance possible. With our marriage, it shoves your chances from slim to none to a strong maybe."

"How do you even know this? Did you go buy a book on *How to Trick a Woman into Marriage to Help Adopt a Child?*"

"I lived it, Siren. My history and your brother's share a similar plot line. I was raised in the system, and that system ended up putting me on the street with nothing to eat, no roof over my head, and no way to survive. Had it not been for Jagger, I would have died there, a nameless child that was the product of an even more fucked up family. Your brother is getting a chance to avoid the fate that I had, and if I had to do this all over again, I would because his life is worth more to you than the piece of paper binding us together."

A flash of understanding flashes behind her eyes, giving me a bit of hope, but the wheels of her mind continue to turn, trying to process this.

"Is our marriage even legal? If the courts find out that it's a fake, they'll throw us both in jail."

"It's not a fake, Siren. It's completely legal. While we may not have said the words in front of a preacher, both of our names on the dotted line make it that way. In the eyes of the law, we are husband and wife until death do us part."

"That last part may come sooner rather than later."

I slip from the chair and settle in beside her.

"I know that this makes me the world's biggest asshole, but you understand that I did this for you and for Asher. Not every child in the foster care system has someone on the outside fighting for them. He deserves a chance to have you in his life. I may not have had the same opportunity, but I want that for you both. That's why I did this, and I do not regret it for a single moment. I meant what I said this morning when I told you I love you. I may not be the smartest man when it comes to relationships, but if I can make you happy for just one second of the day, then I am doing my job right."

She remains silent as the grave while my heart is beating a thousand miles an hour.

"I want to make a promise to you, here and now. If, in a year's time, you want out of our marriage, I'll give that to you. No argument. No fight in court. You can be free and clear if you just say the word. This wasn't a move to trap you in a relationship with me, and I want you to know that. I will take your lead and follow it until you tell me to leave."

I shove the ball in her court, and all I have left is to wait for a sign. A sign of anything between us that can be salvaged. Her muteness continues for several minutes. I can tell that there's something else on the tip of her tongue that she wants to say, but she stalls. Flopping her back against the couch, she lets her head fall against the back of it. She hisses, forgetting her wound, but stays where she is.

"We're married, and I don't even know your real name. How can we be married, and I don't know such a basic piece of information?"

"Jude," I proudly state. "My real name is Jude Azzo."

"Jude," she repeats, testing it on her own lips.

"Does that mean you'll give this a shot, Siren?"

She lifts her head from the couch, locking her beautiful brown eyes on mine.

"I'll give you your year, but this isn't me giving you a free pass from the dog house. You have to work a little bit harder than that to get back into my good graces."

The biggest sigh of relief in my life escapes my lips. While I'm still in deep shit, at least our relationship isn't over completely. She is the first person to who I have ever told my story outside of Jagger, and it feels good to open up more about my past to the woman I want to be my future. Even though we're technically married already, I want to know her more than on a carnal level. I want to know her soul, her body, and her mind like no other person ever has.

Reaching across the couch, I rub my hand across her chin and pull her into a kiss. She leans into me, and for the first time, I truly know what it feels like to be owned by someone completely. I break the contact, and a lingering question pops into my head.

"I have to ask. What were you looking for underneath that bed?"

She smiles back at me, and suddenly I get the feeling that I may not want to know that answer.

"My knife to cut off your balls."

Yep, I definitely didn't want to know that at all.

Was having Voodoo hack the system in California to legalize a marriage license wrong? Maybe. Was having her sign it without telling her what it was worse? You bet your ass, but it's a necessary evil to help her. She would have never agreed to do it, even if it was the best course of action to take. Ricca has lived a life where decisions and choices were never hers to make until now and, being the asshole that I am, I did the same thing. Even if it was for her own good and for the sake of her brother, I'd do it all over again.

Chapter 17

RICCA

IT TOOK me nearly a week to come to terms with the fact that I was married to Ratchet.

Married. To. Ratchet. Not dating. Not fucking. M.A.R.R.I.E.D.

An institution that I never thought would include my name in its ranks. He was the type of man I would have never picked to be the marrying kind, but he did it without a single thread of hesitation or a lick of sense. Typical fucking alpha male bullshit. The fact that he never even asked and just assumed was a decision he's paid for since I found out. It was almost pleasurable to watch him stalk to the couch every single night. Not that he didn't try like hell to convince me to let him back into the bedroom. I wanted him to know just how much he'd fucked up at his attempt at solving a problem.

What woman wants to wake up and find that the

man in her life and his cocksucker of a brother took her from a miss to a missus? Had we been in Vegas, it might make more sense. The absurdity of my life was becoming to be a bit much. I have to laugh just thinking about it. How in the hell had someone not tried to buy the rights to tell my life story on Lifetime or HBO? It might not have flying dragons or vampires in it, but I bet that HBO could make a killing on it.

His declaration of love seemed so genuine, but the issue of our marriage still lorded over me. He chose me, for better or for worse, and to share his name. My heart should have soared at the idea, but it didn't. A part of me wanted to scream for joy, while another sulked at the thought of this being just for the sake of Asher. He did this without either of us ever meeting him. It was about the principle of the idea and the fact that it's what I wanted. This was his way of throwing his support into my corner. I wish he'd have just asked me first. It's really that simple. Just ask a girl, for goodness' sake.

I replay our conversation on repeat nearly every second of the day as I look for hidden answers in his words. Each time I think about his comparison of his life to Asher's current situation, my heart drops. Ratchet has never been forthcoming with information about himself before the club saved him, but the revelation that he nearly lost his life on the streets is utterly heartbreaking.

Much like me, he spent most of his life on his own,

scraping to get by and to survive. To look at him now, you'd think he has it all, but deep down, the skeletons hiding in his closet must be darker than mine, considering his position within the club. Though he has never said it aloud or even alluded to his job, it doesn't take a rocket scientist long to figure out he's the one who makes problems go away. His brothers held him in high regard, and unbeknownst to him, I saw them usher him into a room for counsel. He was their rock in the wake of Jagger's death. He filled the void and cut down their enemies at the same time.

The club whores were even afraid of him, which was a plus for me, but the darkness that shrouded him had always been well-protected until now. I was stunned as he gave me a glimpse of his life before I knew him. Yet, there was something more to it. I watched him closely, and it was obvious that this was just a broad overview. He was holding something back, and a part of me wanted to hear more of his story. But I didn't push. While he had been so patient with me during my recovery and detoxing process, I could give him the time he needed to tell me more should he wish to do so.

Being married, we had all the time in the world to talk. Well, a year at least, but that was all dependent on my feelings when that deadline came around. Had he given me the option to end it the day it started, then my anger and frustration would have screamed yes, but I see his side of the story now. His backward ass gesture of love gave me a better chance to get Asher, and it was something that I would never forget.

So much about him makes sense now. His overprotective nature, his drive to make me happy at any cost, and his surprisingly large want to get Asher out of the system. Not that I want him there either, but I wasn't at the place I needed to be before I dove head-first into the potential of being his guardian. Days still went by when I second-guessed my decision to do this, and self-doubt weighed heavy on my mind.

Would I even be good at this?

My mother's track record spoke for itself, and my father's was non-existent. I just hoped that I was given a chance by the court system tomorrow. All I wanted was just a chance. A chance to meet him and maybe, even give him a life so much better than my own. Asher was innocent in all of this, and he deserved to be raised by someone better than my sperm donor. The fact that my father had custody of him was a shock to me, and I still cannot figure out his angle in all of this.

Why would he choose to be a parent now when he shunned me from my birth? Could he be Asher's father, or was he the product of one of my mother's numerous liaisons for drugs? If he was his biological father, why didn't he claim that fact right off the bat and adopt him? The possibilities were endless, and if I kept thinking about them, I would probably go bonkers. It didn't help the fact that Dr. Matthews was suddenly unavailable for our sessions. The voicemail that she left me a few days prior about a sick relative and leaving town was clearly a bold-faced lie from the sound of her voice, but what could I do? She was the only therapist within a hundred-mile radius. My hope had to lie in the fact that she would return or that she had at least sent her notes to my case-worker before taking off. I needed her reports to help against the odds already stacked so high against me.

The sound of snapping fingers shakes me from my daydream. Missy, the other bartender at Willie's, stares back at me with a look of concern.

"Sugar, you look like you're a million miles away right now. You okay?" she questions.

Shaking the cobwebs from my mind, I try to re-focus on where I am. After a few weeks on day shift, it was messing with me that I was working tonight. I was already planning to be off tomorrow for my shift to attend the court case, but one of the night girls had called off. When Willie called, I couldn't say no for a number of reasons. I needed money, and I needed a distraction. Ratchet was a little less enthusiastic about it, but it took a little convincing to make him go back to the house. With a little loving and a push for him to get my truck finished up, he reluctantly complied with my request. When he was here, I spent more time watching to make sure he didn't get his ass into trouble or worrying that any guy who tried to flirt with me would have their asses handed to them.

"Sorry, Missy. It's been a long week," I offer as an excuse with a shrug of my shoulders. "I haven't been sleeping much."

Not the best excuse, but it's all I could think of on short notice. Her lips crack into a knowing smile as she slips her card from her pocket and slides it into the register to close out a tab.

"If I was up screaming at three in the morning, I bet I would be as tuckered out as you are." She smirks.

My mouth falls agape, and my face flushes as bright as a cherry tomato. This fucking town and the damn rumor mill strike again.

I wonder which of my neighbors sent out the mass message about the noises coming from my trailer. Jesus, did they have someone casing the place for new material to spread? This is like a small town of paparazzi. The next thing you know, our escapades will end up on the front page of the Willow Brancher newspaper with a less-than-savory picture of us. Not that Ratchet would mind. I was a bit of a different story when it came to romantic modesty. Not everyone needed to know our bedroom business, while he would rather I shout my enjoyment from the rooftops. Believe me, he's asked.

"Sugar, you better close that mouth of yours before

something flies right in there," Missy exclaims, still smiling. "You know how this town is. I think Vickie damn near fell over herself when that man of yours told her he was moving in with his wife."

"He didn't," I hiss.

"Oh, he did. Why didn't you tell me y'all were hitched? It would have saved you a lot more trouble with Vickie."

"It was a recent development," I mutter under my breath. A man steps up to the bar and barks his order at me. I slide past Missy and grab a glass from behind the bar, pouring his draft. The man tosses the money down on the bar and walks away.

"Fucker," I hiss as I gather his money. Missy looks over to me as I show her the money in front of me. "No tip."

"Sugar, you know these drunk country boys. They think the only time you should tip a woman is when she takes off her bra and shows them her tits. Don't sweat it."

I look over, watching the man walk over to his table, and I get my second shock of the night. As he passes one of the far corner booths, I see a face that I thought would never step foot into this place. My father. This is the closest that I have been to him in my entire life. I have always kept my distance at school for this very reason. I didn't want him to spot me or know that I was back in town. Nothing good could come of his knowing that information.

His eyes are thankfully not on me, and I take the chance to duck around the corner, where we keep the top-shelf liquor. I shift in the small space and keep my eyes trained on him. His large form sits alone in the booth, eating a sandwich. He looks so out of place in this den of sin. Even the waitress that walks over to check on him doesn't linger long. While most places wouldn't care if their preacher was in an establishment that sold booze, this town had a far mightier opinion of the man who was once responsible for their moral salvation. He was far out of his element, and that meant one thing. He was here for me.

Coils of anxiety begin to tightly wrap around my chest when the realization hits. He has no other business here but me. The daughter he never wanted and lost everything over. When my mother pointed the finger at him as being my father, the whole town, including his own family, turned their backs on him. He had broken his oath to serve the Lord and his community, and to stay faithful to his barren wife. My mother must have been one hell of a temptress to get him into her bed because men like him are supposed to be untouchable. I guess the old saying was right. The higher you are on the totem pole, the harder the fall back down to the bottom.

He sits quietly while he eats. No one stops by to

speak to him or even acknowledges his presence. I continue to hide in my safe space out of his sight, but Willie notices me.

"Ricca, darling, you look like you've seen a damn ghost. Don't tell me that no good Johnny Monroe has stepped back into my fine establishment?" he asks. His body readies for a fight, but I shake my head at him.

Willie moves closer to me, but the sense of my space being invaded makes me shove back farther into the cubby.

Recognition of me being uncomfortable registers in his mind, and he stumbles back.

"Shit. Sorry, sugar. Your man told me how you don't like people in your space. I plum forgot."

"It's okay, Willie. No harm done."

"You look like you need a stiff drink. Why don't you head on home and take the rest of the night off? I appreciate you coming in, but it's not busy enough to keep you and Missy both here."

I look back around the corner and find my father gone from his booth. If I stayed here, I was only giving him more of an opportunity to find me. Something I wanted to avoid at all costs until after my court date tomorrow morning.

"I wouldn't normally turn down a chance for some extra cash, but I think you're right. It's probably a good idea that I do go home."

Willie smiles back and tells me to have a good night before heading back to the kitchen. Checking again that the coast is still clear, Missy is consumed with a few orders, but I whisper over her shoulder that Willie was sending me home. I grab my purse from under the bar and shoot off a quick text to Ratchet to come get me. I glance around the room a third time before heading out the side door to wait for him.

The cool, crisp May air wraps around me like a chilled blanket and sends a shiver down my spine. I chide myself for not grabbing my jacket off the bike when Ratchet dropped me off earlier, but that's on me. Rubbing my hands over my arms, I try to warm myself up as I walk toward the front of the parking lot to wait. As I round the corner, a hand reaches out and grasps me tightly. I shriek, but another hand grabs my mouth, silencing me.

"Hello, Erica," an unfamiliar male voice says against my ear.

I try to shove away from him, but he only jerks me tighter before unleashing his hand from my mouth and spinning me around. My eyes peer up, and the sight of the man in front of me seizes my chest mid-breath.

My father.

"If you touch me again, I will scream for help," I threaten him, still testing his grasp on my arm.

"You do that, girl, and I'll make this a lot harder on you than it will be for me."

His cold, emotionless voice scares me more than his presence. His dark eyes are pools of unmoving darkness with no life to them at all.

"Why are you here?" I ask him, stalling in hopes that Ratchet will arrive. I just need to stall him here.

"I'm here for you," he sneers. "Don't you go getting any ideas about your man. He won't make it in time to save you from this, daughter. The deputy is running sobriety checks tonight, and I may have called in an anonymous tip to have him detained a bit longer."

My stomach drops, knowing that he planned this. The first time meeting my father in person, and he's holding me like a hostage with no hope for escape.

"It's time you and I have a little father-daughter discussion about how we don't touch things that don't belong to us."

Asher. This is about Asher and my court date tomorrow.

"I don't know what you're talking about," I lie as I attempt to pull away from him again.

"You know damn well what this is about. The boy. He is none of your concern," he barks at me. Spit from his mouth splatters against my face. I move to wipe it away, but my father digs his fingers into my flesh deeper.

"He's my brother, and that makes him my concern," I growl. "He doesn't deserve to be with you."

"And you think you're any better? You're a whore, just like your mother. I've heard all about your tramping around town with that biker in tow. You may have everyone else fooled, but I can see right through this farce. He's your pimp."

I laugh back at his absurdity. *Hurry up, Ratchet. Hurry the fuck up.*

"My pimp? That man is my husband and a member of one of the largest motorcycle clubs in this country. If you try to hurt a single hair on my head, he and the entire force of that club will be beating down your door," I threaten him back. I hate having to bring the club into this, but it might be the only way I am getting out of this without Ratchet's presence.

My father flinches but doesn't release me.

"Oh, I know all about his club," he retorts. "I could have him put away right now if I wanted to do it."

The sound of a motorcycle roars into the parking lot, and my father's eyes fill with dread.

"That would be him," I chide. "Want to meet him?"

My father shows a brief flash of panic as the roar of his motorcycle grows closer. His eyes tell me that he's conflicted, but they harden when he notices me watching him. He growls, knowing his time is running short.

"If you show up at that court date tomorrow, I will

make you pay for meddling with the boy. He doesn't belong to you, and I will make for damn sure that you don't get him."

"We'll see about that," I throw back at him.

Ratchet's bike pulls up just a few feet away from us. My father's eyes switch from me to Ratchet and back again as he dismounts his bike, waiting on me.

"This isn't over, Erica," my father sneers as he releases his grip. I watch him run from me and head toward the back, around the corner of the bar.

I breathe again for the first time and take stock of what just occurred. My father not only knows about me but also my intent to take Asher from him. His threats were clear on that fact. At that moment, as I reel from my encounter with him, I make a promise to myself. That no threat from my father or anyone else is ever going to deter me from this course. My father has a purpose for Asher, what that is, I don't know, but I am not about to let that come to fruition.

Straightening my clothes and taking another deep breath, I walk around the corner of the bar and greet my man. As I slide onto his bike, I kiss him and don't mention a word of what transpired today. My father is my problem, and I am going to solve it on my own because Ratchet's solution would be more permanent and a bit harder to explain.

My father deserves to die but at the right moment.

And I am the one to determine when the ribbon of his life is to be cut.

Chapter 18

RATCHET

FROM THE MOMENT that I saw her round the corner of Willie's, I knew something was wrong. She tried to play it off as exhaustion or nerves about tomorrow, but her eyes told a different story. The light that I had grown accustomed to seeing over the last few weeks was all but gone. They were lifeless. No flicker. No flash. Just empty glassy pools. I tried to talk to her about it after we got home, but she made excuse after excuse again. I've seen her exhausted. I've seen her at the highest point of her anxiety. This was none of those things. Every inch of me is on alert as she remains silent.

I hate silence, and I hate that she won't open up to me. Her shutting me out will do nothing to alleviate her distress, and it only stresses me out more. Ricca has never been a quiet woman, and the awkward silence between us is deafening.

"You sure you're okay," I plea as she slips into bed beside me.

She slowly brushes her long hair before tying it up into a loose bun, completely ignoring my concern.

"Okay then," I mutter. "Good talk."

Ricca clicks off the bedside light, pulling the blanket up her nearly naked legs. The darkness of the room feels like a noose around my neck, and the woman next to me feels like a stranger. Is this how she felt when I carried her into the clubhouse and into my room? She shifts over and over again before huffing an exasperated sigh and throws her hands over the top of the blankets.

"I'm scared," she whispers into the darkness. I shift to my side and stroke her arm in a soothing motion.

"You don't have to be scared, Siren. I'm right here, and I will protect you and Asher until the end of the Earth."

The gleam of a tear streaking down her face reflects in the moonlight, peeking through the bedroom window. A second one falls from her other eye before a full stream of them begin to cascade down her face.

Reaching over her body, I pull her into my chest. Her face nestles against my breastbone as she sobs uncontrollably.

"Shh," I whisper, against the top of her head, before I plant a chaste kiss on the top of her. She pops her chin up and gazes at me.

"What if he doesn't like me? Us? What do we do then?"

I chuckle at her, and she stares back in confusion.

"Is that what you are worried about?"

She mutters a soft yes, before burying her head back against my chest.

"You aren't your mother, and you are the only person in the world who understands the hell he's gone through. It may be weird at first, but with time, you'll heal those wounds left by her."

Ricca told me the dirty details of her life with her mother one night after work. Just as we had settled into bed, she started to have one of her nightmares. I held her for hours as she poured her heart out to me about her childhood. I lulled her back to sleep, but I couldn't sleep after that. I lay there thinking of how her mother used her body for currency and gifts, and it sickened me. It takes a lot for someone to shock me, and knowing that she survived that piss-poor upbringing gave me hope that nothing else in the world could stop her from outliving us all. She was much stronger than she realized, and I would make her see that in time.

"You think so?" she questions, wiping her tears against my naked chest before looking back up at me.

"Yes, I am. When someone has the same life experiences as you do, there's this bond between you. It's like a kindred spirit kind of thing, just like the two of us.

Neither of us has had the greatest life but look at us now. We're together and still breathing."

"Maybe you're right," she agrees.

"I know I'm right."

"What if I do end up like her?" she sheepishly asks.

"You won't," I assure her. "You've come too far to ever be like her. Besides, if you do, I'll rescue you like I did before."

She smiles and playfully punches me in the stomach.

"You just think you walk on water, don't you?" she teases, with a flicker of her light refilling her eyes again.

"As long as I have you, I can do anything. Even walk on water."

"You're so full of shit that you might just float."

She begins to giggle, and the sound of her happiness again makes me laugh. Her smile beams brighter than the moon, and since we came home, she finally feels at ease.

"I love you," I whisper against her lips before I lay a kiss on them.

"I love you," she replies. The silence of the room settles around us, and not long after, her breaths become shallow. I hold her while she sleeps and finally allow the darkness to take me under.

"Get up, Ratchet," she yells at me from the bathroom. "We overslept!"

I roll over and look at the clock. Sure enough, it's only

an hour before we're due at the courthouse, and we have at least a thirty-minute drive ahead of us.

Rolling out of bed, I stretch my stiff muscles, and she huffs her displeasure at how slow I am moving. I stalk to the bathroom and find her quickly throwing make-up on her face with her hair still up in the messy bun from last night.

"I like you like this," I whisper against her neck as I wrap my bare arms around her.

"Not now. Go get dressed."

I scoff at her, but she swats me, and I pad out of the bathroom. There's no use in fighting with her today. This is it. Our point of no return. Either we can move forward with the process of gaining custody of her brother, or we're dead in the water.

I step back into the bedroom and grab the new clothes that I picked up while she was at work. Her demand to fix the truck covered my tracks to take care of this one last detail for today. Little did she know, the truck had been done for a few days, but I liked having her on the back of my bike too much to give it back to her just yet. Call me selfish, but that's how I am with her. Every moment I get with her, whether she is chewing me out or giving her body to me, is a moment I cherish.

It doesn't take me long to finish getting ready, and when I step out of the room, her eyes bug out.

"Wow," she utters. "You, um, clean up nice."

I look down at my blue button-up shirt and khakis and smile. The look on her face is approval enough to know that I did okay picking out this monkey get-up. I smile, thinking back to the storeowner's face when I walked in asking for dress clothes. It's not every day that a guy like me walks into a place like that. I also learned that finding a shirt that would fit my larger upper body was not as easy as I thought. This is why I stick with t-shirts.

"I could say the same for you."

Ricca's hair is up in a smooth, sophisticated bun. Her curves are on display in the simple black dress that hugs her in all the right places. The heels on her feet only accentuated her shapely legs and ass. Had this not been important, I would have probably helped her right out of that dress and into my lap. But that will have to wait for later.

"Stop looking at me like that," she demands while grabbing her purse off the bar. "No way."

"I didn't say a thing, but now that you mention it."

"No, Ratchet."

"Later then," I promise her.

She laughs her way right out the door, and at my protest, we take the truck. While I would usually prefer to drive, she needs the distraction more than I do.

We make it to the old grey stone courthouse a few towns over with a few minutes to spare. It takes us less than no time to make it through the metal detectors at the front of the entrance, and before I know it, we're standing in the hall.

We take the stairs up to the third floor, where the family court is located, and find her caseworker lingering in the hallway. As soon as she spots us, she walks right over to us.

"Good morning, Mr. and Mrs. Azzo. Are you ready for this?"

Hearing Ricca being called Mrs. Azzo makes me smile. She notices and throws a sideways glare back at me.

"As I'll ever be," she answers Nicole.

"Is there anything we should know before going into this?" I inquire.

"This hearing will be very basic. The judge will review your application and any additional paperwork that you included. The judge may ask for additional details such as employment or assets, but other than that, it should be pretty straightforward. Judge McCain is pretty evenly fair, so you shouldn't have any trouble."

The doors of the courtroom open, and a large group of people tumble out into the hallway. Ricca's hand comes to her chest as her anxiety strikes.

Coming up behind her, I pull her against me.

"Just breathe, Siren. I'm right here," I whisper to her. "Just breathe."

She practices the breathing exercises that she was given to do back in her California group therapy session, and as the last person exits, her breathing slows.

Nicole waves for us to follow her. Ricca reaches back and grabs my hand tightly.

"Together, nothing can stop us," she repeats from our conversation last night.

She starts to walk into the room with me in tow. The courtroom is completely covered in dark-colored wood. Each side of the room has a table for each party, and the judge sits at the center. An older woman sits to his left with a typewriter in front of her.

A man walks toward us, and Nicole hands him a stack of papers. He flips through them before handing them up to the judge.

"Case Number one-six-seven-nine-two, regarding the custody of Asher Harrison Delmont," the man calls out to the empty room.

The judge reads through our application a page at a time, and with each flip, Ricca grows more nervous at my side. His lips move as he's reading, while his face remains unanimated.

"Everything looks to be in order here, Miss Wild. Are these two the candidates in question seeking to adopt this child?"

Nicole steps forward and waves us to join her at her side.

"Yes, your honor. This is Mr. and Mrs. Jude Azzo. Mrs. Azzo is Mr. Delmont's sister."

The judge looks up and eyes Ricca.

"There seems to be quite an age difference between the child in question and his sister. Could you please explain that, Mrs. Azzo?"

Ricca shakes as he calls on her to answer, but I squeeze her hand tighter.

"My mother had me at a very young age, your honor. I wasn't what you would call a planned pregnancy."

"I see," he observes. "I also see here that you have never met Mr. Delmont and are requesting visitation. Is that correct?"

"Yes, your honor," she answers, gaining confidence with each word. "I did not know about him until my mother's passing. She and I have been estranged for several years."

"Hmm," he mumbles. "This is your husband?"

"Yes, your honor," I answer.

"I don't seem to have any employment information listed for you here, Mr. Azzo. Do you currently hold employment?"

I release Ricca's hand and straighten my posture. The judge watches me, analyzing my every move.

"I do, your honor. I work for a private security company back in California, and I also do mechanic work on the side."

"Good," he utters. "Do you intend to move back to California should this custody motion be granted?"

Ricca looks at me. While we had never talked about it, it has always been my intention to go back. We didn't have a reason to stay here if Asher was going with us. Our support system and lives are back there in Upland, but if she wants to stay, I'd do it for her.

I nod back to her, putting that decision in her court. Whether we stayed or went back, we do it together.

"Yes, your honor. We do intend to go back to California."

The judge nods his head in acknowledgment of her answer.

"I am ready to make a decision."

Ricca reaches out again, taking my hand in hers, as we wait for the judge to read us our fate. This is the moment she's worked so hard for. The moment that decides whether our future is a family of two or a family of three.

"In the case of Asher Harrison Delmont, I order that temporary supervised visitation be granted. With your intent to return to California, I also order that a home study be completed in California, and pending the results of that study and a DNA test, I will make my decision on permanent custody of the child in question. Court dismissed."

Ricca turns toward me, and the biggest smile I have ever seen forms on her face.

"Did he?" she stutters. "Did I hear that right?"

"Yes, Siren," I answer back. "You get to meet Asher."

Ricca leaps into my arms, and I carry her out of the courtroom and straight into the truck. Her jubilation lasts the entire way home, and we celebrate our small victory the only way we know how.

Together.

Chapter 19

"HOW CAN they do a home study if we don't have a fucking home, Ratchet?"

"My answer didn't change from the last time you asked, Ricca. It's taken care of," he responds in a monotone voice. For days, I have grilled him about how this is all going to work.

"And you repeating the same damn answer isn't helping me one bit," I snap back at him. He fucking laughs in return.

"It's not funny, asshole."

"Actually, Siren, it is a little funny. The house inspection is only a part of the study. They'll interview our friends and family; check our finances and our references."

I roll my eyes at him. How can he be so relaxed about this? We are about to invite complete strangers into our lives and have them analyze every single thing about it. Where we live, which he says he has under control, and all the people in it. Who would recommend us as the references to parent Asher? Voodoo? Hero? They'd laugh us right out of the courthouse. Our residence is a biker clubhouse filled with club whores and booze. Those two things alone would cement us in the never going to fucking happen category.

Plus, how does he know all of this crap? He's like the walking encyclopedia of adoption. For every question, he has an answer. It's suspicious.

"And we have all those things?"

Ratchet smiles back as he turns left onto the highway. I know that I didn't agree to this marriage at the beginning, but this laughing bullshit is about to be nipped in the bud. I wonder if he has life insurance?

"Stop thinking whatever you are thinking right now," he demands. "I can see those evil wheels turning, and I don't like that look one bit."

"Get out of my brain," I tease him.

"I know you're nervous, but like I keep telling you, everything is covered. You're going to get your ass on that plane and get things taken care of while I'm on Asher watch."

The thought of flying for the first time alone is nerve-wracking enough, but with everything else compounded in with it, I am on the brink of exploding in a mess of crazy. It was a miracle that we got a home study scheduled so quickly. Apparently, Darcy had a connection with the local child welfare group and used it to our advantage. I don't know what strings she had to pull, but we owe her big time.

"Fine, but you don't miss a day of seeing him at school. I want updates."

"Yes, boss," he mimics me. Ratchet changes lanes like a madman on the road, not caring about the people driving around us. Louisville may be one of the largest cities in this state, but they sure don't drive like we do in California. Traffic lights and lines on the road are merely suggestions that hardly any of us follow. A woman speeds by us in the slow lane, flipping Ratchet off in the process.

"I think she likes you," I snort.

He changes lanes a few more times before the signs for the airport come into view. The dark skies remind me of just how early we had to get up this morning, and after working another night shift at Willie's, I am completely drained. My only hope of sleeping was on the plane because as soon as I land, I want to hit the ground running. The quicker I get this done, the sooner I get back. Without having a return date in stone, we haven't been able to set up our visitation with Asher, and I don't want to delay it a second longer.

From the moment he decided that it would be me

going out to meet the home study coordinator, I began to worry about leaving Asher behind. My father's threats were clear as crystal, and I ignored them. I wavered last night and nearly told Ratchet of his existence in Asher's life and his threats, but he would kill him and then me for hiding it from him. As long as I could get away without telling him, the better off I would be. This would be the last lie I would ever tell him because the wedge its driven between us is suffocating me from the inside out.

"Why do planes have to leave so early in the morning?" I complain. "Why can't they leave at a more reasonable hour? Like noon."

"They do leave at noon, but you said you didn't want to waste a day trying to adjust to the time zone change. No rest for the wicked, Siren."

My eyes narrow at his continuous string of digs at this entire escapade. His chipper attitude at this time of the morning was already annoying me the moment we left the trailer, but the steady stream of jokes and jabs are wearing my patience thin.

"We're here," he announces as it appears in front of us. The glass dome sparkles in the reflection of the terminal lights, but the entire place is much quieter than I expected for a Wednesday morning. My phone vibrates in my pocket, and when I look down, I see the alarm I had set to get up to be at the airport. Son of a bitch. We're over three hours early for my seven forty-five flight.

"Are you kidding me right now?" I bellow. "Ratchet, we're way too damn early for this flight. The check-in counter probably isn't even open yet."

Ratchet realizes I'm right and smirks. He eyes the parking lot signs and sharply turns off to the right onto the exit ramp, away from the departure terminal sidewalk. We twist and turn in the parking garage until he eyes a spot on the very top level and pulls in.

"Could you have gone any higher up?" I complain. "There's hardly anyone here."

"I know," he notes with a knowing smile forming on his face. "Seems like the perfect place to give you a proper goodbye."

"Here? Are you kidding me right now? We'd be arrested for public indecency if they caught us. You're crazy," I mock him.

His grin doesn't change.

"Get over here, Siren," he demands. "I want to tell my wife goodbye, and I will not take no for an answer."

I consider his proposition, and I have to admit the thought of it turns me on a little bit. It seems so juvenile, but at the same time, it feels so forbidden. It is also something that I have never done before. Most people lose their virginities in their first car on an old country road while they pray someone doesn't drive by and see them. But not me. My sexual awakening was a completely different nature, and this is a chance to do something normal couples would do. Maybe he isn't crazy.

I unbuckle my seatbelt and watch as his chest begins to move much faster than before. His eyes never leave mine as I shimmy across the seat and find myself next to him. My hand moves onto his leg, and I give it a few tender squeezes.

"There's something a bit farther up that would like to be squeezed," he suggests.

"Not yet."

"Are you teasing me, wife?"

"I might be," I giggle.

"I might just like it," he responds. My hand slowly inches up his thigh before landing on the hard erection growing in his jeans. His head falls back at the sensation of my hand on his cock. My fingers trace the outline of his hardness, teasing him more.

"That look on your face is positively evil, Siren. I like it," he growls.

I allow my fingers to roam toward the fly of his jeans and slowly pop the button. He grows harder as I tug the latch of the zipper and start pulling it down. He looks down at my hand with a quizzical look on his face as if this isn't really happening. What likely was his idea of a joke is about to become a reality.

My hand reaches inside and strokes his cock. He shifts in his seat, giving more access. He audibly moans when all of my fingers wrap around his length and rub against him.

A sound in the garage jerks my hand from his jeans and my eyes to our surroundings. We both scan the area but find no one or a single car coming into the area. The idea of someone seeing us sends thick streams of excited arousal straight to my core.

"As much as I like where that was going, this isn't about my pleasure. It's about yours," he growls.

A mischievous look forms on his face as his hands shift from his legs to mine. They slip below the maxi skirt I had picked out to wear on the plane and cup the edge of my panties. He tugs them off my hips and painstakingly inches them down my legs until they reach my feet. Ratchet tosses them onto the dashboard before returning his fingers underneath. His finger swipes against the outside of me, and a shiver shoots up my spine from the contact.

"Do you like it when I do this, Siren?" he asks before slipping a finger inside of me. "Does this make your pussy wet?"

"Yes," I sigh and spread my legs wider for him.

"So responsive," he comments, plunging a second finger inside my wet entrance. His fingers crane and a jolt of electricity spreads across my body. His other hand reaches up the length of my body, pulling up my shirt and exposing my thin bra. My nipples are pebbled against the coldness of the cab. He leans forward and pushes one of the cups of my bra away, exposing my breast completely. He dips and takes it in his mouth. His tongue swirls around the sensitive numb, and my body goes into electrical overload. His fingers begin to thrust in and out of me with every lick. He releases my nipple and then devours my lips. I moan against his lips, and he smiles at my pleasure.

"Please," I beg him. "I need you inside of me."

He breaks the kiss, and that mischievous smile returns.

"I have an idea," he tells me, leaning back against the driver's side door. "Just go with it."

Ratchet swivels in his seat and pops open the truck door. I watch as he steps outside with his cock popping out of the top of his jeans. I fix my shirt, trying to cover myself. He reaches in and pulls me out along with him, and leads me to the truck tailgate.

"Oh god," I exclaim.

"Trust me, Siren."

And I do. Ratchet lowers the tailgate and turns his ass to it, hopping up on the gate like a seat. He scoots back until he's midway to the front of the bed and motions for me to follow.

Gathering the length of my skirt in my hands, I hoist my leg up and barely make it in. I crawl up to his side, and his mouth returns to mine. His tongue caresses mine like two partners dancing. Our kisses are a mixture of lips and tongue in perfect union.

"Ride me, Siren," he murmurs against my lips. I pull away and stare down at him, trying to decipher if I really heard him right.

"Out here?" I nervously question.

"Yes, out here. Let go and feel freedom, Siren."

I try to convince myself this is crazy, but I want this as badly as he does. I hike up my skirt again, and his hands slide his jeans down to his hips and expose his cock. His hardness is ready, and my pussy is screaming at me to find my release.

Shifting my weight, I slide a leg over his hips and settle myself above him. His cock rubs against me as I find my center, and we both groan. Releasing my skirt, I use my hand to guide his tip to my entrance and lower myself down onto him, impaling him inside of me. My walls relax as I lower myself farther onto his length and fully sheath him.

His hands fall to my hips, and I begin to rock my hips across his pelvis. My back begins to arch, and my head falls back in quick succession as his motions combine with my own.

"You are so fucking beautiful like this, Siren. So exposed, and so mine," he hisses as I increase my speed.

"Ride me harder, wife," he demands. "I want to feel your pussy come all over my dick."

Arching my back more, I deepen his reach, and the edge of my release begins to blossom. Each repetition sends my arousal branching out in my body until it hits the wall, and my orgasm hits me hard. My body feels as if I stuck my finger in an electric socket, with sparks tingling up and down my flesh. As I ride out my pleasure, Ratchet's balls clench as he finds his own release. I fall forward against his chest, and we both heave, trying to catch our breaths. His arms come around my middle, pulling me into another deep kiss. The lights of a flashing security vehicle begin to illuminate the parking garage walls, and we both laugh. I slide off of him, and we both bolt out of the bed of the truck and back into the cab. Ratchet smiles as he turns on the ignition, and we peel out of our not-so-secret hiding spot.

Taking a peek at my phone again, I see that it's actually time for me to head into the terminal. My high from our time together fades quickly back into dread. It's been over six months since I left California, and here I am, going back empty-handed, without Ratchet. The strangeness of it all rattles me.

As he pulls back onto the road toward the departure drop-off lanes, I try to calm my nerves. Ratchet reaches over and places his hand on my thigh.

"It's going to be fine, Siren. Stop overthinking this."

"I know it will be," I reassure him and lie to myself.

Ratchet pulls up to the curb, hops out, and circles

around to open the door for me. I take his extended hand and slide from my seat. With so much of my stuff still back in California, I didn't need to pack more than a few items that easily fit in my purse, along with the iPod shuffle that Ratchet had picked up for me for the flight.

He pulls me into an embrace, and my arms wrap around his neck. I didn't want to let him go, but the terminal officer blew his whistle at us and told Ratchet he couldn't park there at the terminal.

"Time for me to go," I fretfully admit.

"I love you, Siren. Call me when you land," he says, planting one last kiss on my lips.

"I love you."

We reluctantly release each other, and I hitch my bag over my shoulder, heading into the terminal. As I make it through security, I have to force myself to shake off the feeling that I am making a mistake by leaving them both behind. My father could strike at any moment, and I am leaving them both exposed without telling Ratchet of his threats.

You have to do this, Ricca. It's not the right time to tell him. Get the paperwork signed, and then unleash the hellfire down on him. Be patient.

The pep talk to my subconscious barely helps, but the call for my flight to board dishes up the distraction I need from my wavering thoughts. Settling into my seat, I keep my eyes trained on the window. The expansive

Kentucky bluegrass fields fly by in an instant as the plane takes off and, within a few hours, are replaced with the brown, dusty remains of former manicured lawns that make up most of Southern California. My hope to sleep on the plane was thwarted by the screaming baby directly behind me. Even hard rock turned up to eleven wouldn't have drowned out the noise.

After I disembark from the plane, I make my way to the outer terminal to call a cab, but as I step outside of the automatic doors, I see an unexpected sight. Dani and Darcy stand with an outstretched banner, welcoming me home. Their excitement to see me eases my nerves about how much my time away would affect my relationships with the people back at the club. Maybe this won't be as awkward as I thought it would be. The taxi traffic is heavy in the terminal. It finally clears, and I make my way over to them. Dani squeals and quickly draws me into a hug. Her arms around me are a welcoming embrace instead of a panic-inducing motion.

She squeezes me tighter when she notices that I don't resist her embrace. Darcy just smiles from the sidelines, but I pull her into the group hug.

"I'm so happy you're back," Dani declares. "You've missed so much." My eyes fall to her rounded belly, and my mouth falls open in shock.

"I know, right? He's insatiable."

I look over to Darcy, and she shakes her head.

"That is so not an option for me anymore. Five kids between us are enough for me."

We all laugh, and Dani points toward the SUV waiting at the curb. Following around behind them, I take my first real breath of California air, but it doesn't feel as much like home as I thought. But the biggest piece of my home isn't here. Only a few hours apart, and I already miss him. Remembering his request, I slip my phone from my pocket and shoot him a quick text to let him know I made it.

He responds right away, and I stow my phone again as I slide into the car. A driving beat of Justin Bieber powers out of the car stereo, and I cover my ears, pretending to be tortured until they switch the station. Not that he's a terrible artist, but I can only take so much of a man singing like a damn girl.

Darcy steers the car off the curb and onto the freeway. The familiar rush of the cars soothes my homesickness a little. Darcy and Dani chatter along as we drive, but I notice that suddenly we're not taking the right exit for the clubhouse.

"Uh, I know it's been a few months since I lived here, but did the clubhouse move or something?"

Dani peers over at the passenger seat and just smiles.

"It didn't, but we have a surprise for you. Ratchet wanted us to get you settled in, but we're impatient,"

Darcy declares as she turns off the main drag into the newer part of Upland.

"And I need to pee again," Dani adds.

Home after home zips by before Darcy pulls off on a quiet side street and parks the SUV on the curb.

"And where are we exactly?" I ask, peering out of the window at a modest home nestled on a corner lot. The house's stonewalls are beautiful and accented, with large bay windows in the front. The yard is pretty tiny, but that's the norm for this part of town.

"Welcome home, Ricca," Dani squeals as she opens the passenger side door. I follow her outside and just stare from the sidewalk up at the house.

"Who's home? I don't live here."

"Uh, yes, you do. This is Ratchet's house."

Chapter 20

RATCHET

RICCA'S ABSENCE hits me harder than I could have ever expected. After years of living on my own, this woman tumbled into my life and reset the delicate balance of everything. Not that I minded, but to miss someone like this was not something that I anticipated. I barely slept the first few days, but the repair work that I had put onto my plate to make this place livable again was ahead of schedule. I couldn't classify myself as a professional handyman, but installing new cabinets, updating the bathroom, and even laying new carpets was simple enough.

With the intent to move back to California, once this was all said and done, I wanted to make this place good enough to sell. With our marriage, she didn't need to worry about a cash flow, but I don't want her to feel completely dependent on me. She needed a nest egg of her own, and if she wanted to work, I wouldn't stop her. It just wouldn't be back at Red's. He had expressed an interest in my wife far before she shared my last name, and I'll be damned if I allow her to go back to that kind of workplace. Willie's was bad enough, but at least her boss and I had an understanding. While I hadn't given him all the information regarding her past, I let him in enough to know that she walked a thin line of both sobriety and panic. His agreement to move her to the day shift was a welcomed one, as was his promise to keep an eye on her. His only stipulation was that he got the first shot at Johnny Monroe or any man that crossed a line. I agreed, but I can't say that is something that I would be able to honor. She is my everything, and I'd die to protect her.

Setting down my tools for the night, I settle onto the couch with a few slices of pizza on a plate while I wait for her nightly call. I won't lie and say that she gave me hell for hiding the fact that I had a house already set up and even accused me of doing this alongside our surprise marriage. But the truth was that I had owned the place for years prior. I just hadn't told anyone about it until I needed it. It had been my private project and a way to decompress after years of working for the club. A couple of beers, a hammer, and some nails were the closest thing to therapy that I had found to soothe my mind until Ricca.

I employed Dani and Darcy's help to get the furnishings and home shit in order to make the place ready, but with Ricca there, I insisted that she make the place her own. It was going to be our home for our family. Our private space to just be us, without the weight of the world trying to kick in the door and screw it all up.

As I take a bite of pizza, my phone rings. With my mouth still full, I grab it and try to answer it.

Her intoxicating giggle fills the phone as I choke on the food in my mouth, trying to answer her.

"You're supposed to chew first," she chastises me. "Bite, chew, then swallow."

"I'm aware, *wife*," I tease back. "Hearing your voice was far more important, though."

She giggles again, and I picture her beautiful face smiling back at me across the miles that separate us. Only a few more days, and she'll finally be home to me.

"I'd much prefer you'd still be alive when I get home, *husband*," she responds back.

Tucking the phone between my ear and shoulder, I sit up from the couch and grab the plate, tossing it in the trashcan. She remains silent, and the fear that the house inspection today didn't go as planned sinks in. Silence and my wife aren't a combination that has boded well for me in the past.

"Everything go okay, Siren?" I hesitantly question.

"Hmm," she responds. "Oh yeah, it was fine. The inspector checked everything out and was out of here in less than an hour. She said she would be conducting the reference interviews later this week and that we should have her final report by the following week."

"That sounds promising."

"It does," she concurs before the silence returns. "Can I ask you something without you getting mad?"

"Depends. Do you think I will get mad?"

"You might. I did something that I probably shouldn't have done without asking first."

My mind runs with what she could have possibly done to suggest such a reaction out of me. There's only a few skeletons left in my closet that she hasn't been privileged to, and most of them were club business. Not something she would have just found on her own. Our bylaws are clear on that fact. While Raze did stretch the rules around to allow Darcy to be involved somewhat with our dealings with the cartel that killed Jagger, he didn't want the women involved. It was too dangerous for them, and any kind of danger to our families affected the group as a whole. We couldn't protect them and ourselves at the same time. It was better that way.

"Go on," I instruct.

"I found a photo today in a box from your room at the clubhouse. I was trying to see if there was anything there that I could maybe put up in the house, and it slipped out from a book."

In an instant, I know which photo she is referring to. While I had given her a glossy overview of my past, there were pieces that I hadn't told her about. She may have faced her demons and her mother alone, but I didn't.

"I can't believe I am even asking this, but who is the girl in the picture? Is she someone you were close with?"

I sigh before answering her. This wasn't how I envisioned this call going. My expectations of discussing the inspection, her time out there, or hell, even how she has decorated parts of the house were shot out of the water. Instead, I was about to divulge to her a piece of my past that only one other person had known about, and that was Jagger. His act of salvation came with a stipulation and a price. The loss of her.

"You could stay that," I begin. "The girl in the picture with me is my sister, Genevieve. I called her Ginny for short."

"Oh," she murmurs. "You've never mentioned her before."

"There's a reason for that, but I need to start at the beginning, Siren. If I am going to tell you about her, I need to go back to where it all begins."

"I'm listening."

"Our mom died giving birth to Ginny when I was a

few years old. My dad decided to cope with his loss by drinking himself to death."

"Oh, Ratchet," my wife declares. "I'm so sorry."

"That's just the beginning, Ricca," I mention. "Ginny and I bounced around from foster home to foster home until our caseworker placed us with the Wilson family. I was about fifteen at the time, and Ginny was thirteen. For the first year, everything was great until our foster mom died in a car accident. After that, everything went to shit. Like my real dad, my foster father also started drinking, and before I knew it, he started looking at my sister completely differently."

"He didn't," Ricca gasps, realizing where the story was about to turn. I know I need to tread lightly on this part of the story because Ricca herself had lived in this kind of hell. Bringing back those nightmares was not something I intended to do.

"He didn't get the chance. He tried to break his way into her room one night, but he only found me. I could tell by how much he was throwing back that he was fixing to do something bad. So, I sent Ginny to my room and told her to pack our backpacks and slip down into the kitchen to get food before hiding outside near the old shed. I waited for hours, and then I heard his heavy foot-steps coming up the stairs. As he jiggled the locked door handle, I readied myself. The moment that he broke the plane of the door, I smacked him with one of the bats, which his wife had gotten me for my first Christmas under their roof. He yelled and tried to fight his way to get me, but I hit him harder a second time. He fell to the ground, and I just ran."

"Oh my god," is the only thing that slips from Ricca's lips before I finish.

"Ginny was scared that he'd come after us, but I had already taken care of that. On my way out the door, I grabbed the gas can that he kept by the backdoor and doused the entire kitchen with it. I lit the place on fire, grabbed Ginny, and never looked back."

"That's how you ended up on the streets, isn't it? That's how Jagger found you."

"That's right. He brought us both back here and put us to work. Ginny worked in the kitchen, and I worked in their mechanic shop until I was old enough to prospect. Things were good for a while, but club life really started to affect Ginny as she grew older. The guys looked at her just like my foster father did, and I knew I had to get her out of there when one of the guys made a play for her. The club decided her being underage was too much of a liability and sent her away to live with one of the former old ladies, whose husband had just passed."

I pause, trying to ready myself for the last bit of my story. As much as I want to pretend that I am tough as nails, Ginny, much like Ricca, was the light of my world.

I lived to protect her. Ricca must sense that I am nearly through because she doesn't say a single word on the other line.

"A few years after she left, I became a full member. She begged me to let her come back now that she was of age, but I just didn't want this kind of life for her. The woman that she lived with had homeschooled her and given her a life that she would never get living the club life. I got a call not long after that she had taken off. I searched for her for over three years, but when I finally caught up with her, she was heavily addicted to drugs. The day I convinced her to go to rehab, I bought that house, but she would never live in it. She committed suicide after a week of going through withdrawal. The pain was just too much for her."

A stray tear gleams down my face, and I am thankful that Ricca can't see me this way. There are only two things in this world that would make me shed my hardened exterior and actually give into the coiled emotions buried deep inside of me. My sister and my wife. While I could not save Ginny, I would save Ricca and Asher.

"That's why the house has been empty all this time, hasn't it?" her voice finally answers. "You couldn't live there because that house was never supposed to be yours."

"Somewhat," I offer her. "Being alone in that house, I

felt like I was suffocating. It was meant for a family, and at the time, I never thought that I would deserve one."

"Oh, Jude. My heart is breaking for you right now."

Her use of my first name makes me pause, and she notices it immediately.

"Sorry, I didn't mean to call you that," she backpedals with an obvious note of nervousness in her voice.

"Say it again," I plead. "I need to hear you say it again."

"Jude."

For the first time since I lost Ginny, I loved hearing my real name spoken out loud. In my mind, the right to use that name was only meant for my sister, but now that torch has been passed onto Ricca. Hearing it may have brought back memories of Ginny, but she was gone. Most might think that I traded one damaged woman for another, but they would never understand my reasoning. I needed someone like Ricca in my life to ground me.

"From now on, when it's just you and me, I want you to call me that. In public, we'll have to stick to my road name, but alone, I'm your Jude."

I can feel Ricca's smile beaming from my phone, and for the first time in my entire life, I feel absolved of my past. My misery of losing Ginny was long fading away, and in its place was beginning to fill with my happiness of Ricca and hopefully Asher.

Ricca's silence returns, and I know that I need to push

this conversation back to a lighter topic. I couldn't have her self-doubt trying to overanalyze the story I just told her because it wouldn't help her or me. We needed to keep our relationship away from the bullshit of our pasts and only look to the future that was to come.

"So, what are you wearing?" I ask, bringing her giggles back to life.

Chapter 21

RICCA

MY TIME in California has been eye-opening. Even with the distance, I feel closer to the man who holds the title of my husband. Ratchet let me into his past far more than I think he even intended. Yet knowing what I did now, I think that I love him even more. Despite the blood on his hands for the club, he was a man that had experienced the worst of what life has to offer discarded children. He protected his sister the best he could, but when someone is so far gone, there's nothing more you can do. While his words told me he didn't fault himself, his voice told a different story. His sister was everything to him, but no matter what he did, the outcome would have likely been the same. I lived through addiction for years, and I barely survived the detox and withdrawal process. Countless days of hot and cold flashes, the feeling of my insides burning and rotting from the inside out, and then the dark thoughts that screamed inside of my mind to end it all. Only the strong could survive it... and someone with a good support system, like I had with him. He may not be the hero that you read about in books, but my savior came equipped with a motorcycle and a blackened heart of gold.

Though the weeks dragged on and on while I was back home in California, it seemed that time moved much faster here. Ratchet had done so much work on the trailer in the two weeks I was gone that I barely recognized the place. This is what I can only surmise kept him busy in my absence. He surprises me at every turn, and this is one of the things I like best about him. The point you think you have him pinpointed is the moment he pulls a bait and switch and reveals a completely different side of him. Much like a priceless gemstone, he is multi-faceted.

The days after my return, Ratchet filled me with satisfying the ache of our separation, and we began to learn more about each other between my shifts at Willie's. He was resistant at first to let me go back, and frankly, after my father's visit, I nearly let him convince me, but I needed something to pass the time. Where he had his renovations, I had nothing to occupy my mind and body besides him. Something he didn't mind, but the days of waiting to find out when I would finally get to meet Asher, were killing me.

Until today.

Nicole called me shortly after my shift ended last night to give me the good news. She mentioned that the foster family wasn't cooperating with them and that she had to pull rank in order to make this happen. What Nicole didn't know is that I knew this would happen. For whatever reason, my father didn't want me to interfere with Asher's place in his home. Having Asher in his custody was the last thing that I wanted. I would rather give up my custody battle and for Asher to be placed with someone else than for him to remain under the same roof as that man. My father may seem like a reformed holy man on the outside, but the cold emptiness of his eyes told a different story. A story with an unhappily ever after for us all. Was I scared of what he would try to do out of retaliation? Of course, I am, but my fear is not keeping me from doing anything, despite the consequences that may be coming my way.

"You ready to go, Siren?" Ratchet yells around the corner of the bathroom doorway. My eyes move from my reflection in the mirror to his face, and in his eyes, I find my peaceful center. The dark storms may swirl and churn inside of me, but he's like the lighthouse calling me home. All I need is his call to bring me back safely.

"Almost," I mutter while swiping another layer of mascara over my lashes.

"You know that you don't need that clown make-up shit, right? You're more beautiful without it."

I swivel and swat him away.

"You're biased," I holler back at him. His chuckles reflect off the walls as he stalks back to the living room.

Today is, by far, the most panic-inducing day of my life. Forgot the Tribe dungeon, my father's threats, Ratchet's surprise marriage, or the day in court. Meeting Asher tops them all. He's grown up so much in his life without me in it that I am afraid he'll hate me. His reaction could run the gambit, but I was willing to try to connect with the one person on this earth who shares at least half of my genetic sequence. The DNA test results were still pending, but I knew that no matter the percentage of blood we share, he will always be my brother. Whether he is in my life or not, I will make damn sure that my father is not a part of the equation.

I glance back in the mirror one more time and check my appearance. My hair is slicked back in a long ponytail, and my make-up is minimal. The last thing I want is for Asher to take one look at me and think I'm fake. This is the real me, and I want that to shine through. No frills. No pretensions. Just me.

Slipping from the bathroom, I find my husband spread out on the couch with his arm draped across the back of it. Like me, he chose to be casual today with just a t-shirt and jeans. We had a brief argument about his insistence on wearing his cut, but it was quickly solved with a promise of making it up to him later. I didn't want my brother to see him and run for the hills from the scary biker. Ratchet was intimidating enough on his own without all of his pomp and circumstance. Today he was just a man, driving his wife to meet her little brother.

His eyes remained trained on the car auction that is blaring from the television set that suddenly appeared when I got home.

"Earth to Jude," I tease him. "Come in, Jude."

His head cranes around slowly, and he beams up at me.

"I love it when you call me by my first name." He smiles back. "It sounds so different rolling off those beautiful lips.

"You know, I did a little web search yesterday to see what your name meant. Do you know what I discovered?" I giggle.

"That saying it three times will get you the best orgasm of your life," he offers back with a hint of arousal in his voice.

"Nice try, but there's no time."

He frowns and reaches for the remote to flick off the show he was watching. He rises from the couch and saunters toward me with a mischievous gleam in his eye.

"As I was saying," I start, grabbing my purse. "I found out that you share a name with a Catholic saint."

"That so," he dares. "The saint of good fucks?"

I laugh and squeal when he grabs me and pulls me against him. I let him feel like he's winning before shoving him away and pointing him out the door.

"It couldn't be farther than that. Saint Jude is the patron saint of lost causes."

"Well, that's not even remotely right," he offers, stepping out the trailer door. "I can't be lost when I am with you."

My heart swells at his sweetness. For a man who can be so rough and vicious, he is a completely different person with me. He balances his light and dark sides so well that there are times I forget the side of him that I should be scared of. The side I hope I never have to see him use again for my sake or the clubs.

His mouth forms into a line of disapproval. Thanks for getting me in trouble, Google.

"Don't blame me. I'm just the name meaning messenger."

"Come on, wife. We have places to be, and once we're done, I'll show you the patron saint of lost causes."

The promise of his show and tell later is enough to make me move even faster out the door. While most women would tire of their husband's overwhelming need to fuck all the time, I will never have that reaction to him. Sex with Ratchet is far from boring and predictable.

He opens up the truck door for me and ushers me inside. Rounding the truck, he slides into the driver's seat. We take off toward the park, where we are supposed to meet Nicole and Asher. Each mile makes my heart beat faster and faster while my nerves fray into tiny shreds of sanity.

"It'll be fine, Ricca," he reassures me. "Just be yourself."

"That's easy for you to say," I snap back. "If he's anything like I was at his age, everyone is a potential enemy. He'll have his guard up."

"Then I guess you'll just need to figure out a way to knock those walls down just as I did with you."

"You didn't knock them down, Jude. You chiseled a hole and found my weak spot before you brought in the wrecking ball and demolished them with one blow."

My husband answers back with a garbled satisfactory moan, which makes me immediately roll my eyes. Subtly and pride in his work aren't exactly his strong suit. Our romp in the airport-parking garage was enough proof of that. His request for a repeat was promptly tabled for a later time.

The pine trees that line the park dot the horizon. With the weather finally turning more summer-like, young families flood the area. Family car after family car line the parking lot that surrounds the playground. I say a silent prayer that we were getting to avoid that stage of my brother's life. I liked kids, but not being in the same vicinity of tons of them screaming and yelling as they play.

An open-sided pavilion comes into view with two people sitting underneath its metal roof. Nicole is staring at her phone when we pull up and doesn't notice us.

I take the chance to study my brother for a few minutes before Ratchet reaches over and unbuckles my seatbelt.

"Stop stalling, Ricca, and just go," he orders, reaching past me and unlatching the door.

"Wait," I hesitate. "You aren't coming?"

"As much as I want to meet him, Siren. This is your time with him. I'll have my chance the next time. This is for you and him. I don't want to intrude."

His gesture and words nearly send me melting into a puddle of happiness. How could this man understand me so well? It just isn't possible.

"What will you do while I'm with him?"

Ratchet unbuckles his own seatbelt and nods to the truck pulling in next to us. My boss sits in the driver's seat and waves to us both.

"Why is Willie here?"

"He's my ride home. I don't want you to feel rushed thinking that I am waiting in the truck. So, I am leaving it here for you whenever you're done and heading back home. Text me when you're on your way."

He exits the truck and comes around to my side, helping me out. His eyes peer down into mine with one last calming moment before he kisses me and heads toward Willie's awaiting vehicle. I watch him walk away before I start toward the pavilion.

Breathe. This is what you wanted. Stop acting like a damn chicken, Ricca. Go meet the piece of you that you didn't know was missing.

Nicole spots me when I get a few feet away and stows her phone away. She leans down to Asher and speaks to him. His eyes lift from the ground and meet mine. Nicole waves for him to stand, and he does so just as I make my way inside. For the first time, I am standing face to face with my little brother, and I have no idea what to say.

Nicole must sense my nervousness and jump-starts the introductions for me.

"Asher, this is your sister, Erica."

"Hi," he quietly says, outstretching his hand to me.

"Hi," I respond, taking his small hand in mine. My body doesn't instantly throw me into a panic with the contact of his hand. The clenching of my muscles and chest remain dormant, and his hand feels so right within mine, like a missing puzzle piece that is finally found to complete the puzzle.

He breaks the contact first and returns his gaze to the ground.

"I am going to go sit over here and answer a few e-mails while you two get acquainted," Nicole interjects. "Take your time," she whispers to me as she passes us.

"Do you want to sit down?" I offer.

"Sure."

Asher turns to the table he once occupied and slips his legs over the bench. I settle in on the other side, and the awkward silence continues to reign.

What do I know about a kid his age? What do they like? Dislike? My lack of childhood was seriously hindering my communication skills right now.

I study his face up close and notice how similar his features are to mine. His tousled curls are like dark tendrils on the top of his head. The deep brown hues of his eyes match the lightly tanned color of his skin. Even the slight upturn of his nose reminds me of myself. I didn't need the results from my DNA test to know that he is my brother.

"Are you really my sister?" he nervously stutters.

"I am."

"Why didn't Mama tell me about you if you're my sister?" he asks, looking into my eyes with sadness clearly painted in their dark hues.

"Mom and I didn't exactly see eye to eye on a lot of things. I hadn't spoken to her in a long time."

"Oh," he adds. "Mama could be like that sometimes."

"Yeah, she could. I may not have good memories of

her, but I bet you do," I state, in hopes of him giving me a glimpse into his relationship with her.

"Mama was always busy," he offers. "I spent a lot of time alone."

Those few words shatter my heart. My mother's parenting skills had obviously not improved the second go around. I observe him for a few moments as silence settles between us again, looking for signs of further abuse by our mother. The skin on his arms, neck, face, and hands are unmarred. I let out a breath of relief.

"Can you tell me a little about yourself?" I hopefully inquire. "Do you have any hobbies?"

"I guess so," he answers. "I like to watch Marvel movies and play video games. And I like to watch WWE when my foster dad lets me."

The mention of my father in that capacity sends an instant coil of rage into my hands. I try my damnedest to keep it at bay in front of Asher.

"I like watching wrestling, too. Who is your favorite wrestler?"

"I like John Cena. He's pretty cool," he offers with a flicker of promise in his eyes.

"I like Roman Reigns."

Asher's eyes light up when he realizes that my interest in something he likes isn't fake. Like me, I could see a fraud from a mile away.

"He's kind of a jerk. How could you like him?" he

protests. "John Cena is a good guy. You should be rooting for him."

"Why don't you tell me more about him? Maybe you can convince me to change my mind."

Asher smiles and starts in on all of the wrestler's attributes that should make me like him, including his hot girlfriend. I could only smile back at his animated reasoning for liking a man portraying a fictional character; it also helped drop his guard. For nearly two hours, we talk about wrestling and some video game that I could barely follow his explanations about. I didn't care that our small talk was about silly things because I was here with him.

Before long, we were laughing at the jokes he started to tell me. His silliness was a breath of fresh air in my life. His smile and laugh were addicting, and each second I was able to listen to him chatter on or laugh was a blessing. But, like all good things, it had to come to an end.

"It's time to go, Asher," Nicole tells him, and his frown returns. He looks at me, and my heart sinks. The time we were given was far too short, and I didn't want it to end.

Nicole waves for him to get up, and I follow suit. We start for our respective vehicles, but Asher stops and runs back to me. His small arms encircle my waist as he grips me as hard as he can. Nicole watches from the background and taps her watch impatiently.

"Hey, Asher," I whisper to him, pulling him away from me. "This is just the beginning. How about next time we play that video game you were talking about? Maybe you could let me win."

He smiles up at me and nods. Without another word, he pivots and goes toward Nicole. I watch as they pull away from me. The piece of my heart that wasn't with Ratchet was now attached to Asher, and I was forced to watch it drive away from me.

"Soon," I whisper to the world around me. "Soon, we'll be together again."

Gathering all my strength, I force myself into the truck and head home. My mind remains focused on every single thing Asher said to me to the point that I don't even notice the flashing red and blue lights behind me.

"Shit," I exclaim, pulling over to the side of the road. "Don't tell me that I spaced a stop sign."

The officer pulls up behind me and walks to the driver's side of my car. He taps on the glass, and I hand crank down the window.

"Can I help you, Officer?" I politely offer. "Was I speeding?"

"Get out of the car, ma'am," he demands. "Leave the keys in the ignition, and step out with your hands up."

"What is this about?" I question.

"Are you not obeying my direct order?"

Thinking about how badly this could go should I resist, I comply with his orders and step out of the truck. His hands roughly spin me around and plaster me to the side of the cab. The officer forces my legs apart and pats me down roughly before jerking my hands down and cuffing them.

"Hey, why am I being cuffed for a traffic stop? This isn't necessary."

My pleas fall on deaf ears. The officer leads me to the back of my truck and shoves me against the tailgate.

"Do not move from this spot," he gruffly commands. "Do you have any weapons or drugs in your vehicle that you would like to declare?"

"Are you kidding me right now? Of course, not."

A second officer pulls up behind his squad car and exits the vehicle with a German Shepherd leashed behind him. The officer with me steps away and talks to the man out of my range of hearing. The canine officer opens the cab of my truck, and I watch as the dog jumps onto the seat. Within seconds, he growls, and the officer handling him pulls him away from the truck.

The original officer returns to me with my purse in hand.

"What do you think you are doing with my purse?"

"Shut up," he orders and dumps out the contents in

the truck bed. Using his pen, he flips through my personal belongings and retrieves a Ziplock bag with white crystals inside of it.

What the fuck is that, and why is it in my purse?

"You lied to me."

"No, I didn't. I have no idea where that bag in your hand came from. It isn't mine," I loudly protest.

"The drug dog hit on your purse, and here I am holding what looks like to be a bag of crack cocaine, but you have no idea how it got here."

"No, sir," I plea. "It's not mine."

"Unfortunately, I don't buy it."

The officer sets down the bag into the bed with my other belongings before grabbing me by the cuffs on my wrists.

"Erica Delmont, you are under arrest for the possession of an illegal substance. You have the right to remain silent," the officer starts before shoving me into the back of his squad car.

How did one of the best days in my life lead to me being arrested? The officer shuts the door, and from the window, I see a familiar face on the sidewalk watching my arrest.

My father.

Chapter 22

RATCHET

"YEAH, V, she's with him now."

Voodoo cracks a joke as I look down at my watch. It's been over four hours since I dropped her off, and not a peep from her yet. That I will take as a good sign. As much as I wanted to be by her side today, this needed to be between the two of them. Two lost souls damaged by their upbringing seek solace and peace in this world. Unlike Ricca, Asher had no one except for her. This was their chance to start over together and my chance to give Ricca something that no one else had done before. A family.

"How's Thor doing?"

"He's doing alright. The sister, not so much. She has been a joy to live with," he declares. "I'm positive she came from money, and this kind of lifestyle isn't exactly her cup of tea, if you get my drift. I wanted to do a background search on her, but Thor threatened my manhood."

"Yeah, I'd leave that one alone, brother. Is she clashing with the other old ladies?"

"Not exactly. With helping Ricca with the house, Darcy, Dani, and the others have been pretty busy. It's the club girls that are the problem. They all apparently wanted a piece of Thor, and this chick isn't exactly on board with their type of nursing. It's like Fight Club with less bikinis and mud."

This news isn't surprising at all to me if V is correct in his asset of the girl. Those who come from privileged lives aren't good fits for club life. Being an old lady isn't an easy position in the club. They hold no official titles, aren't privy to club business, and have no say in most of our dealings. Raze tries to give the women more wiggle room than most other clubs, but it's for their own protection that we keep them out of it.

"Let me guess, Daisy and Bubbles."

"You hit that one on the head, but the problem has been solved. Raze blew his top this morning when he came in to find the place trashed."

"I take it the sister is gone."

"The opposite, actually."

I almost gasp. Club whores are a dime a dozen for us, but these two women had been with us a long time. Ruby depended on them when it came to keeping the clubhouse in ship shape, but if you cause trouble, you'll be doing it from the outside. There's enough drama and bullshit in the world to deal with bad-behaving pussies.

Voodoo babbles on about some woman that he had met online. Leave it to him to find pussy on the Internet that he loves so much.

"You sure she's real? And not cat-baiting you?"

"Cat-baiting?" he chuckles. "Dude, it's catfishing, and do you seriously think I didn't check on that shit right off the bat? Hello, computer genius here."

"Hey, I barely function with my phone and a Google search. I leave that other shit to you."

"She's real, trust me."

The confident tone of his voice tells me he's serious about this crazy ass shit. Meeting someone online is a dangerous business these days, so I really hope that he did, in fact, do his homework. I'd never let him live it down if he went to meet this chick and it turned out to be a dude.

"Are you going to meet her anytime soon?" I question, prying to see just how far he's gone down the Internet dating rabbit hole.

"That's the problematic part," he confesses with disappointment clear in his voice. "She's not local, but I hope that once you're back and she's still interested that I can get a few days off to give that a try. So hurry up, asshole."

Jesus, he does have a hard-on for this chick. As long as I have known him, I've never seen him stick to just one woman. He was a favorite amongst the club girls, and he wasn't afraid to flaunt that fact. The only steady relationship that he'd ever had was the computer that sat in his office and probably a bottle of petroleum jelly.

"I'm trying my best, brother. If today goes as well as I think it is right now, we could be able to fast-track the paperwork."

An idea pops into my head that might just help us out even more.

"Say, how hard would it be for you to hack a government computer again? Like you did for the marriage license?"

Voodoo lets out an exaggerated sigh before answering me.

"Dude, that was child's play. The State of California really needs to hire someone who actually knows how the dark web works. One link click, and the ransomware going around, would shut them down for weeks."

"I don't need the play-by-play, V. Is it possible?"

"Of course, it is. What are you thinking?"

The idea I have teeters on the edge of my tongue. If I go through with this and V gets caught, this could hurt our case. Meddling with court documents could land us both in jail. The devil on my shoulder is screaming for me to ask, but the lesser evil version on the other is telling me to rethink this. A thing that I had never done before meeting Ricca. My mind used to be so clear on my path. I never second-guessed myself once, but when it's not just you anymore that you have to care about, it's completely different. I had made a mistake in giving Ginny her space to protect her, but all it gave me was the painful memories of her death. A mistake that I wouldn't deal with again.

"I need you to hack the caseworker who did the home study for us and find out where we stand with her recommendation to the court. Think you could do that?'

"Dude, I am already ahead of you. She told Darcy and Raze that they were her last interview and that she'd be finishing her report soon. I've been remotely monitoring her computer for it since."

"I would tell you that I love you, but you might just take it the other way."

"Awe, Ratchy," he teases. "I didn't know you felt that way about me."

Voodoo laughs, and I pray that this asshole doesn't have the phone on speaker again. I listen for the roar of laughter in the background, but it remains silent. Thank fucking god for that.

"I'll let you know as soon as I do, brother," he interjects between his snickers. "Shouldn't be too much longer."

"Thanks, V. I owe you. Say, how did Ricca react when she was out there? She try to kick your ass?"

Voodoo starts to answer me, but a large boom comes from outside the trailer. The thin trailer door flies open, and a canister is shot into the void. It thuds against the wall before ricocheting to the ground. An explosion of gas flashes before me before I can make a move. With my phone still in my hand, the noxious gas fills my lungs. I sputter, trying to breathe in clean air but fall down off the couch onto my knees. Two dark figures break through the plane of the door and head straight for me. The cloudiness in the air blocks out their identities. Two pairs of hands grab and pull me forward toward the door. As soon as we reach clean air, I gasp. My lungs heave, trying to inhale fresh air into my burning lungs. The water pouring from my irritated eyes still blurs the scene, and my ears ring from the explosion.

"Up," a muffled voice demands. I shake my head to try to recover my hearing, but the ringing continues.

"I can't hear you," I yell out.

The people holding me jerk me to my feet but don't free my hands.

"Get up, motherfucker," a voice finally pushes through the high-pitch squeals.

I rub my eyes off my shoulders and squint. Two men in dark blue officers' uniforms are holding me up. Their faces are obscured with black gas masks. Only their eyes are visible.

"What the fuck?" I bellow. "Was there a gas explosion?" I question, trying to rationalize the scene before me. One of the men's muttered voices goes unheard, and before I can stop it, I am being cuffed and shoved into the back of an awaiting squad car. As I am shoved inside, one of the officers rips my phone out of my hands, canceling my ability to call for help or record the intrusion.

"What the fuck is going on?" I scream. My blurry vision finally clears as I watch a group of men enter the trailer.

Is this a fucking raid? Why the hell are they doing this? This must be a mistake. There's no cause for this.

I try to call out to the officer standing outside of the car, but my pleas fall on deaf ears. He doesn't even turn to acknowledge me.

I watch in horror as an officer tosses item after item out of the trailer. Anger flourishes within me as I am forced to watch them destroy our home.

"Where's the warrant?" I yell. "This is illegal!"

"Shut up in there," the officer orders.

Two hours pass by, and I am still stuck in the squad car, waiting for answers. Minute by minute, I become a ticking time bomb of rage on the brink of explosion.

Ricca's absence tells me that this isn't a coincidence. Something has happened, and I need answers now.

Finally, an officer approaches the car and throws the door ajar. He reaches in and pulls me out of the car, making sure to shove me against the warm, metal exterior of the squad car. My joints ache from the cramped backseat of the car, but I fight through the discomfort.

"Where are the rest of the drugs?" the officer barks at me. "Where are they hidden?"

"Drugs? What drugs? We don't have that shit here. You've got the wrong place."

"Don't lie to me. Your wife was picked up with them. They have to be here," he tells me.

"The place is clean, sir," a different officer says, stepping up beside us.

"Are you sure?"

"Tossed the entire place, sir. No hits from the dogs. If she had drugs here, she's cleaned up her tracks."

"Fuck," the officer holding me exclaims. "Fine. Get everyone out. We're done here."

"Bullshit," I respond through gritted teeth. "Where's your warrant, and where's my wife?"

"Your wife, Mr. Azzo, is currently where she belongs, in the Hancock County Jail. She's been charged with a Class D felony of possession of cocaine."

Fuck, Ricca had drugs? Had she slipped off the

sobriety wagon and started using again under my nose? Did this start in California?

My body roars in rage over this bullshit charge. I would have known if she was using again. Her body would have shown the signs of it. Track marks, dilated pupils, or even a bloody fucking nose. Absolutely nothing. Besides the fact that cocaine was never her drug of choice, this was nothing but bullshit. Something else is happening here.

The officer clicks the cuffs on my wrists open, and I rub them to relieve the pain from the metal biting into my skin.

"You're free to go, but I'll be keeping a close tab on this place, don't even think about trying to bring drugs in here after we leave."

I sneer at the officer, but as much as I want to take a swing at him, I can't. If I am in jail, that doesn't help Ricca if she really has been arrested. The men clear out of the scene, and the officer who took my phone from my hand gives it back to me. He no doubt put a tracker on it, and I know that I may need to ditch it for a new one.

I wait for them to leave before I start back for the trailer. The scene in front sends a growl screaming from my mouth. Every inch of this place is destroyed. The new wood panels and carpet has been ripped up and torn away. The furniture has slashes in each cushion with stuffing scattered around the floor. Even our bed has been torn apart.

All for the sake of searching for drugs that aren't here and probably never were. The dark side of me roars to life from its dormant state. This may not be California, but even I know that to do this much destruction that there had to be probable cause. The officer never issued me a warrant for his search, which tells me right off the bat this was illegal as fuck. Nothing about the situation seems right.

Securing this place should have been my first priority, but it's not. Ricca is in trouble, and that trumps every-thing. Looking down at the phone in my hand, I know what I need to do.

I hit the button next to Raze's name and call in the cavalry. If it's a war they want, it's a war they'll get. No one messes with my family and lives.

Chapter 23

RICCA

THE YELLS and pleas of the other inmates surrounding me echoes off the walls. My head pounds from them, and they remain unanswered.

My head hangs in my hands as I try to wrap my mind around my current situation. In one fleeting moment, I thought that I had it all, only for it to be taken away just as fast.

This was my father's doing. The smirk on his weathered face told me the truth as I watched him from the squad car. He did this to punish me. This was the price that I had to pay for that moment with Asher. Remembering the smile on his face is all I'll have now. The deputy that booked me assured me multiple times that bail and freedom were two words that I should just forget the meanings of.

How he had access to my truck boggles my mind. I

never left it unlocked, despite the low chances of it being stolen or ransacked in this town. Too many years of having everything I owned stripped away from me taught me that lesson. Protect yourself and the things you cherished most. Yet, here I was. Alone in my own agonizing memory with only hope left to pray for. Hope that the man I love would see through the farce of these charges and free me. Even with that hope, self-doubt took over my thoughts. Would he run for the hills, or would he be the knight in shining armor after all? Only time would tell, and I had plenty of time to kill in here.

Heavy footsteps ricochet off the walls as they move toward my cell. A female officer steps into view, and her hands fall to the lock of my holding cell.

My heart pounds with the hope that this madness is over already.

"You have a visitor," she bellows, fiddling with the lock.

As quickly as my heart raced, it now slows in a slow beat of despair. Visitors within a few hours of imprisonment meant only one thing. My court-appointed attorney was here, and with his or her arrival, my hope of leaving any time soon diminishes.

The officer slides open the door, and it clangs against the bricks as it stops. She motions for me to step forward with a pair of handcuffs dangling from her hands. I outstretch my wrists as she shackles me. The cold metal sends a shutter throughout my body.

"This way, inmate," she orders. I step out in front of her, and she follows closely behind me. Each cell I pass, the faces of those inside are hardened or fearful. A combination that I, too, have felt here.

We reach the end of the cellblock, and she shoves me to the left down a hallway. The shackles at my wrists clink and clang with every step. A second shove leads me into a room with mirrors on all the walls. An interview room. Just great.

The table in the room has one of the two chairs occupied. The occupant is not the lawyer that I had hoped to see but that of my father. His eyes twinkle with delight at seeing me this way. The product of his handiwork on display for his entertainment pleasure.

"Sit," the officer orders. I comply, and she connects my shackles to metal hoops bolted to the table. Why this would make more sense for a more violent criminal, it doesn't for me. Drug charges are a dime a dozen, especially in this part of the country, where meth production runs rampant in the quiet country suburbs. Most first offenders were issued commuted sentences of community service and a hefty fine, so for me to be treated like this tells me that there's something more to this. And that something more is sitting right across from me.

The officer finishes the task of shackling me and steps

out of the room, closing the door behind her. For the first time since Willie's, I am alone with my father and completely at his mercy. I have nowhere to run and hide from him.

"I tried to tell you, girl, but you didn't listen," he starts, clasping his hands in front of him on the table. "Just like your mother."

"I am nothing like my mother," I sneer back at him. His face remains unchanged from the pure look of delight since I entered the room. He's enjoying watching me squirm.

"My mother was nothing more than a mindless whore whose biggest mistake was fucking you," I argue.

"No, your mother's biggest mistake was opening her slut mouth and ruining my life. I was happy until she brought you into the world. No matter how much I offered to pay her, she wouldn't give up her fight to name me. You were born out of pure greed. You were her meal ticket when her tap from me ran dry."

I growl and pull against my bonds. Their bite into my wrists takes me back to the Tribe dungeon, and my stomach churns at the thought. The cusp of my anxiety begins to build, and my throat attempts to seize when my lungs restrict my airway.

Force it down, Ricca. You can't go back there right now. This isn't them. This is your father trying to punish you in a different manner. Fight. Do not let him win.

"My mother was a monster, but you ruined your own life. You slept with her. You got her pregnant, and when it was time to own up and take responsibility, you didn't," I berate with my eyes glued to his. He could try to tear me down, to keep me imprisoned here, but he would never break my spirit. That is something that he would never have over me. His words were only an instrument to cut me down even more. Brutal realities of a life that I had already lived. A life he had nothing to do with until he decided that the breath coming out of my chest, which he helped create, was disposable in his pursuit.

"My mother may have been a monster, but you are the bigger one. You let your own daughter be raped, starved, and tortured for those financial gains. You sat on your throne of righteousness and let it happen. Punish me all you want, but over my dead body will I let Asher live that kind of life."

"Oh, Erica," he explains, "that's where you are already wrong. I've already won. Look around. You're in jail, and I still have him. There's nothing you can do to change that fact."

"Never underestimate me, Father. I may be in here," I declare, motioning to the room around me. My restraints jingle with the flicks of my wrists. "But you will never win. Asher will never be yours."

I push up from the chair and get as close as I can to

him. He leans back to avoid contact, and I laugh in his face.

"I may be out of the game, but there are other players still left in it."

"Look at you," he smiles, "so much piss and vinegar. Posturing yourself when you can't even leave this room without someone unhooking you from the restraints that bind you. You're helpless here. Just like your brother. You've both fallen into my web, and neither of you will escape."

His smug demeanor beams more, and I want to rip these chains off the table and strangle him with them. The officer raps on the door and steps inside. My father leans back in his chair, knowing that his chance is over for now.

The officer removes my additional shackles and starts moving me toward the door. I stop and pivot back toward him.

"Even if I have to sell my soul to the devil himself, I will never let you win."

The officer jerks me back, and the cracked smile on my father's face fades out of my view.

"Officer Mentone," a male voice calls out from down the hallway. "Azzo has another visitor. Take her down to room four. Give her ten more minutes, and then take her out."

Another visitor? Could this actually be the lawyer I so desperately need right now?

Shuffling down the hall, the other room's door is wide open. A gasp slips from my lips as I find Ratchet sitting at the table. As soon as I step near the door, he's up and out of his seat, charging toward me.

"Shit your ass down, sir," the officer with me orders. "You can't touch the prisoner."

Ratchet bites back the response I know is on his lips, but he does as she demands with wavering. The officer repeats the same motion as before and steps out with a warning of our limited time together.

I outstretch my hand toward him, and he grabs it quickly.

"I didn't do it, Jude. The drugs weren't mine," I blurt out. Tears begin to stream down my face.

His hand squeezes mine, and the damn of my tears breaks.

"I know, Siren," he reassures me. "I would have noticed if you'd started again, and cocaine was never your thing. What I don't understand is why this happened? Who would have it out for you to the point of planting drugs in your truck?"

I waver on revealing the truth to him. If I am going to escape this, all of the cards need to be on the table. No more lies. No more secrets. He was my last chance, and I need to let him in completely.

"I lied to you about something, Jude. Asher isn't being fostered by some random person. He's in the care of my father," I confess. He remains silent, almost knowing there's more to this. With the likelihood of the room being watched, I have to closely guard my words. I don't want Ratchet or I implicated further, should this go the way I suspect it will. With my father's blood being spilled by Ratchet. It will be a justified killing if there ever was one.

"The night before the court case, he came to me at Willie's and told me to drop the case to get Asher. He didn't tell me why he wanted him, but he threatened me that if I didn't, he would take matters into his own hands."

Ratchet's eyes flash with anger, and his entire body tenses with the truth of my betrayal exposed. At this moment, he could see my soul, and only he could decide what to do with it.

"Say something, please," I beg him.

"You lied to me, Siren. Something we promised each other never to do again, and yet, you did. Why?"

My heart sinks as his face falls into a deepened frown. He's angry with me, and rightfully so, but this isn't the way I envisioned this going.

"I'm sorry, Jude. I wanted to protect you from all of this. I thought my father's threats were empty ones, and yet again, he's proven me wrong."

He huffs at the thought of me protecting him. The look on his face is clear as day as he processes the words about to leave his lips.

"My job is to protect you," he growls. "Not yours. Not anyone. *Mine.* You had no right to hide this from me. I thought we were in this together."

"We are, but it's not that simple," I try to spit out before the officer returns.

"Time's up."

She releases me from the table, and Ratchet stands as she drags me from the room.

"Just know that I love you," are the last words he speaks to me before I am taken back to my cell. Those were words laced with a promise that I knew would have dire consequences. My lies may have driven us apart and lost Asher forever. Just like everything else, this is my fault, and there's nothing I can do to take it back.

Chapter 24

RATCHET

SHE FUCKING LIED to me after all the promises that we made to each other. The lies were supposed to end, yet, here I am in, seething in fucking anger that she broke that promise. They say a leopard can't change its spots, and neither can my wife, apparently. The betrayal of her trusting me hurt like a knife straight to the heart.

I waited like a fool for hours in that waiting room of the jail, only to be turned away until the morning. The pain that I felt about abandoning her there nearly killed me, but it is nothing compared to what I feel now.

Why didn't she tell me about her father having Asher right off the bat? Was I so unworthy of knowing the full truth?

The veins in my arms bulge as blind rage courses through them. So much of this could have been avoided had she told me the truth. Without the knowledge of her father's existence or threats, I couldn't protect her. The semblance of a life that we had built here has been shattered the moment she admitted to knowing about this being a possibility. I have no doubt her arrest and our home being torn up like the aftermath of a tornado were all connected.

I wasn't stupid enough to say what I really felt in that room for fear that it could be used against her in court. Any admission on my part of threatening her father in any way could make her an accessory to the evil thoughts running through my head. The beast inside of me was readying for a fight, and it would have it.

After leaving the jail, I went straight back to the trailer. The makeshift repairs that I attempted on short notice to secure it were haphazard at best. I tried to clean up the mess as much as I could, but nothing was spared. Without a bed to sleep in, I was forced to sleep on the uncomfortable floor. My body ached from the lack of support, but that ache fueled me.

Just as I pull into the driveway, two familiar faces stand on the threshold of the trailer. Raze and Slider, my brothers-in-arms, had answered my call for help.

Parking my bike near the rental car that occupied the driveway, I cut the engine and slide off. Raze meets me before I even make it off the porch with a look of deep concern in his eyes. He knows there's more to what I told him on the phone last night, and his weathered look, in return, tells me that he has gone without sleep to fly here. Flying meant one thing. That he was ill-prepared in terms of hardware, should this go badly.

"Prez," I greet him, extending my hand toward him. He takes my hand in his, gripping it tightly. "Thanks for coming on such short notice. I really appreciate the help."

"That's what brothers are for, Ratchet. Let's step inside and talk business out of the public eye."

I nod and unlock the simple padlock I used in haste on the door. The lock clicks open, and we head inside.

"I like what you did with the place, Ratch," Slider utters. "It's so you."

Both men's eyes scan the room and take inventory of the damage done by the deputies who raided the place. Even with a quick cleanup, it looks more like it did when I first got here.

"It was a welcome to the neighborhood gift from the county mounties," I answer with a shrug of my shoulders. "They do roll out the welcome wagon here."

"You could say that," Raze adds.

His usual booming and demanding nature is different, and his eyes sweep from the room to me. While this would usually be his lead and his club, the fight here is mine. I am the leader, and he and Slider are my support. The leadership change feels odd after so many years.

"Tell me what you know so far," Raze inquires, and I

tell them of the recent developments. As the story unfolds, neither of them says a word until I finish.

"So what's the plan?" Slider interjects. "Do we have any solid evidence of her father's involvement other than some back alley threats and her word against his."

"I don't, but I'm hoping that V can find out something about it. On my way back from seeing her, I called him with the new information she fed me."

"So all we have now is to wait and see if we can prove her innocence and his guilt," Raze surmises.

"Unfortunately, yes. I may have been a bit premature in calling you both in. This is going to have to be a wait-and-see kind of chess game."

"Is she worth all this trouble?" Slider asks. "No piece of ass should bring this much trouble on you or the club."

I roar with rage. And start for him. Raze steps between us, cutting me off from my target.

"She is not a piece of ass, Slider. She is my fucking wife. It may not seem like it to you, but when you make a fucking commitment like that, it comes with the good and the fucking bullshit."

"Jesus, dude," Slider backpedals. "I was only asking."

"You don't have the fucking right to ask something like that until you can fully understand what it means."

Raze just watches the back-and-forth pissing match between Slider and me before he finally backs down from me. This is the worst time for him to find his balls. One more fucking word out of him, and he'd end up like one of those army men from *Game of Thrones*. Unmanned and unmatched.

"What can we do while we wait?" Slider asks, steering the conversation back to where it should be.

My thoughts race to how I can prepare for what's ahead. There are so many different angles that one wrong move before we know anything could cook us. The waiting game is our only ally.

"I don't know, but I do have something you can do in the meantime, Slider. With Ricca's brother being the common factor in this all, I need eyes on him. Do you think you could handle that?"

Slider looks to Raze, who nods in return, then back to me.

"I may be young, but I doubt I could pass for an elementary school student," he jokes, trying to lighten the mood.

"I didn't mean infiltrate the school as a student, dumbass. I want you to watch him. Think you can handle that?"

"Yeah, yeah. I got it."

"He will be getting out of school soon. There are signs on the main drag through town. Just follow them to the school, and stay out of sight."

"Yes, boss," he chides me before stepping out the

door and on his way to his task. With Slider watching Asher, I could have an early alert system should her dad try to run.

With Slider gone, it's just Raze and I left to twiddle our thumbs.

"How are you managing this, brother?" he asks me.

"Is this your version of a man-to-man talk, Prez? Because you really need to work on your intro a bit more before you have this with one of Darcy's boys."

"Shut up, asshole," he fires back. "I know this can't be fucking easy for you. She took off, and you followed her into this mess."

"That I did," I acknowledge. "I thought this would be a simple dash and grab, but nothing is easy with her. Just when I think I have her figured out, she changes her damn mind or lies to me. There's never common ground with her. I spend every single day second-guessing myself on if I made the right decision."

Raze slaps his hand on my shoulder while I pour my heart out to him. Of all the people who would understand, it's him. His first wife was a cunt who knew more about betrayal than how to be a wife and mother to his two kids. Because of her, his best friend is dead. Yet, his death brought something else into his life… Darcy and her kids. I was against the union at first, but seeing them together made more sense after I realized how much they needed to lean on each other. It helped that Jagger posthumously consented to the match. Call him crazy, but Jagger was the kind of guy that would sacrifice everything to keep her safe. And that's exactly what he did. He saved her, and through it, he gave her a second chance at happiness with his brother in arms. Strange as it might be on the outside looking it, it worked. Raze was happier than I had ever seen him, and the addition of her kids made his new house the home it was truly meant to be.

"Women will never be a simple fix, brother. They are like the rarest of cars. The parts are either hard to find or non-existent. No matter how many flaws you find, you just have to live with them as they are. The chinks and dings in them give them character and doesn't take away from their value."

His wise words sink in. As much as I want to condemn Ricca for her lies, I can no longer fault her for them. When you spend your life trying to keep yourself safe from the world, you learn to survive on your own and in your own way. What she saw as protecting me was actually hindering my ability to help, but it was also shielding herself from the onslaught we're currently facing now. With her father in the equation, we would have always ended up in the exact same position as we are now. I just had to find a way of putting the pieces back together again. For her. For Asher. And for myself.

Raze's phone rings in his pocket, and he retrieves it.

He answers it with muffled tones before pulling it away from his head and flicking it on speakerphone.

"Hello, Sunshine," Voodoo's voice rings from the phone. "Miss me yet?"

"I miss you like a damn toothache," I fire back at him. He chuckles in response. "What have you found?"

"You were right about one thing. Her father is a fucking douche canoe."

"He had his daughter thrown in jail. Tell me something I don't already know."

Raze hands me the phone before searching the room for something to write on. He shuffles around some of the debris and finds a discarded paper towel and one of Ricca's make-up pens. Not a notepad and paper, but desperate times call for desperate measures.

"Her daddy dearest is about to be in some pretty hot water," he starts. "Finding out his contact information wasn't the hard part. I did a little digging in his financial and court records, and you're not going to believe what I have on him."

"Seriously? This suspense thing again? Just spit it out," I order him. Raze shakes his head at V's theatrics and waits to take down notes.

"Fine, Buzz Killington. Her father, one Ronald Boatman, has filed for bankruptcy three times in the last twenty-odd years. The most recent of those files was last year. But what's interesting to me is that his bank account doesn't appear to be empty. The secret one, that is."

"Dude, how in the fuck do you even find this shit out," I blurt.

"Magic. Stop interrupting me. About four years ago, her dad started working for the local hospital, and that's when the large deposits of cash started showing up in this other account. The funny thing about this account is that his name isn't on it. It's Asher's."

"Son of a bitch," I exclaim.

"It gets worse. Not only does he have this bank account in Asher's name, but there is also a corresponding life insurance policy for over a million dollars. Looks to me like daddy is planning a one-way ticket to the six-feet-under hotel for little Asher."

"That's why he wanted him so badly. He has all this money in his name, but for what purpose? Where did the initial sum even come from?"

"Boatman is about to be served with a summons to appear in court regarding a missing drugs case at the local hospital. He worked part-time as a chaplain there during the period in question."

"You don't think?" I ask Raze, who nods in return.

"It would explain the drugs. If he's selling prescription drugs, he would have access to non-controlled substances. It makes sense to me."

"The part I don't understand is if he has a bank

account with Asher's name on it and a life insurance policy, how did he get those without claiming the kid? Don't you have to be a legal guardian to set that shit up?"

"That's the other part of this. He didn't set them up. The mother did."

You have got to be fucking kidding me. Ricca's mother is the reason this wheel of insanity started rolling. Was this all her idea, or did he play a part in it? The only way I'm going to find that out was to ask him myself.

"Give me that address for him, V. I think I need to make a house call."

Chapter 25

RICCA

IT'S BEEN two days since my arrest, and with each day, my will to fight starts to slip away. The confidence with which I came into this hellhole has been stripped away from me piece by piece. I had hoped that my stay here would be short-term, but even the backwoods lawyer who sits before me thinks I'm fucked.

The case against me is a mockery of the judicial system and has been orchestrated by my father's drive to ruin my claim on Asher. The false charges that are listed next to my name mean nothing but jail time to the buffoon representing me.

"Mrs. Azzo, I understand that you want to enter a plea of not guilty, but you have to understand. In the eyes of the law, you are. The drugs were found in your purse, in your vehicle, and in your presence. Even with the lack of fingerprint evidence and the negative drug test results, you still are being charged with possession with intent to sell.

I slam my shackled fists on the table in front of me. Possession with intent to sell? How in the fuck have they fabricated such a claim against me? Intent implies that I had buyers, and to have buyers, I would have to be a dealer. None of which I did, nor I am. I'm not sure who educated the man in front of me, but he needs a re-education on simple terms in the dictionary. None of this makes sense.

"Mr. Gibbs," I start.

"You can call me Leroy, Ma'am."

"Whatever. Listen, Leroy. You went to law school, right?"

"Of course I did. I am a licensed public defender for Hancock County. How could I be sitting here with you if I didn't have a license?" he throws back into my face.

"It seems to me, *Leroy*, that you should be more attentive to the truth instead of trying to get me to admit guilt when there is no guilt to be had. I am innocent, and no matter what you or anyone else says, that is the truth. There's no evidence that I intended to sell. You just admitted that my fingerprints weren't even on the bag. It could have been easily planted by someone else. Explain to me how I didn't leave a shred of evidence behind on the bag. Were rubber gloves found at the scene?"

"I do admit it is quite odd that there is no DNA or

fingerprint forensic evidence that links you to the bag of cocaine found in your car. But you still were in possession of it, and that in itself is against the law. The judges in this area are hard on first-time offenders, and I just want you to be aware that a guilty plea may be the better odds of staying out of jail."

I want to reach across the table and strangle this incompetent asshole. The evidence says I'm guilty? Not in my fucking book. It's as if this man watched *Law and Order* and called that his education. His ineptitude is going to get me locked away without a doubt. Is this all a running joke that no one has let me in on yet? How is any of this even legal?

"Admitting guilt to something I didn't do is just as bad as falsely admitting to doing it on the principle that it would be easier for you. Furthermore, what was the reason for the officer pulling me over and searching my car? Was there suspicious activity involved? Do your fucking job, and get me out of here," I demand of him before calling for the guard.

He shoves his papers back into his worn leather satchel and sneers back at me.

"Fine, you don't want to listen to your attorney, then you can represent yourself. I will not work with someone who chooses to do things in the most difficult way possible. Good luck with your case, Mrs. Azzo."

Leroy stomps past Lydia, the guard waiting in the

doorway. She shakes her head at me before stepping in and releasing me. Unlike the other guards, Lydia is gentler when she un-cuffs me and doesn't shove me at every turn. Had I been more of a noncompliant inmate, I would understand the rougher treatment, but this is fucking ridiculous. Nothing I have done has warranted such brutality.

"If it's any consolation, Mrs. Azzo, you convinced me of your innocence. The man is an idiot, and you're better off without him."

"At least you don't think I'm crazy," I offer to her as she ushers me back into my cell. The door shuts with a clang and locks me into the tiny space that may end up being my temporary home for several years. Just the thought of calling this home sucks the air right out of my lungs.

This will not be it for me. I will show them.

Lying back on the paper-thin mattress, my thoughts drift to Ratchet. The way things ended is still haunting me. He may have said that he loved me, but the tone of his words had something lingering just underneath the surface. A promise. A threat. Maybe a combination of both. The endless possibilities of his intended words are enough to drive me crazier than I already am. What is it about a jail that makes those who inhabit it less mentally stable than when they arrived? Is it something in the air?

The fact that I had betrayed the trust that we had

agreed upon ate at me. Why did I think keeping him in the dark was going to spare me from my father's wrath? It has only made things more divided. Where we would have stood together and fought against him, we now stand on either side of the battle lines. Together we are strong, but together may not be the right word to describe our situation after my lie.

I took my father's threats and Ratchet's pride for granted. Two mistakes that I never intend to make again.

My head falls back, and soon, sleep takes me. My dreams are filled with horrors, just like they have been since my first night here. The veil between real and imaginary is the hardest to see in the dark spaces of one's mind, and today's nightmare show is the worst yet. Asher screaming for my help as my father drags him away. Ratchet destroying my love for him by fucking one of the club whores in front of me. But the worst comes in the last dream. The swirling fog clears and reveals the scene that has haunted me for years. Not even the desert dungeon could touch the disgusting visions playing in my unconscious mind. I watch, as a ghost that is still watching their living family, as my mother sells me to a man three times my age. She sells me for his pleasure and for my virginity. I could hear my own screams and pleas from the room, but as I moved closer, a sound startles me from my sleep.

I shoot up from the bed, covered in sweat, and gasping for air. My eyes are wild as I try to convince myself that it was just a nightmare and it's not real.

"Inmate," one of the guards barks.

I groan when I see someone other than Lydia standing outside my cell bars and flop my body back onto the bed. For days, it has been an endless slew of moving in and out of my cell. Between the visits from my father, Ratchet, my attorney, and the investigating detectives, I have hardly slept. It's almost as bad as being admitted to the hospital with the constant round checks.

"What now?" I groan.

"Doctor is here to see you," she offers, opening up my cell yet again.

I want to ask her again to make sure that I heard her correctly, but I don't. Why would the guards call a doctor for me? I wasn't sick or injured. The guard leads me down a different hallway into a regular room instead of being placed into one of the interview rooms. No windows, no mirrors. Just a table and chairs.

"Hello, Mrs. Azzo," Dr. Matthews' voice rings from inside. I nearly jump for joy at the sight of her. If anyone would believe my story, it will be her. I hope.

I immediately place myself in the seat across from her and send the guard on her way. As soon as the door closes behind her, I sob.

"Erica, are you okay?" she gasps.

"No," I solemnly answer.

Dr. Matthews shifts in her seat as I cry uncontrollably in my hands against the desk. Everything I had held back comes flowing out of me as I force myself to choke out the story of my incarceration.

"I'm innocent, Dr. Matthews. I swear that I am. I wouldn't jeopardize my chance with Asher for this."

Dr. Matthews reaches out toward me and takes my hands into hers.

"I have been helping people for many years, Erica. Many of those patients lied to me on a regular basis and continued to abuse their vices. You are not like them," she assures me, squeezing my hands at every word.

"You believe me?"

"Yes, Erica. I do."

I don't know what to say to her, and the urge to hug her comes over me. Not a single person has taken my story at face value and seen the bullshit that clouds the truth underneath the murk.

"What about the new man in your life? The one from your past. Where does he stand in all of this?" she questions.

Dr. Matthews has obviously taken note that I had left him out of my story. I did it intentionally because that is not a can of worms I want to open up with a potential lynchpin in my fight for my brother. The less she knows about him, the better off we both are.

"I think he believes me, Doc, but he's seen me at my worst. He knows I wasn't using, but we didn't exactly leave on the most solid of terms. He was here the first day, but I haven't seen or heard from him since."

"The ones who love us the most are the quickest to condemn us when their feelings have been hurt. Be patient with him, and I believe, in time, that he'll see things your way."

"God, I hope so. What can I do to make others see that I'm not guilty, Doc? The evidence is sketchy at best, yet they are trying to just throw me straight into the fire."

"Continue to stand your ground, Erica. When the world seems the darkest, the brightest light will always shine through. Do not let this place take away from all the progress you have made over the last few months. They cannot define you. Only you can do that."

"Thank you, Dr. Matthews. I needed to hear that more than you know. After a few days in this place, it's like the fight and life are being sucked right out of me."

"I know, Erica. I wish I would have been here sooner," Dr. Matthews announces to me. "Maybe I could have stopped this from going so far."

"There was nothing you could have done to prevent this. Trust me. I have my suspicions about who is really at fault, and with any luck, that is going to be taken care of soon enough."

The doctor goes silent, and I realize that what I just told her could be interpreted in so many different ways. Thankfully, this room doesn't seem to be as monitored.

"Is your sick patient better now? I know you probably can't tell me, but you look really exhausted."

The doctor is visibly curious about my inquiry. I, the patient, am asking the doctor questions. It may be unorthodox in the practice of psychiatry, but even therapists need a chance to talk about themselves. How they stay sane listening to the problems of the world, I will never know.

"That's not exactly why I was gone. I have a special patient that I have to see immediately when an appointment is requested. The call came shortly after our last session, and when I met with her, I knew that this wasn't a quick one. She needed more time with me."

As Dr. Matthews speaks, I sense fear inside of her. This patient may be special, but there's something more to the story. I know that there's laws preventing her from telling me anymore, and I respect her for following them. But she seems troubled by her admission.

"Are you sure that you are okay?"

Dr. Matthews hesitates again but quickly regains her composure. She steers her questions back to my case and away from her other patient. In doing so, she piqued my interest more. For someone who is tight-lipped about her personal life, why would she share this with me? As our session continues, she never brings it back up again, but I cannot shake the feeling that this conversation is going to come back and haunt me someday.

Chapter 26

RATCHET

WE PLANNED for two more days before I was finally ready to make my move. My first priority was to make sure that Asher was out of harm's way. If things were going to go as far south as I anticipated, I didn't want him to walk in and see what was left of the man housing him. I would call him his father, but the jury was still out on that fact. If he was Asher's sperm donor, it would make his intentions even more nefarious. How someone could plan to take his or her own son's life is beyond me. A child should be cherished, and not a means to collect cash. Had Ricca's mother still been alive, I would have likely broken my no-women rule just for her. A mother's job is to protect their children, not to throw them into the pits of hell for their own gain. The pair of them deserved death. Her father was just not there yet, but I might just change that fact today.

Death was the only way to ensure that he would never come back for Asher or for Ricca. It was the permanent restraining order and the only option I may have to protect them both. He was evil, despite his former religious inclinations that Voodoo discovered. A man of the cloth he may have been, but the harbinger of death was coming for him.

Raze and I planned while Slider watched Asher. It was a divide-and-conquer approach, and so far, it was working out in our favor. Voodoo's information gave me the motive, but without a confession from the asshole's own lips, it meant nothing. It was only connecting the dots that even a shitty lawyer could defend as a mother trying to ensure her son had the means to live after her death.

The day was set in stone, and with any luck, so would the man who drove a wedge between my wife and me. After today, no one would ever come between us again. I will make damn sure of that.

Raze sits in the trailer, checking the few weapons we were able to scrounge up. Thank god for buy-and-sell sites on Facebook that skirted the rules. A few fistfuls of cash, and we had more firepower than we did to begin with. While I didn't plan on just outright shooting him, I didn't want to be ill-prepared. Never go into a shootout with just your dick in your hand was something I had lived by for years.

Raze blows into the chamber of the gun, clearing away the dust as he finishes checking it over. He locks in the magazine and racks one in the chamber. He shoves up from the table, which dwarfs his large frame, and hands the gun to me, butt first.

"Just in case," he offers before slipping the other magazines he filled into his back pockets.

"Thanks."

I stow the gun into the waistband of my jeans, pulling my t-shirt over it. Not wearing my cut onto the battlefield feels so weird to me, but we can't have the club's name associated with this if we get caught. Today we are not the Heaven's Rejects motorcycle club. We are brothers in arms.

"Ready?" Raze questions, and I answer with an affirmative nod. The text from Slider that Asher is safe comes in just as we step out of the door toward the car we also purchased through Facebook. No records or traces of us. We will be ghosts in the wind once this was finished.

The tiny compact car barely holds the two of us. We swing by the school, grab Slider from his hiding spot, and head toward our target.

Boatman's house isn't far from the school, but it is remote enough from the town that it would take time for someone to notice something is amiss. Raze pulls off onto a side road that is parallel to his modest brick home.

On the outside, it looks like the American dream home that everyone wishes they had. It's large but not overwhelming. The front porch is wrapped with a white railing, with flowering bushes cascading around its curves. Though it looks perfect on the outside, it's what's on the inside that is not.

A black town car flies past us, and we duck down, appearing as if the car is just abandoned. It doesn't even slow down, so we know we haven't been spotted. At least, that seems to be the case. This guy is either stupid or doesn't pay enough attention to his surroundings.

Boatman pulls his car into the garage and shuts the door behind him. We give him a few minutes to settle in before we begin to make our move. Exiting the vehicle quietly, we give the perimeter a wide berth. Each step that I take closer to the house, my mind focuses on another way I can make him pay for this intrusion into my life.

Would I make my point with my knife? The gun at my waist? Maybe my fists. Whatever method I use, it's almost a guarantee that he won't like the results as much as I will.

Raze waves for Slider and me to break off, and head toward the back door. Raze has too much to live for with his newly expanded family, and I made it abundantly clear that if this went to shit, he was to leave me behind.

Slider knew the risks of being on my team, but he was ready to take the plunge. After this, he might get his full membership status. Prospects need to prove themselves worthy of the title, and he was doing that by being here. I would make sure of it if we made it out of this alive.

Taking either side of the back patio door, I peer in through the blinds and see no one in the vicinity of the room. Taking my gloved hand, I try the lock, and it pops open.

Dumbass should've known to lock the doors when he's doing illegal as fuck shit. Apparently, no one taught him protection skills, or he's just that fucking cocky.

I nod to Slider, who readies his weapon. I quietly shove open the door and step inside, gun drawn. Slider follows directly behind me and mimics my every step.

The room is quiet, and it reassures me that there isn't a guard dog that is about to tear my face off. Slider scans the room, and at this point, our risk-taking is about to go up another notch of crazy. Voodoo was able to secure the house layout from the general contractor plans that were provided to the zoning board for the building contract. It was just another reason why I owe that guy big time when I get back. The hall directly in front of us is diverged into two sections of the house. Slider steps forward into the hall and waves me on that the coast is clear. I wave back, and we separate.

My piece of the hall is nothing but a series of closed

rooms, one after another. The first room on my left grabs my attention when I see a large padlock panel on the outside of it. Without even having to look, I know this is Asher's room. His forlorn look of dread when he saw this man makes more sense now than ever before. He was a prisoner here, just as his sister was in her jail cell. The same man being responsible for both deeds.

A growl of anger tightly coils inside of my stomach, but I force it down.

Save the rage for him. He is about to get everything he deserves.

I clear another set of rooms before I finally hear signs of life coming from the one at the far end. A muffled voice comes from the crack in the door at the end of the hallway. I peek inside and see my target. Ronald Boatman is seated at a large desk with his ear plastered to a phone. His face is filled with irritated anger as he begins to scream at the person on the other end of the line.

"I am trying to get you your money. I just hit a snag, is all," he bellows. His hand rubs his brow as he listens to the response of the other person on the line.

"I promise this is the last delay. I didn't expect her to actually go through with the filing. Once she's convicted, the heat will be off the boy, and we can take care of the situation."

The coldness in his voice as he talks about his

daughter and likely his own son is unfathomable. There is no caring, no concern, and no love present in anything that he is saying for two people who share a piece of him. The lack of any emotion toward his kids is sickening as fuck.

Every word that comes out of his mouth enrages me even more. It's fucking torture listening to him speak while waiting in this hallway. I want to jump in there and end it now, but the caller might just call back or show up. Something that I can't have until we're done here.

I lie in wait like a predator until he gives me what I need. He dismisses the person on the other line and tosses the phone down on his desk. I watch as his head falls back and his eyes close.

I slowly push open the door, staying as silent as I can. It isn't until the door creaks that he's aware he's not alone. He jumps in his desk chair, scrambling to leave it.

"Don't move, motherfucker," I order with my gun trained on the center of his forehead. "You shift, and I shoot."

His hands come up into the air in a show of surrender. His eyes flicker to the phone on his desk, and I can already see the wheels turning in his head. He starts to lower his hands toward his one lifeline in the house. In a few short strides, I reach his desk before he can make it and snatch up his phone in my gloved hands. I slide it into my back pocket and end his plan dead in its tracks.

"What do you want?" he mutters. "Money? My car? Take it!"

"I'm not here for your money, Ronald. I'm here for much different reasons."

I can visibly see him shaking as he tries to decide my motives. It isn't until he focuses on my face that I finally see the recognition that I have been waiting for. I don't want to hide behind a mask of fear. I want this asshole to feel everything that I do to him. Maybe then he'll realize an ounce of the pain that he's caused my wife. His narrow gaze and furrowed brow form in realization.

Go ahead, motherfucker. Try to posture yourself up to me. No angry glare is going to save you from this. You sealed your fate. Not even the devil himself can recall the contract on your life.

"You," he announces, "you're her fucking pimp."

"Pimp?" I laugh. "You couldn't be more wrong."

"If you think this scare tactic will get me to help get her out, you're delusional. She deserves to be in there."

The rage stored inside of me unleashes. I round the desk, hitting him twice directly to his temple. He cries out with each strike, and blood begins to pour from the cut over his eye. Boatman slumps in his chair as I hear a heavy set of dragging footsteps coming down the hall. Slider's face comes around the corner, his gun drawn.

"Rest of the house is clear, Ratchet."

"Good. Get over here and keep your gun on him. The fun is about to begin."

The man I tower over looks up at me with a flash of fear in his eyes. I turn back to Slider and nod. Pulling a few wire ties from my pocket that I had stashed away, I bind his wrists tightly to his chair. He will not escape his fate.

"Will a thousand dollars help end this now? I can get that for you in less than an hour. If it's money that you need, just let me help you, and this can all be over."

"Are you trying to bribe me? And how could you help, Ronald? Are you going to admit to me that you were the one who planted the drugs? Because that's the thing that you can *help* me with," I bait him. He remains silent. I shake my head at him and spin his chair to face me. The smell of piss wafts toward my face. What a fucking pussy. Two headshots, and he's already pissed himself. How could someone like him take the life of his son?

Give me part of what I came here for. Squeal, little piggy. Squeal. No one is coming to save you from me.

"I'm waiting, Ronnie," I bellow, drawing the knife out that's strapped to my leg and placing it against his throat. He gasps for air when I apply just the tiniest bit of pressure on the blade. "Tick tock."

"Yes," he gurgles. "It was me. I planted the drugs."

"Good boy," I goad him while I remove the knife from his throat and pat his head like a dog.

"I'll kill you. You will fucking die. Let's make a deal," he pleas while jerking against his restraints. "You want her out? I can do that."

"A deal? Just like the deal you had with the mother of your children?"

"I don't know what you're talking about," he scoffs.

"Lying to me isn't going to save you. I know all about the bank account and the life insurance policy. Killing your charge and what I can only guess is your son over money. How fucking pathetic."

"I didn't want to do it. It was all her idea."

"While that may be true, here you sit, preparing to finish what she started."

He starts to utter yet another excuse, but I cut him off when I plunge the knife into his leg. He screams out in pain, and the sound brings a smile to my face.

"What did I tell you about lying to me?"

I sit on his desk and observe the gushing trail of blood streaking down his piss-stained pants. He squirms against the metal buried in his flesh, only deepening the wound further.

"Try again. The truth this time, if you please."

"I don't know what you mean," he calls out with tremors of panic and fear lacing his voice.

That's it. Fight me more. It will only make this last longer.

He cries out in pain and feigns ignorance again. My hand wraps around the hilt of the knife, yanking it from his leg. He watches me spin the blood-covered blade in my hand before I repeat the action into his other thigh. Thick streams of blood now run down both of his legs. His eyes tell me that he's finally getting the gist of why I am here when he starts to flicker his gaze between Slider and I looking for a way out. He is in deep shit without a canoe or paddle to get himself out of it.

With what I have in mind, I have to keep my knife as far away from his bones as I can. The way I have envisioned his death in my mind over the last few days only end one way. My way. Striking the bone would leave evidence behind, so I stick with the meaty flesh to do my damage.

"Tell me, Boatman. Tell me why you want to kill your son."

He spits at me and tries to wrench his arms free again. The wire ties dig into his flesh, drawing more blood from his body. With the way things are currently going, he'll die from blood loss before I get the chance to kill him myself.

Even as his instincts call for him to fight, I can see his will to keep on going ebb. His continued silence irritates me more.

I rear back and pound into his face and stomach in

quick succession. The impacts are clearly making him dizzy and incoherent even more.

"Tell me why," I order him again. His silence is excruciating to my ears, and even Slider is bothered by his lack of compliance. He has to know that this is only going to end in one way.

"Just fucking kill him already, Ratchet. He's not going to tell you anything," Slider interjects, just as I told him to do should this happen. When someone is cornered, and in his position, they are desperate for an ally. Stalling may extend his shelf life, but it does nothing for them in the end. Slider's act of playing devil's advocate would give him a reason to speak. A reason to try to fight back.

"Shut up, asshole. He's going to talk. Just point the gun at him, and do your fucking job."

"I don't like this," he continues on with the charade. "It's taking too fucking long. Someone is going to notice our guys outside."

"Shut up or get out. I'm not leaving until I finish this."

Slider adds a slight tremor to his stance, and Boatman takes the bait.

"Your friend is right," Boatman finally croaks out. "This doesn't concern you. Why don't you run along and go back to being a fucking loser? My daughter should be out in five to ten years. She might even wait for you."

I let him regain his confidence and hope that this

ends differently. His attempt at baiting is giving me the fuel I need to let the final piece of my plan play out.

Slider turns his gun on me. His eyes are filled with the anger-induced fury of someone who is on the edge of loyalty. His entire body screams I want out of this mess, and he'll do it at any cost, including killing his partner-in-crime.

Keep it up, Slider. Sell it.

"I'm over this bullshit," he declares. "I don't want to be your minion anymore. Drop your gun and slide it over to me."

"Are you fucking kidding me?"

"Smart move, son," Boatman sneers. "Untie me, and I'll help you kill him."

I do as Slider asks, cussing him the entire time. He circles the table and presses the barrel of his gun to my head.

"On your knees."

I comply and growl the entire time as my knees touch the ground. The smell of urine and blood fill my nose, and I wretch from the smell of weakness coming off the man next to me.

"Son, you kill him and then release me, and I might just have some business for you to do," Ronald repeats with an added sweetener to his deal.

"Like what," Slider inquires.

"Let's just say that I have a small problem that needs to be taken care of. I'll give you fifty grand to do it."

"You want me to kill the kid, don't you?"

"Yes," Boatman replies. I try to stand up and strike out at Slider, but he presses the gun barrel harder against my scalp.

"Why do you want the kid dead? Why not bring in that free state money for watching him?"

"I have some financial investments currently in his possession. His mother fucked up my plan, and now I need to remove one more complication. Once the boy is gone, the money is mine. What do you say, son? You in?"

"As generous as your offer is, there's just one problem," Slider declares, pulling the gun from my head and pointing it directly at Boatman. He hisses, realizing that his own pride has just revealed his true plans to us both, and now he sees the mic currently strapped to Slider's chest, recording his confession. "Unlike you, I don't betray my family."

Game. Set. Match.

In a sweeping motion, I rise from the floor and retrieve my knife from his thigh.

"My wife sends her regards, motherfucker," I announce to him before plunging my blade into his throat, slicing it open.

The blood pours from the open wound, and I stay still, watching as the last ounce of life leaves him, drop by drop. Satisfaction rolls over me like a rogue wave hitting the beach. My girl is safe and will soon be free.

Slider retracts his gun and holsters it, putting his hand on my shoulder.

"Time to light the place up, Ratchet. Let's finish this."

A demented smile forms on my face. "Let's burn this bitch, and go get my girl."

Chapter 27

RICCA

"PLEASE RISE," the bailiff calls to the courtroom. "The honorable Judge McKenzie Chaplain presiding."

The entire room lifts to their feet as the judge walks up to her bench. She wears a hardened look on her weary face as she descends to her throne of judgment. Her black robe flows behind her like the rags on the grim reaper. She may not have a scythe in her hand, but her gavel would serve as her instrument of my impending damnation.

I have to admit that I never thought my case would get this far into the process as I stand here in the middle of my arraignment hearing. My diminished hopes and doubts convinced me that this day would come, while the other half of me thought my husband would save me. The man who, besides the first-day visit, has been all but absent.

Was he even still here in Kentucky, or did he cut his losses and go back to California? If I had been in his shoes, the latter might have been the option I considered the most, but it would have been a far more difficult decision to make. Why would you wait for someone who may spend the next several years as a resident of the Kentucky State prison system? It was a dead end, and there was no guarantee that I would even be freed once convicted of the false charges that lay against me.

Much to my dismay, the public defender that I was sure I fired showed up when I was ushered into court with my hands and feet bound. This man standing next to me would all but assure that I was going to be calling the gray bar hotel home.

"You may be seated," the bailiff declares. "Your honor, this is case number one-zero-one-three-one-seven, the State of Kentucky versus Erica Azzo. The defendant is charged with a class D felony of possession of an illegal substance with the intent to sell and resisting arrest."

"I did no such thing," I blurt out before my attorney jerks me down into my seat and orders me to be quiet.

"Control your client counselor, or I will be forced to charge her with an additional account of contempt."

"Of course, your honor. Excuse my client's poor manners," he drawls, shooting a glare at me for my outburst. I nearly flip the man off, but I doubt the judge would go for that. "She's from the big city and doesn't know how to keep her outbursts in check."

Yep. Leroy is about to get a slap to the back of the head before he has me dragged off to jail. Maybe even a couple more for good measure.

The judge's eyes turn back on me, and I shrug a sorry to her. It's hard to keep quiet when your fate lies in the hands of a man who probably couldn't tell the difference between his own dick and a Cheeto.

"How does the defendant plea?" the judge calls out to my attorney. He looks down at me, urging me to say the words he wants. But I am not guilty, and I will not let my father win by admitting to something that I didn't do. That's not how this story will end for me or for Asher.

"Not guilty," I stammer out before a sheriff's deputy busts through the closed chamber doors. His feet drag against the wooden floors of the courtroom, and the judge's face instantly turns to anger at the intrusion. The few people scattered in the court chamber turn in a flurry to see what is going on. I mimic their motions and sigh when I don't see Ratchet sitting behind me. I guess that's my answer about whether or not he stayed. It would have taken an act of God for him not to be here prior to my keeping secrets about my father. It goes to show that even when I'm happy, I can still fuck up my life.

"What is the meaning of this, Officer? This court is in

session. How dare you interrupt this case," she reprimands him, smacking her gavel down. "Order in the court!" she cries out. "I will have order!"

He steps forward through the swinging wooden gate that separates the onlookers from the Judge and the tables for the plaintiff and me. Bead after bead of sweat drip down his forehead and onto the collar of his uniform. His body quivers from the spotlight being on him, and it makes me wonder if he lost a bet to have to be the one here doing this. The officer's hands shake as he musters up the courage to speak to the judge.

"Permission to approach the bench, your honor." The officer holds up an envelope in his hands for the judge to see. "I have evidence that Chief Moulton thought you might want to see before you proceed any further."

"Proceed, Officer," she advises him. The man slowly walks toward her with carefully calculated steps. He's on edge, and the entire courtroom can see it. He hands off the envelope to her, and the judge reaches into it, retrieving a shiny, circular disc.

My heart begins to race at the sight of it. Could this be another gift from my father? What other evidence could he have on me to warrant this kind of display?

"What is this?" the judge asks the officer, holding up a CD encased in plastic for the courtroom to see. "Is this a joke?"

"Your honor, that disc was found alongside a written

note of confession inside a vehicle of a burned home we found yesterday morning."

Burned house? Why would a burned-down house have anything to do with my drug case?

The answer suddenly flourishes within my mind, and my stomach rolls. This can't be happening. My father has faked his and Asher's deaths to take off with him. That's the only reasonable explanation for him to confess.

The judge cocks an eyebrow at him and waves for him to expand on that thought. Either this judge is a badass, or this guy is a pussy for her to have to push him into speaking. Every fiber of my being is on edge, and wants to scream out for him to spit it out already.

"Have you listened to the disc, officer?"

"Yes, your honor. The recording that it contains is that of a confession," he stutters.

"Bailiff," she calls, considering his words carefully for a few seconds. "Please play this disc."

"Objection, your honor. This new evidence was not provided to us," the state district attorney argues. "The State would like a chance to review it before it is presented as evidence in this case to prove the authenticity of its origin. This could be a fake piece of evidence spearheaded by the defendant's attorney for shock value."

"Overruled, counselor. Neither party has been given the opportunity to review this supposed confession, and it has been reviewed by the police department. I highly doubt that Chief Moulton would send this man here with fake evidence. He's not that stupid to interrupt my court sessions with something trivial. My ruling stands. Bailiff, please proceed."

"Yes, your honor," he scoffs, flopping down into his seat like a child about to start throwing a tantrum. He makes a show of shuffling and fidgeting in his seat, announcing his displeasure with the ruling.

The bailiff retrieves the disc from the judge and places it into the audio-visual equipment near the side of the room.

A gruff voice begins to blare out of the speakers in the courtroom. I gasp as I listen to my father's voice confess to planting the drugs in my car and conspire to kill my brother. My body grows weak, and I nearly black out, but Leroy catches me.

"I take it from Mrs. Azzo's display of shock that this voice belongs to someone she knows. Do you have an identity, Officer?"

The recording concludes.

"Yes, your honor," he murmurs. "The note was signed by Ronald Boatman, and the name matches that of the homeowner."

"Do you have Mr. Boatman in custody, Officer?" she questions him.

"No, your honor. Mr. Boatman's remains were found inside the burning building."

Oh fuck. He didn't. Please tell me that this wasn't his form of a last goodbye to me. If my father was dead, why wasn't Ratchet here?

The judge looks to both of the attorneys and calls for a sidebar. Leroy settles me in the chair and heads for the judge's bench. Each of the attorneys talk in muffled tones and animated waves of their hands with the judge before stepping back toward their respective tables.

"In light of this new information, I am dismissing all charges against Mrs. Azzo. Case dismissed."

The judge bangs her gavel onto the wooden platform, and my heart soars.

I'm free.

The only thing that could make this better would be for Ratchet to be here. As the thought crosses my mind, a prickle of tiny tingles roams my body. Pivoting to find the source, a smile forms on my face. My husband stands at the bar behind me.

"Hello, Siren," he says to me. "Sorry, I'm late."

Without a word, I jump over the bar into his strong arms, wrapping my own around his neck. For the first time in nearly a week, I feel at ease with him near. The fear and doubt that ruled me faded as soon as his lips descended on mine. I didn't care that the judge, attorneys, or onlookers were viewing our display. Hiding away from the world was something that I was never going to do again. I would celebrate the little things and the second chance at life that I was given by the grace of God. Maybe there was someone upstairs looking out for me after all.

"I love you, Jude," I tell him before pulling him into another kiss.

"I love you, Ricca."

He carries me out of the courtroom, still in his arms, never breaking the contact between us. It's not until he sets me back onto my feet outside that I let all of the emotions from my incarnation out of me. I cry, I laugh, and I take my first real breath of freedom. Ratchet holds me and lets me get it all out on the lawn of the court-house. As the last bitter piece of darkness that has had a hold of my life flows out of me, an indescribable peace fills the void left behind.

I am happy.

I am loved.

I am safe.

When I settle, he takes my hands in his and pulls them against his heart. The rhythm of it beating beneath my outstretched fingers.

"This heart is and always will be yours, Siren."

"As mine is for you," I declare, repeating the same motion with his hand on my heart.

"Your heart may be a little full for me to hold it all, Siren."

"What do you mean?" I question him, but he points behind me, and I see Asher leaning against a car with Raze and Slider flanking him.

"How?" I ask, quickly looking back to my husband. "How is this even possible?"

"I went to the judge this morning. That's why I was late. I explained to him that your incarceration was false and that you'd be cleared of all charges today. Considering his legal guardian was no longer living, he granted our application to adopt him."

"Wait," I croak out, "are you saying what I think you are? Asher is ours?"

"He's ours."

I jump into my husband's arms. Tears of the purest joy that could have been made on this Earth fall from my cheeks as I hug him. My brother is ours. Never again having to be apart from me. I could give him the life that I never had and maybe, in doing that, find my own last bit of happiness.

"I thought that we needed to have the home study back and the DNA test? How did you get him to agree to all of this?"

"The home study report came in this morning. The day you were arrested, the lab received the results.

Nicole tried to call you, but it was after they picked you up. I also told him about your father's plan."

"His plan?"

Ratchet divulges to me his intentions and motives for wanting my brother still in his possession. My stomach heaves at the thought of my mother being involved in it too, and I am even more thankful she is dead because I would have killed her for it.

"What if my father tries to come after him after the fact? What will we do?"

"You don't have to worry about him anymore, Siren. He's not going to be a problem."

The words fall oddly off of his lips. I'm missing something buried underneath his words. I try to process everything that has happened today, and that's when the realization hits me. My father wasn't going to protest my adoption of Asher because he couldn't. My husband did the only thing he knew what to do to protect our family. He killed my father, and the last piece of my past still walking the earth.

"It was you that got him to confess on that CD, wasn't it?"

"There is nothing that I wouldn't do for you, Siren. Believe me when I say that he will never bother you again," Ratchet promises me.

I could have asked more questions, but I didn't need to do that. My husband had done something that no one else ever had. He protected me and gave me the best gift of all, a family. A family that loves me. We may not be the most picturesque group, but not all love looks like a Hallmark card. My family may have come at a cost to my own father, but that was his sin to bear for his plans and misdeeds. I hope that he and my mother enjoy their reunion in hell.

Looking at him, I smile and take his hand in mine.

"Let's go home."

Epilogue

3 MONTHS LATER

RATCHET

BEING home with my family is a feeling that I don't think will ever grow old. In all my years of living alone after my sister's death, this felt right. Ginny was my home for so many years, and in her death, a piece of me died with her. The guilt that I felt had been washed away and, over time, replaced with Ricca and Asher's happiness.

The transition here for Asher was tough at first. Much like my sister, he was reserved. He didn't want to play with the other kids running around the club and preferred to be alone. Until Wes and Colt, Darcy's boys, finally found common ground with him. After that day, they were inseparable. And trouble all at the same time. Jagger's personality ran wild in his boys, and add in a bit of Ricca in Asher, and you had a volatile mix. The mischief was only yet to come for our families.

Peering in on my sleeping wife in our bed, I smile. The dreams and nightmares that had haunted her for years drifted away, and she was finally sleeping through the night. Her panic attacks still happened from time to time, but they, too, were beginning to fade.

I listen down the hallway and find the house still quiet. Asher sleeps like the dead, but he's an early riser. If I was going to make my move on my wife without interruption, it had to be now. I missed having her all to myself, and this may be my only chance today.

I quietly pad to the dip and try to get in without waking her, but I fail miserably. Her eyes snap open and lock onto mine as soon as my weight shifts the mattress.

"Good morning, Siren," I whisper to her, placing a kiss on her lips.

She returns the greeting and stretches her muscles. Her smile beams in the early morning rays, peeking into the room through the blinds.

My finger traces her exposed collarbone and travels down to her breast. Her nipples pebble as my thumb brushes against them lightly.

"What are you doing?" she giggles, trying to pull the covers back over her naked body. One of the best things she adapted to in our marriage was the rule of no clothes in our bed with the doors securely locked. With Asher in the house, I need to take all the chances I could get to fuck my wife. This just eliminated one of the steps.

"Can't a man love his woman?" I tease back.

"What about Asher?" she protests.

"The kid is out cold in his room. And before you ask, yes, I locked the door. I need you, Siren."

She smiles at my candid request and rolls onto her side. Her tiny hand shifts underneath the blanket and wraps around my already hard cock.

"Mmm," she moans as she strokes me, "you're so hard already."

"Siren, I am always hard when you're around. The damn thing always salutes whenever you walk into a room. You're like a homing beacon to my cock."

She giggles at my confession and strokes me harder. My head falls back, enjoying the sensation of her hand pumping me. The scent of her sex fills my nostrils, and I know that she's already wet for me. My lips dip to her exposed neck, and she shudders as I lick and nip her collarbone. I can feel her pulse quicken underneath my mouth as I tease her favorite spot. Why kissing her collarbone turns her on so much, I will never know, but if that's what gets her motor running, I'll do it.

She turns to look at me with my erect cock still in her hand and bites her lip.

"Touch me, please," she asks sweetly.

She adjusts her body, half rolling onto her back, and

invites me to touch her. Not that I needed an invitation to touch my wife, but she likes to try to hold power in the bedroom. And, of course, I always let her.

My hand slips underneath the sheet covering her lower half, and she shivers as I graze her cleanly shaven pussy. The soft skin glides with my touch, the wetness spilling out of her. She softly moans at my touch, and I slide a finger inside. Her clit is a hard, swollen nub of arousal, and I circle it once. Her soft moans turn louder, and her pelvis begins to move against my hand. I dip a finger lower and penetrate her. Her walls clench around me, and her hips increase their speed.

She's as worked up as I am. Living with Asher had come with unexpected challenges, and finding time for things like this were becoming fewer and farther between. I had to make a point of sneaking off on my lunch hour from the security firm when I could to catch her alone. Who needs food when I have her to feast on?

"Just like that," she moans. "Don't move your fucking hand."

"So demanding, Siren."

She growls at me when I disobey her, but arguing isn't on the menu right now. As much as I want to draw this out, I can hear Asher stirring in the room next door. If I don't speed this up, my cock will be screaming at me for the rest of the day in protest.

"Hey, I said not to move," she protests as I pull her body

across mine. Her perfect fucking pussy sits across my groin, and my aching dick can feel her wetness straddling him.

"And?" I rebut. "You'd rather my hand make you cum over my dick. Siren, I am shocked," I pretend to gasp.

"Asshole," she fires back, smacking me in the chest. "I was so close."

"I can do better than close, wife."

"Oh?" she challenges me. I shift beneath her and press my dick into her wetness, reminding her of what she nearly missed out on. My hands grasp her hips and angle her apex at my cock. Her hands fall from the tops of her thighs and help guide me inside of her. I'm not sure what it is about watching her take control and put my cock inside of her cunt, but it is the hottest fucking thing on this planet. It's weird, but it's my kind of weird.

Her back aches as she adjusts to fit me in.

"You feel so fucking good wrapped around my cock, Siren."

She smiles and grinds her pelvis against me, trying to find her rhythm. It doesn't take long before she leans forward, shoving her perfect tits in my face. The visual of her dominating me is fucking stunning. No strip club or sex club has anything on the woman who is riding me. Nothing compares to her.

"Fuck my cock," I moan. The sensation of my orgasm

begins to vibrate. Ricca can sense I'm close and starts increasing her rhythm.

"Just like that," I demand her. My hands dig into her luscious hips, forcing her pussy down harder on my cock. Her body stiffens as she finds her release. Her beautiful face glows as she rides out her pleasure on top of me. So fucking beautiful. Watching her enjoy herself and the pleasure rippling through her brings my own orgasm. My cock twitches and spills my cum inside of her. Ricca smiles and leans in for a kiss when the door handle begins to turn.

"Ricca, are you okay? Did you fall out of bed?" Asher questions. "I heard yelling."

Ricca's face flushes the instant that she hears Asher's voice on the other side of the door.

"I'm okay, buddy," she reassures him while stifling a laugh. "Jude was teaching me a new dance move," she lies.

"Can I come in?" he asks with a nervous tone to his voice.

"NO!" we both yell in unison and scramble off the bed, looking for something to cover ourselves with.

"Oh," his voice drops.

"Why don't you go turn on the morning cartoons? I'll be right out to watch them with you while we make breakfast for your sister. What do you say?"

"Okay," he agrees, and we hear his feet pounding down the hallway in a trot.

"Oh my god, that was too close," she exclaims.

"We've still got a few minutes before he comes back, you know," I suggest, trying to incite a second round of fucking my beautiful wife.

"Dream on," she rebukes. "You made him a promise, and I am going to go take a bath."

I sigh in defeat and smack my head against the frame of the doorway. Pulling a pair of plaid pajama pants over my hips, turning to her to offer one more time. She swats me away as she makes her way into the bathroom.

"At least send me a selfie," I call out to her.

"Maybe," she teases before I hear my phone ding on the counter in the kitchen. Asher's feet trot to the kitchen, and I hear a gasp from his mouth.

"What was that?" Ricca yells out from the bathroom.

"Nothing!" I respond back.

She didn't need to know that her little brother may or may not have seen his sister in a compromising situation. I think our breakfast meal prep is going to come with a few life lessons. Don't open someone else's phone, and maybe the birds and the bees. Parenting is a bitch.

A little while later, Ricca, Asher, and I head over to the clubhouse. It's become our normal Sunday routine. Sleep in, breakfast, cartoons together, and then time at the club. With so many kids in our ranks, the brothers decided to make Sunday a permanent family day. The club girls disappear, and our families enjoy time together. Not that the club girls were a problem with the ladies around. Most of the troublesome ones had moved on the more the guys settled down.

Pulling up to the clubhouse, I see all the usual vehicles in the parking lot except one. A two-door green sedan sits near the back door with an out-of-state license plate.

"Who's that?" Ricca asks, noticing the same thing as I did.

"Not sure," I reply, keeping an eye out on the place. It's been a few months since our club had any visitors. Quiet months I'd been relishing in as Asher settled into our routine. I eye the car as I park.

"Why don't you and Asher go around the front?"

"Everything okay?" my wife asks with a touch of worry on her beautiful face.

"It's probably nothing, but I want to check it out first. You two go on, and I'll meet up with you in a bit."

She agrees and takes Asher along with her as I asked. I normally wouldn't be so suspicious of an outsider here, but something doesn't feel right to me. If there wasn't anything happening, then why is the hair on the back of my neck standing up at attention?

I slide from our new SUV and stalk quietly to the back door, only to find Voodoo leaning against the wall next to Raze's office. Now, I know something isn't right. I slide up next to him, but his eyes don't move from the doorway.

"What's going on, V? We got problems?"

"You could say that. Remember that woman I told you about that I met online?"

"Yeah. You never shut up about her."

"She was Ricca's therapist you had me check out."

"Okay?" I answer back. "I don't think Ricca would mind you seeing her if that's what you think, but Kentucky isn't exactly just down the street. Not going to be easy to see her."

"That's going to be a problem, Ratch. She's here."

"Are you fucking kidding me? Did you invite her here?" I hiss. Inviting strangers into our home? I knew V had issues with following the rules, but this is fucking new. He, of all people, knew better than this. Strangers have no place here. Not until we can clear them. The fucking job this asshole does.

"Nope," he says, exaggerating his words with a loud pop at the end of it. "I didn't even tell her where I lived."

"So, she tracked you down and showed up then. That's fucking creepy."

"That's not exactly it. She showed up this morning with another girl in toe, demanding to talk to Raze."

I stare back at him in confusion. Why would this woman

want to talk to Raze? It doesn't make any sense. How would she even know about the club, for that matter? The only way she would even possibly know that is if she is either familiar with the club, Voodoo told her, or she's a fucking crazy ass stalker. With him, either could be a possibility.

"She's his fucking sister."

"You've got to be shitting me. Ricca's therapist is Presley Sanders." I laugh. "All this time, you've been web fucking Raze's baby sister."

"Laugh it up. She apparently lied about her name. I saw her walk in here, and I about died where I was standing."

"Not before Raze kills you first," I blurt out. "God, I hope I get to watch. Wonder how much popcorn we have in the storage room. You and that stalker shit you do online is finally coming home to roost."

"Not funny, asshole."

V smacks me, and just as he does, the door opens. A tall woman steps out of the doorway, and I know in an instant that this is Presley. Her time away from the club has done wonders for her, and the skinny little girl who left here with her mom so many years ago is finally grown into a woman. She must be only a few inches shorter than her older brother now. V stiffens up next to me and smacks me hard.

"Who's that?"

I look back to Presley as she steps aside and reveals the other woman who came in with her.

She is smaller in stature than Presley, but there's not saying much for the Sanders genes. All it takes is one good look at Raze, and you realize that no one in their gene pool is tiny. His old man was over six feet tall from what I knew, and their mom wasn't exactly short herself.

"Do you recognize her?"

A cascade of black hair masks her face, but as she shifts it out of the way, I freeze. It can't be. I rub my eyes, shaking my head in the process to clear the thought going through my mind.

"The fuck," I mutter under my breath. "It can't be."

She's gone. There's no way this woman could be her. She's dead.

"Hi, Jude," the woman declares with a soft, sheepish wave of her hand.

My fucking sister is alive.

Ginny Azzo is alive.

Did you enjoy Absolution?

Read more from the Heaven's Rejects MC Series.

Heaven's Rejects MC Series

Heaven Sent

Angels and Ashes

Absolution

Lies and Illusions

Resolution

Song List

My Happy Ending – Avril Lavigne

Can't You See – Black Stone Cherry

Hell and High Water - Black Stone Cherry

All the Same – Sick Puppies

Sound of Silence – Disturbed

Coin for the Ferryman – Nickelback

Broken Bones – Rev Theory

Careless Whisper – Seether

FMLYHM – Seether

Wrong Side of Heaven – Five Finger Death Punch

Breathe No More – Evanescence

Hollow – Breaking Benjamin

Hail to the King – Avenged Sevenfold

Hurt – Christina Aguilera

Outside – Staind

Simple Man - Shinedown

Acknowledgements

It's been a year since I released a full length Heaven's Rejects MC Novel, and I know what you're thinking. Why did it take so long? The truth is that my muse disappeared. My driving need to write went along with her. It took time for me to find my place again, and when she came roaring back, I was ready. I knew when I had decided to put Ricca and Ratchet together that their story would be the hardest story to tell. Ricca's past was heartbreaking to write about in Heaven Sent, and as the muddy waters cleared, I realize that the darkness was still yet to come for her. Sometimes it's necessary to put your characters through hell for the sweet, innocent moments to really be cherished. Ratchet was her safe place, and like so many others in reality, helped her find her center again. Their story isn't pretty, and it was never meant to be that way because out of the darkness, the light will come again.

I want to thank each and every one of my readers who have patiently waited for this book. Without you, I wouldn't have been able to finally write the words "The End". Thank you from the bottom of my heart.

There are a few people that I would like to acknowledge in their efforts into making this book possible.

To my husband: For the past seven years, our lives have drastically changed. The day we pledged ourselves to each other we made a promise to be there in sickness and in health. Last October, I thought I lost you for the second time, but you fought. You fought harder than I have ever seen you fight, and nearly a year later, you are the strongest person I know. Our life together has had its ups and downs, but when we are together, nothing can stop us. I love you with all of my heart, and I want to thank you for giving me the gift of your presence in my life. As crazy as a ride that it has been over the last few years, I am happy that I get to do it with you by my side.

To everyone who had a hand in the creation of this book: The team of people who are behind me with every book amazes me. I am nothing without the team of people who support me from behind the scenes. Their dedication and hard work takes my words and makes them into a stunning piece of literary art.

And lastly, my readers,

Thank you for giving me this opportunity to give you

a part of my soul, and loving the characters as much as I do. Each book is an extension of myself, and allows another part of me to heal from the loss of my father. I do this all for you.

Avelyn Paige is a USA Today and Wall Street Journal bestselling author who writes stories about dirty alpha males and the brave women who love them. She resides in a small town in Indiana with her husband and three fuzzy kids, Jezebel, Cleo, and Asa.

Avelyn spends her days working as a cancer research scientist and her nights sipping moonshine while writing. You can often find her curled up with a good book surrounded by her pets or watching one of her favorite superhero movies for the billionth time. Deadpool is currently her favorite.

———

Want to talk books? Join Avelyn's Facebook group to learn about new releases, future series, and to hang out with other readers.

ALSO BY AVELYN PAIGE

The Heaven's Rejects MC Series

Heaven Sent

Angels and Ashes

Sins of the Father

Absolution

Lies and Illusions

The Black Hoods MC

Dark Protector

Dark Secret

Dark Guardian

Dark Desires

Dark Destiny

Dark Redemption

Dark Salvation

Dark Seduction

The Bastard Boilers MC

Property of Azrael

The Dirty Bitches MC Series

<u>Dirty Bitches MC #1</u>

<u>Dirty Bitches MC #2</u>

<u>Dirty Bitches MC #3</u>

Other Books by Avelyn Paige

Girl in a Country Song

Cassie's Court